GW01402793

A DEADLY QUEEN

LARKIN'S BARKIN'
BOOK 2

PETE ADAMS

Copyright © 2024 by Pete Adams

Layout design and Copyright © 2024 by Next Chapter

Published 2024 by Next Chapter

Edited by Elizabeth N. Love

Cover art by Jaylord Bonnit

This book is a work of fiction. Names, characters, places, and incidents are the product of the author's imagination or are used fictitiously. Any resemblance to actual events, locales, or persons, living or dead, is purely coincidental.

All rights reserved. No part of this book may be reproduced or transmitted in any form or by any means, electronic or mechanical, including photocopying, recording, or by any information storage and retrieval system, without the author's permission.

"Everything has been figured out, except how to live"

— *JEAN PAUL SATRE*

Sub Rosa:

First recorded in 1650–60; from Latin sub rosā literally, "**under the rose**," from the ancient use of the rose at meetings as a symbol of the sworn confidence of the participants. However, the rose has held a deeply symbolic significance in many times and cultures as a symbol of maternal creativity and of feminine generative power. It is also thought by some to indicate that all life stemmed from woman, even the Gods, and thus, power should rest with women as a *Divine Union*.

Stepney Myrmidon - Dead, Dying or Gorgeous:

Drop 'em Blossom, Mickey One-eye, Snotty Oliver, the Rinso Kid, Harry Horse Collar, Scats Edwards, Silly Boy Eric, and Flan Milkman.

To Jacinta Murphy of Crumlin, Dublin, who inspired the Myrmidons. A warm-hearted and lovely woman who never fails to make me laugh.

To three wonderful ladies I met on a train to London – they were going for a day and night out on the town. I indulged my love of people watching and banked many notes of so much conversational joy. They each bought one of my books in exchange for the following acknowledgement: 'Three menopausal ladies and a socialist'. I have to say I have also banked that as a future book title.

PREFACE

This is a sequel to the first book in the Larkin's Barkin' series *Black Rose – A Midsummer Night's Chutzpah*. Following the popularity of Black Rose, I am considering a Larkin's Barkin' series, taking the characters established in book one, and many more as they join the journey, through the ages, from 1966 to, maybe, modern day, and to explore some of the incongruity of life through an idiosyncratic narrative that may bear an uncanny resemblance to real life?

> *"Something unknown is doing we don't know what"*
>
> — *SIR ARTHUR EDDINGTON*

But first, the 2 Larkin's Barkin' books are to be seen as an historic note for my compendium of separate mini-series: Kind Hearts and Martinets, The DaDa Detective Agency series, The Rhubarb Papers and finally, An Avuncular Detective. It will be an anthology of 14 books, with a cover-all title of *Divine Breath* also the title of book 14 – even in Larkin's Barkin', set fifty years in the past, the seeds of what occurs in the above series are sown, a tale of the establishment, benign or malignant? Self-serving or beneficial to society as a whole? Well, you can make your own mind up on that and, is violence if perceived as 'for the greater good'?

Following on from Divine Breath, each individual series will make its own way – maybe enjoining again, who knows? You can never really know where a story is going to take you once you have penned the first words. For me, that is the excitement of writing, and this story? Well, you will just have to read it and see, because it surprised me.

INTRODUCTION AND AUTHOR'S NOTE

Summer 1966 saw a not particularly peaceful revolution in the East End of London. No surprises there, in what was billed as a gangland turf war, but the result...? That was a surprise. Read: Black Rose – *A Midsummer Night's Chutzpah,* and now... *another war?*

Both Black Rose (set in London 1966) and A Deadly Queen (continuing the story in 1969) takes as a backdrop the political situation in Northern Ireland in particular the IRA and how it grew in prominence in the minds of the British people, and how they came to understand the, 'Troubles'.

I do not claim to fully comprehend the historic accuracy and this novel is, of course, a work of fiction, but I am sure that as history reveals itself over time we will discover more than the media and government allowed the people to know. This is not a real history, or faithful even to the narrative portrayed and known by many.

However, it could be, or, it could have been.

PROLOGUE

1969 – STEPNEY, THE EAST END OF LONDON - SUMMER

THE DARKNESS: WHAT CAN THE DARKNESS TAKE FROM YOU?

Love? perhaps the most precious commodity, can be dangerous, deadly even. Love can lead or abandon. Can be all-seeing or blind. Whatever it is at any time, it can also be an excuse, a reason to tread where good sense does not prevail. Academic inquisitiveness can also disguise so much. For Wendy Richards, consultant psychiatrist at the Royal London Hospital in the East End of London, never was a truer word said. Danger stalked and it was nearer than Wendy could ever imagine.

Love: Wendy loved Detective Sergeant Flora Wade, the chalk to her cheese, and it transpired that Flora was not the solid, steady Eddie lady she thought she fell in love with. Flora was now an MI5 agent working with a maverick Irishman wrangling with a potential IRA threat to London, or was the Irishman, Padraig Casey, the threat, and what did this mean for Flora, and for that matter Wendy herself?

Curiosity: Wendy Richards was counselling *public enemy number one,* Chas Larkin, head of the gangster Larkin Saint family, and she had to agree with the prevailing thought, Larkin was barkin' mad. However, his history and his *current* evolved personality made him a fascinating study. Add to that he also, *tacitly,* works for MI5, and you have a crucible in which to fuse so many nascent factors, any one of which could flare phosphorescently; oh so dangerous, and Wendy had not the street savvy to see what danger she might be *creating,* let alone, stepping into.

Danger: How aware was Wendy that she may have placed herself in a precarious position? Why? Because unknown to Chas Larkin, and even Flora, Wendy's central focus was on the two women who, day to day, ran the gangland family: Maude Larkin and Bess Saint, though they reputedly deferred to Chas and most times they did, but in Maude's case, not always. Maude was dangerous. Sometimes uncontrollably violent; a scary woman. Bess Saint, however, was intriguing. An enigma. Domestically docile in her *marriage* to Maude, however, Bess was the brains of the gangland empire, and Bess could control her erstwhile spouse; at least this was the accepted thought. But lately...?

Life force: For Wendy, it was a fascination as to how these people survived and lived their lives, seemingly okay with their existence. It was not just the danger of street violence because ironically, since Chas Larkin wrested control, and under the guidance of Bess Saint, a quasi-peace reigned. What Wendy did know was that when the *danger* of everyday life was removed, or at least not so preoccupying, this allowed the mind to play tricks, and this was the kernel of Wendy's research. So many of the people in this sphere of East End life had lived a nightmare childhood, and when you no longer have to look over your shoulder for your safety or death, you can sometimes dwell on that damaged past and the shadow of the *Grim Reaper* could dog your heels; ever present, but now in your head; the *Black Dog.*

Used and abused: The life that many children grew up with, often with absent or no parent, or abusive parents, meant that they were ripe to be plucked by unscrupulous and cunning predators. The safety net of welfare services was not so safe for many of the waifs and ragamuffins who grew up in the nineteen fifties and early sixties. It was about escape for most of these children, escape from the *system,* and sadly, escape from the *establishment,* because in amongst the still bomb-damaged buildings and abject poverty of the East End of London, predators felt safe to maraud and to feed their vulturine appetites; there was nobody to stop them. It was *life,* and you just lived with it. It had always existed, hadn't it?

———

Cherchez la femme – look for the woman. Would that be Maude Larkin or Bess Saint? Would it be Wendy? Or would it be the Black Rose?

1

Saturday, 21ˢᵗ June, 1969 – London's East End swelters in a stifling heat wave. Feelings effervesce and contention sizzles inside and outside Incubator Street School playground.

REPUTEDLY THE MOST COLD-BLOODED GANGSTER IN THE EAST End of London, Chas Larkin, wept. He was ruthless. He was, or could be, kind and generous. He was no doubt damaged goods, and even with all of that, he quite possibly had saved London in 1966. I suppose you could say he was an enigma, but without doubt, Chas Larkin was barkin' mad.

Blossom Temple, Chas Larkin's common-law wife, wept. She was inconsolable as she stood behind the lead milk float; she refused to ride. She would walk to the cemetery alongside other prominent local women and men mourners, crowded in by soldiers; only the elderly or infirm rode. Head bowed out of respect, her red raw eyes stared through her forehead, all she wanted to do was wrest the body of her son from within the coffin and hold him, one more time. Blossom, like so many other children of her time, now grown, was also damaged goods, but a survivor. Her son was damaged physically but loved, cared for, cherished. He had not survived.

'You okay?' Chas asked. He loved Blossom but did not have the where-with-all to comfort her in this harrowing time. Chas had come a long way thanks to the counselling from Wendy Richards, but still, he had difficulty expressing his innermost emotions, aside from his occasional violent rages, and you wouldn't want to be around him then.

The petite and cherubic Blossom looked up to the no longer crooked Chas, no longer the hunch-backed cowering shell of a young man; he was tall, six foot and handsome. 'What do you think?' She answered with a sideways glance. She saw him struggling to know what to do, so once again she rescued him, pretty much as she had always rescued Chas when he was a much-bullied runt of a child; his sanctuary, the bombed-out shells of buildings and his enduring love, Blossom. 'It's okay Chas,' she touched his hand, 'I'll be okay after today. You know...'

'I love you, Bloss.'

Blossom felt even more tears flood her cheeks, if that were possible. Since the killing of her 8-year-old son, she had barely stopped crying, but she did have Chas as a stalwart lover, companion. Husband? Would he marry her? She knew he loved her. She knew she was his one and only love. He had told her so many times, but was this was enough? Blossom had never known emotional security, she just offered it to so many in need. Was this as good as it gets? You cannot push a man like Chas Larkin. 'I love you too, Chas.'

Standing beside Blossom, offering the occasional comforting stroke of her hand to the grieving mother, Bess Saint wept. She in turn was held fast around her burgeoning pregnant belly by her more *stoical* wife, *in all but law*, Maude Larkin. Maude took every opportunity to feel for movement from the baby; she hoped it would be a girl. For Maude, life held the risk of being fleeting, and this awareness as an imminent parent worried her, not that you would know it. Maude wanted to change, but couldn't, and in her mind she believed that she dare not. This was who she was and what people expected of her. It was her life, and Bess made her complete.

Maude was mad. Stark raving, some said. Furthermore, she was enraged at what had happened, and combined with being mentally unbalanced, which she would deny and few would challenge her, this made Maude certified loony bin material, a fact that the *trick cyclist* Wendy Richards would very likely concur. Yes, Maude was dangerously mad, at least this is what people thought, and they would not be too far off the mark. However, today, on this sad but tinderbox occasion, Maude knew she had to hold her emotions in check; this was not the time for revenge. Chas had said she needed a clear head. She needed to martial her thoughts in order to later martial her troops, and, well, Bess had also told her to. So she would.

'She moved,' Maude remarked hardly able to disguise her joy. She rapidly reinstated her sad face.

'How do you know it's a girl?'

'It had better be.'

'It's hard to feel joy about our baby in this sad time, but Maude, I do feel a great happiness, you, me, and the baby in a few months' time. But then, the worry will start.'

'Worry? What worry?'

Bess looked at Maude and wondered sometimes how she could love such a dozy cow, but she did. 'Worry for the bairn's safety, dipstick.'

'Shush.'

'Shush yer fuckin' self, Paddy,' Maude railed back, irritated by the Irishman, mainly because he was a man, but mostly because he was right. She should shut up; Bess had said.

This contretemps did, however, amuse Blossom, and for this Chas was grateful to his lunatic cousin.

7

Detective Inspector Paddy Casey chuckled, but still he wept. He was weird and a true enigma; who was he really? He also hugged his love, his arm encircling the waist of Dr Naadhira Khalid, known as *Nadia*. She had done all of her crying, and today she held Paddy together. Bloody men, she thought. But, she did love him. Theirs was a powerful love born out of extraordinary circumstances. An awkward and alien relationship, an Irish police detective and *quasi*-MI5 agent, a lapsed catholic, in love with and living with a Palestinian surgeon, a Muslim woman. Yes, they loved each other, and he wept for both of them. He was a hard man and an emotional Irish drip, but they shared a mutual pain. Nadia had lost family in Palestine to the Israeli army, and Paddy, his father and one of his sisters had perished in the *troubles*. She understood his pain, his desire to unify his country and to do it peacefully. She suspected, but never knew for sure, that Paddy had been involved with the IRA. She had not asked, afraid that one day he may tell her.

'Come here, you dozy sod,' and Paddy cuddled into his woman. She was tall with an elegant beauty and was emotionally stronger than her limp-lettuce Paddy.

Casey did not return to Ireland following the midsummer events of 1966 as was his original intention. He had stayed in London after completing his mission. Why? Because he loved Nadia. Nadia stayed because she had fled the violence to her family and her people. London was a new life for her, fraught with social land mines, dangerous territory, but she did love her Padraig (O'Neill) Casey. And there it was, Paddy was not just a dangerous conundrum, what was his name? O'Neill or Casey? He never went by O'Neill, so Nadia, now familiar with her lover's smoke and mirrors, believed he was an O'Neill. But, was he MI5 or, and most perilously, IRA? This she could not fathom; did she *love* the danger? Something Wendy Richards had suggested to her.

'Who are you?'

'What?' Paddy answered, always confused when interrogated by Nadia. She had this power over him whereby his mind went to mush and he could never think of an answer, and then he did. 'I'm the man who loves you.'

'Fuck you...'

'Yes, please.'

And discreetly amused, she settled for that; this was not the time. 'I love you too, whoever you are,' and she enjoyed the look of confusion on his dangerous, and not particularly handsome, face.

Detective Sergeant Flora Wade wept. Beside her stood her *trick cyclist* lover, Wendy Richards, consultant psychiatrist at the Royal London Hospital, the same hospital where Dr Nadia worked. Wendy comforted her tough partner whilst monitoring her patients, Chas Larkin and Blossom Temple, two people who carried substantial emotional baggage, but her eyes rarely strayed from Maude Larkin; what was it about that woman? That woman gangster? The Queen of the East End of London. A woman who scared the living daylights out of her. Had scared the living daylights out of her, and in just one consultation, for anger management of all things. All had later been explained, but still, and despite her fear, Wendy could not resist the perilous fascination, and if truth be told, Maude Larkin offered more intellectual depth to her research into life in the East End of London than all of the other players. It is about survival. Of the poor? The choices for the poor? Living always with the threat of death; often a violent death and this applied to Maude also.

To say this was an incendiary situation may be an understatement, and for so many reasons. Just about everyone attending the funeral had cause to worry, cause to look over their shoulder.

2

THE CORTEGE OF MILK FLOATS HAD BEEN PREPARED FOR THE
journey to the cemetery. The route would be lined with people,
most genuinely distressed at the murder of the eight-year-old
Tommy Temple, known affectionately as Tommy Little Legs.
Others would be there because the Larkin Saint criminal
family would expect it, and there were many informers. People
lived on the edge in Stepney, the East End of London borough.

The electric milk floats were quiet and excruciatingly slow,
but this suited the mood of the cortege. The vehicles had a
driver's cab with no doors; if you fell out at the *governed* speed, a
maximum of ten miles per hour, you were not likely to be hurt.
The back was an open platform for the milk crates with a hard
canopy. For the occasion of the funeral, there were ten floats,
eleven if you counted Flan's specially modified lead float; he
could do sometimes up to fifteen miles per hour, but he would
only use this racy speed if his mum had not woken him in time
to start his delivery round. Yes, he was back living with his
mum, arguably safer than the times he had spent in the *homes*,
having been, notionally, *saved* from neglect by welfare services.

Flan's Achilles heel was he was a lovely-looking boy, after he had been cleaned up, and he had grown into a most handsome, though emotionally retarded and damaged man. People said he looked like Clark Gable and that they had a Hollywood star for a milkman. However, of all the local kids now grown, Flan was likely the most screwed up. Learning impaired, people said, offering sympathy for the young man. He had developed a shell of impenetrable hurt. Wendy could see it, but even she could not get into Flan's head and imagined she never would; he had suffered too much.

For the funeral, each float of white with blue flashes had been respectfully draped in black cloth. The dressed flatbed to the rear had a central raised plinth of upside-down milk crates, cloaked in black, upon which were an abundance of flowers. This left a space on the left and right edges where the frailer mourners could sit, except for Flan's vehicle; his box was designed to take the small and unpretentious coffin, flowers atop. Alongside was Tommy's *Space Hopper*. Immediately behind the float, Blossom Temple, his mother, walked with Chas Larkin, Blossom's de facto husband, an unconventional relationship born out of a tragic childhood. They walked to the cemetery and after the interment, followed the milk floats back to Incubator Street, to await. To await what? The wake? More...?

The disrespectful noise from the school playground was difficult to zone out. It was a contrast of emotion; in the playground, celebration, and Incubator Street, deep sadness. The women, mourning: mother, doctor, psychiatrist, copper, gangsters, Bess Saint, Consort to Maude Larkin, Queen. In the East End, homosexuality was accepted as a part of life, and everyone would acknowledge the two women as wife and wife. Even if you disapproved, you kept that to yourself. Bess was the calmer of the two gangsters, gentile in comparison if you screwed your eyes to look, and if you dared open them, Bess was an attractive, bleach-blonde bubbly woman with the look of a mature Rubenesque *Shirley Temple*. However, she was most certainly the brains of the outfit. In contrast Maude, the muscle, was tall and sinewy, lean, a long narrow face dominated by a Roman nose, black hair slicked back, dark threatening hooded eyes. She wore masculine black suits, and the ever-present sunglasses concealed those menacing eyes. If she removed the glasses, most knew it signalled Maude was angry and you wouldn't want to be in the vicinity, and there had been a lot of that lately, so much so the violent reputation of the East End had been well and truly re-established. The knowledge spread far and wide and never more so than in the territories of the west and north where, strangely, it was received with undisguised pleasure.

The Larkin Saint men and women soldiers formed up behind and alongside each float, armed and prepared; recent times had become volatile. The cortege had followed the well-publicised and well-known route, and the residents of this Stepney borough had lined the pavements to say their farewells. Farewells to a much-loved boy, a cripple who had a warm and loving disposition, as well as, ironically, the *protection* of Incubator Street and the Larkin Saint family. They remained lining the route to pay their respects on the return journey. Respects for the Larkin Saints; violent revenge was to be expected, and they stayed waiting in order to display whose side they were on, many followed and now crowded into Incubator Street.

On the return from Tower Hamlets cemetery and upon reaching Incubator Street, the cortege stopped in the pre-arranged places to allow the men, women and children to retire to several houses that had been prepared to temporarily receive the *civilian* mourners. The top front bedroom sash windows of four of the terraced houses had been thrown open and provided a strategic viewing gallery over the school play-ground, and below those windows, it was a short hop onto the roofs of the milk floats, if necessary.

The wake would take place in the late afternoon or evening, in the playground of Incubator Street School. It had been a case of intense irritability that the formal opening of the new Church of England Orphanage and Youth Club was timed to coincide with the already arranged funeral. The *great unwashed* mourners of Incubator Street would have to wait while the *great and the good* displayed themselves, bathing in their self-perceived importance and ensuring everybody knew about the largesse they had provided for this, one of the poorest areas of London. A facility for the *deprived children*, except the locals knew the real reasons. Although the facilities were much needed, the people who ran and frequently visited similar establishments elsewhere in the neighbourhood were not welcome. Their type would not be received gladly. The agenda unwelcome, but what could the people do about it? These were powerful and famous people, and *the people*, especially the children, were at their mercy, not that they received merciful treatment.

A great brouhaha had been made of the proposed development and those who had contributed funds: Film and TV celebrities, churchmen, senior police officers, politicians. And to rub salt in the wounds of helpless poverty, the opening ceremony was to be headlined with the Bishop of Stepney alongside the constituency Member of Parliament. The MP was a local boy *done-good*, now Secretary of State for Northern Ireland, the Right Honourable William Creepe, known by the people of Stepney as *the honourable little Willie*, which annoyed the MP, especially as people doubted the *honour* bit. He was a born and bred cockney boy with the gift of the gab; he made people laugh, it was his *trademark,* but that was where anything benign ended. Little Willie was ambitious. He was headed for the top and he didn't care who he had to walk over to get there, especially the people of Stepney and Whitechapel whom he represented in Parliament, and let's face it, who on earth cared about Northern Ireland, even if he had traded favours to get onto the bottom rung of the ladder?

The mourners of Incubator Street now safely ensconced in the two-up two-down, two-storey, terraced houses, not so much slums anymore, not so much bomb-damaged anymore. Habitable at least because they were taken over and run by the Saint Larkin family; they looked after their own. The first-floor windows within the tight terrace of houses were reserved. The mourners would play no part in the playground celebrations. These festivities, on such an emotionally dark grieving day, were not for them. Their wake would have to wait, the mourning put on hold.

Their part would come later. Revenge would come later, how late, nobody knew, but they were ready.

The line of milk floats, now empty of passengers but with their respectful soldier followers, men and women dressed in black suits, were now in their sentry positions lined up along the frontages of the terraced houses, upon the flat roofs to the carts just below the top floor bedroom windows, and also from these windows, they watched. Prepared, but what for? From these various advantageous positions, the sentries could see that the gates to the playground were now blocked by another strategically placed milk float. The perimeter to the Incubator Street school playground railings, to keep the kids in, now formed a benign enclosure for the dignitaries; they would feel safe from the ire of the peasants.

The wall to the side road completed the enclosure. The third perimeter was the school hall and the final edge was formed by the new Orphanage and Youth Club enclosing the open playground where the dignitaries sipped chilled champagne; a signal that these people were way above those who lived here and for whom the *benefaction* had been expended, provided they did as they were told, which was, shut up and keep schtum.

The school playground where the planned remembrance of Tommy Temple was to take place was occupied by these self-important dignitaries and their toadying and complicit hangers-on, here to witness the opening of the new Church of England youth club and orphanage. To share in reflected glory, or so they thought. They declared they were *giving back to the community*. Self-deluded and self-inflated pomposity and *self-aware* denial, much worse than ignorance.

The local people, however, knew exactly what this was: institutional paedophilia. It had always gone on. It was, sadly, a part of life. The *people* had no say. The *people* were the downtrodden poor and told to appreciate the philanthropy of the Church and the generosity of Celebrities, unaware that the *people* knew what they were about. Unaware that the *people* would no longer stand for it because they now had a true Queen and not a posh tart on a throne who could not give a toss about the people of the East End. The *people* knew that this queen, with her consort, would act and was already acting. Already the Saint Larkin family had set up alternative youth clubs, alternative refuges for the poor. This notorious East End of London gang looked after their own and now, they had a *mad* Queen. They had a barbarous Queen. People feared their Queen, and she was *their* Queen.

The lead float, the one driven by the *beautiful* Flan Milkman, did enter the playground, causing the dignitaries and their retinue of sycophants, in their Sunday best and sweltering in the heat waiting for the ceremony to commence, to shuffle, to make way while they simultaneously elbowed and barged to secure more advantageous positions. Some tried to move the barrier set up to form a protective corral, a safe space for the big knobs to circulate unhindered and to be viewed before they mounted the stage for the formalities. The crowd of hangers-on elbowed and jostled not just for a better view of the ceremony but also to ensure they were seen by the TV cameras and newspaper photographers, to be at the front, squashed against the metal barriers; it mattered to them. Why else stand in the stifling heat?

They resented the intrusion of a milk float with the dozy sod driver. Flan the Milkman steered his vehicle to park in the spot as instructed and he had committed to memory, even if he had to use his float to nudge people out of the way, which he did because he was told to do just this. This float, Flan's float, was to be a statement, not that Flan appreciated this, and he was used to being shouted at anyway. The funereally bedecked milk vehicle now stood sentinel in the middle of the playground as a defiant marker. As a reminder. As a focus of the street's grief, and a challenge to the establishment Church and Council who refused to postpone their celebrations; what was the sorrow and bereavement of this street to them? Nothing. It meant nothing. They offered only a passing glance at the spectacle of the milk floats as they lined up along the terraced houses opposite the playground and outside the school gates. The electric vehicles had glided silently to their agreed positions, unnoticed, until now.

The *Express Dairies* provided the cortege of open-back milk delivery carts; they had no choice, the request coming from Maude Larkin, Queen of the East End herself, and even in less fomenting times you did as Maude asked. Maude had a rep, and just lately, had appeared to have *gone off the rails*, if she had ever been on them. Flan was the only milkman prepared to service this notorious bandit territory. He was a resident of Incubator Street, born here and would likely die here; people did. He was, in the parlance, simple, *special needs*, but the people of this street and the gangsters who ruled *looked after their own* and everyone knew of Flan's history, used and abused, but he knew he was loved by the Incubator Street people, and Chas Larkin had given him and his mum a home. Flan had always wanted to be a milkman, had even learned to whistle, so when he left school and was released from the clutches of the Church Homes for wayward boys, the Larkin Saint family paid a visit to the Express depot and he was given the job that nobody wanted anyway.

Every day, except Sunday, Flan did his round. Nobody knew how it was received by Express management, because Flan didn't do so well in school, and adding up and taking away was a little beyond his reach. It was widely thought that the Larkin Saint family covered the cost of the milk that Flan delivered because he never collected the money and people had free milk. You could say he was untouchable, and add to this, he loved Tommy Little Legs, his only friend, apart from the Stepney Myrmidon: Drop 'em Blossom, The Rinso Kid, Snotty Oliver, Mickey One-eye, Harry Horse Collar, Scats Edwards and *Silly Boy* Eric. What the Myrmidon had in common was that they had all, at various times, been at school with Flan and all, but Snotty had been used and abused by the system and those who ran the system. Now, they all lived in Incubator Street, apart from Snotty Oliver who lived with the Bishop of Stepney, being the son of the *fallen* housekeeper for the Bishop. Snotty had been used and abused in his posh knob public school, so he could relate to the Myrmidons; he shared a latent anger with his *friends*.

It is fair also to say that the Myrmidons did not know what a myrmidon was, but clever bonce and posh snotty Oliver assured them it was a cool name. It meant, Snotty had confidently expounded, warlike people of ancient Thessaly who accompanied Achilles to the Trojan wars. Well, that was good enough for them, and war was expected, wasn't it? It was talked about often, so the populace could prepare, and prepare they did.

And so it was that Flan's float took centre stage in the middle of the playground and around this gathered the only residents inside the playground, Tommy's immediate *family and close friends*: Blossom Temple, Chas Larkin, Snotty Oliver, the Rinso Kid and Mickey One-eye. Flan stood to attention beside the cab of his float his role important; well, it was to him, and he looked the part in his milkman uniform, white coat, horizontal blue and white striped apron and his bus conductor's hat; he'd lost his milkman hat. Wandering around, lonely as a cloud on this cloudless day, was Silly Boy Eric who took photos with a camera he had found that didn't work and had no film, but he thought it made him look important. The people of the area protected the boy. Now, he was safe, nearly eighteen, his abused past behind him, if it is possible to do this, he lived in relative harmony with his demons.

Eric had a minder, an equally intellectually challenged mate, 'Arry 'Orse Collar, a lad who had been at the back of the class for as long as anyone could remember, his mum sending him to school in shirts with collars too big for his scrawny neck, (*he could grow into them*), in the vain hope he might learn something, but mainly to get the boy out from under her feet. She had a living to make and her gentlemen callers didn't like to be watched, even if it was from the back of the class with photos taken by Silly Boy Eric with a camera that didn't work. She also never gave a toss when 'Arry had been taken into *care,* and this grated within the heart and soul of the boy, but now he was accepted, this new refuge given by the Larkin Saints, even if it was back living with his mum.

3

THE PRESENCE OF FLAN'S MILK FLOAT, ONCE PARKED, WAS NOT challenged, because Chas Larkin was there; Chas had a rep and serious back-up if needed. Everybody knew that.

'Fuck, he came?' Chas exclaimed on an exhaled breath, his body noticeably stiffening. He was alert anyway, and who wouldn't be, even the best of laid plans can go wrong. Chas had learned a long time ago that you never spring a trap until you are completely ready, and he had been taught by the very best since he had been taken under the wing of the Black Rose. He was ready, everyone was ready.

Blossom followed the direction of Chas's stare and offered a mumbled grumbled reaction, 'Fuck's he doin' 'ere?' Chas knew, but daren't say. However, he never expected Tanner to come; arrogance he presumed, and Tanner had it in spades.

Aside from the baking temperatures, the playground environs were already a hotbed of galvanised anger; the Church steadfastly refusing to postpone their opening ceremony arranged to suit the diaries of dignitaries, regardless of the conflict with the local funeral obsequies. The obstinate refusal of the Church to recognise the sensitivity of the situation for the local people, fuelled the resentment, the playground or school hall was the only facility available to the people of Incubator Street to use for their vigil. The undercurrents were palpable, this had to be a deliberate act of asserting power to demonstrate, yet again, that the people should know their place.

However, there were probably more dangerous feelings that lay close to the surface for the main players in this internecine pantomime, and the arrival of Tanner to join the period of observance for Tommy could be the match to set fire to this tinderbox of potential violent emotion. Tanner was convinced he was the father of Tommy. He wasn't. He didn't even care for Tommy, and it was widely believed it was he who had arranged for the gunmen, intending to kill Chas Larkin, who had tragically machine-gunned Tommy as he bounced along the street on his *space hopper*.

Chas knew for sure it was Tanner, because Ruth Golding, *bookkeeper* for the Tanner Empire, had told them so. And, in amongst these malevolent machinations was the undercurrents of the aspirations of the IRA, all of which Ruth had also informed them, which was confirmed by the Black Rose. It was all that Chas could do to restrain himself from killing Tanner right there, and he felt for his shoulder holster.

Blossom knew her man and stayed his hand from reaching into his jacket. 'Hold off, Chas. We have a plan. Let's stick to it, and isn't it like Tanner to pull a stunt like this?'

Chas knew Blossom spoke sense and he looked up to the top house windows, flicked his head to indicate the approach of Tanner, signalling no reaction required, yet. He looked to Blossom, 'Sorry. You're right,' and they both watched as Tanner sauntered to Flan's milk float, no respect and with his trademark, devil may care, broad grin on his strong Jewish face; he was enjoying the situation. Tanner cared not for the boy, but he did care for Blossom, and he cared for the East End of London.

His goal: to take Blossom from Chas Larkin and take over the East End of London territory for himself, to add to the West he already controlled.

This Chas knew. The authorities knew. What they also knew was that Tanner had enlisted the support of the George family who controlled North London, and the IRA were complicit in all of it; they supplied the funds; information thankfully supplied by Ruth, but nobody expected it so soon, and especially not while they were saying goodbye to Tommy. However, it made sense.

The old niceties, such as they were, had long disappeared. The previous respect for a grieving family a distant memory of lost times. Would this wake be the showdown? The confrontation between East and West London, even the North, that everyone could see coming, and ironically, Chas Larkin, with Maude and Bess, had *engineered* it so. However, life, or death, had intervened. Blossom's crippled son, Tommy Little Legs, beloved by all in Incubator Street, a street of villainous families who up until recently presumed to protect the boy who always had a smile and not a malicious bone in his deformed body, had just been buried.

So now what?

The danger signals were all there and the fires stoked, for it was only a week or so ago, the naked bodies of three boys, used and abused and dumped, had been found intertwined and stuck in the mud of a small tributary to the River Thames, nearby the Tower of London.

The people knew but were powerless to do anything about it. The police? What was the point? Corruption was rife, and ironically, it would fall to the Larkin Saint gangster family to sort it and they were about doing that, along with the most unlikely of allies. Combine this with a real risk of attempts to topple the Queen of the East End along with the Larkin Saint family, threats from the West, Tanner's territory, and the

Northern quadrant of London and the George family, meant that a battle *Royal* was expected, but now?

However, here was Tanner, as bold as brass walking across the playground toward Blossom and Chas, the crowds of dignitaries parting like the Red Sea; Tanner was a known villain, a dangerous man, and he would not be here if he didn't have back-up. Well, he did, because following him was the obese Queenie George, now Queenie Saint as she had married and brought with her 'Opalong Saint, her new husband.

'Chas.'

'Tanner.'

'Blossom.'

'Tanner. What the fuck you doin' 'ere?' Blossom made no show of welcome. She now addressed the approaching 'Opalong with Queenie who cast more than a metaphorical dark shadow. 'And you 'Opalong, and with yer fat slag...' It looked like Queenie was about to steamroller the occasion taking Blossom first, but 'Opalong managed to control her by passing her a sausage sandwich.

Tanner answered to break the stultifying atmosphere that could only get worse in the oppressive heat. 'Me, darlin'...? Well, I'm not 'ere for the funeral. Knew I'd not be welcome...'

'Well, you got that right,' Blossom interrupted, making no attempt to disguise her anger and hurt. 'So why are you 'ere?' and she looked to 'Opalong, trying to ignore Queenie as she had a mouth full of sausage sandwich with tomato ketchup trailing from her revolting bloated lips.

Again Tanner answered. 'Me, 'Opalong and Queenie, we're dignitaries, ain't we. Put dosh into the Youth Club and Orphanage, and it was one of my builders, twice removed of course, didn't want you sticking your club foot in and messing fings up for me, did I, Chas, and I gave 'em a good price, see.' Chas fumed, and ironically Blossom once again calmed him.

'Anyway, must dash, TTFN an' all that posh codswallop,'

Tanner said as he strode off to be greeted by first of all, Little Willie MP and then many of the other celebrities in the safe space between the stage and the barrier. He waved to the crowd and they cheered back. 'Opalong waved and Queenie wiped her hand down the side of her bell tent dress.

'Well, I didn't see that coming,' Chas said to Blossom. 'I think we should call our people in and talk things through.' Blossom agreed and the small gathering around Flan's milk van left the playground, except Flan. He stayed. He had a job to do and he knew how to keep a secret; this was his time.

4

*The unlikely first line of defence: The Myrmidons -
friendships and allies - Mickey One-eye, The Rinso Kid,
Blossom Temple, Silly Boy Eric, Snotty Oliver and Co and,
Flan Milkman.*

THE MYRMIDONS? WHAT THIS COHORT HAD IN COMMON WAS
that in the past, as a disparate group of misfit children, used
and abused themselves and surviving on the street, they helped
Chas Larkin in his young life as a cripple, half-blind and seriously bullied runt.

Many a time these comrades in survival would squirrel
Chas away in the bombed-out ruins of the East End of London
to prevent yet another beating from Mickey Saint, his playground and street, gangland tormentor, or from Chas's cruel
mother. Apart from maybe one or two, even his teachers offered
him no respite, piling on the pain, both physical and emotional,
and encouraging just about anyone else who fancied a pop at a
defenceless cowering boy, to fill their boots. And, in a roundabout way, this motley *gang* of hopeless nobodies, escaping into
living in their own world of make-believe heroes, compatriots,

acting for the greater good all to help Chas Larkin, would save London in 1969. Maybe with just a little help from MI5, and not forgetting the Black Rose, of course.

There was Mickey One-eye, who played marbles with his glass eye. A lanky, skinny streak of gnat's piss who was never short of friends, the curiosity alone enough to attract followers. However, his best mate, though of necessity distant, The Rinso Kid, was relegated to the sidelines. He stank to high heaven and even in this part of the deprived East End of London in 1957, the ragged, rancid lad, equally as tall, though more bloated than Mickey One-eye, and named, ironically, after the washing powder, *Rinso*, was a pariah. Discouraged from being a musketeer, Rinso had to settle for being Cardinal Richelieu, although he only had a ragged cowboy suit, black with sparkly bits and knotted tassels. He said he was Cardinal Cisco Kid, but he was fooling nobody. However, from the quarantined sidelines, Rinso played with those kids who had robust stomachs and one of those was Blossom, *I'll show yer me knickers for a penny*, Temple; soft heart, this girl, and destined for beauty.

Standing aside, but most definitely an associate of the tripartite of friendship, was Snotty Oliver, the posh kid. What this Lord Snooty, hale there, well met old bean and all of that posh tosh, was doing in Stepney, was a set of circumstances that would be the stuff of a Dickens novel, and equally believable. Suffice to say, Snotty's mother, Lady Clarissa Owseyfather, had divorced the Lord Bernard Owseyfather, and in an acrimonious settlement, which meant being left with nothing as Bernard had taken it all when he disappeared with Boozy, his erstwhile bedfellow when at Eton, Snotty's mum had ended up as the Housekeeper to the suffragan Bishop of Stepney. The Bishop had tenuous connections with Clarissa via the Archbishop of Canterbury where she was at one time assistant to the keeper of the Episcopalian bikes and robes, her brother being Sir Sturmey Archer, who supplied the gears for the Bishopric bicycles and accessories such as mitre cycle hats and handlebar shopping baskets. So, Clarissa fitted in well, even though she had not a fucking clue about how to run a household, but she could mend a puncture in the Bishop's new *Raleigh RRA Moderne, FM triple speed*, in seconds flat and without tyre levers, simply with judicious use of her oversized equine false teeth.

Lady Clarissa was, though, more powerful than even her impressive cycling pedigree would suggest. She had been, and some said still was, the Archbishop of Canterbury and York's Appointments Secretary, the keeper of the *Appointments List,* sometimes known as the *Oven-ready list.* It was she, *the power behind the throne,* who recommended the next Bishop in line for ascendancy, and her current boss and casual bed fellow, Spiffy Smiffy of Stepney, aspired to be Bishop of London and as everyone knew, if your face did not fit, or in this case your ability to satisfy the rapacious Lady Clarissa in carnal gratification and pedal interests, then you had no hope of rising to the stratosphere within the Church of England. Stepney Smiffy could and did do both, so likely, he would, though his proclivities were more wide-ranging than Clarissa's fat arse, so it might be best to not talk about a fondness for the bathing of small boys that he saw as sanctimonious caring; for them?

The Bishop of Stepney being a renowned miserly cleric, Snotty Oliver was therefore no longer at boarding school, where he would have been nurtured with cold baths, buggery and flogging, and thus groomed for the Establishment hierarchy, he now was left to fend for his education in Incubator Street School and on the dodgy cockney streets of the East End of London; the Bishop and his housekeeper were compelled to live in the Borough of Tower Hamlets, Stepney. This Bishopric posting and residence did, however, suit the Bishop's desire to accommodate the shared penchants of his powerful chums, along with many other big kahunas, who had a keen interest in the local Boys Clubs, but that would be another matter. Lady

Clarissa was broad-minded in her views on the Bishop's friends and their perversions, and she was determined to get her Smiffy into the Bishop of London's Palace; she was on her way back up the Church of England slippery pole. Clarissa was single-minded, and nothing would stop her.

The trinity of musketeers, Blossom, Mickey and Snotty Oliver, with the malodorously distant Rinso as Cardinal Stinklieu (he had to eschew the Cisco Kid epithet as someone had nicked his titfer tat, hat), therefore grew up together suffering the abuse as a part of their lives and in sublime ignorance of the poverty and the squalor in which they lived, apart from Snotty, of course. Oliver just grew up in ignorance, being what in posh circles would be known as an aristocratic divine puerility, apart from his knowledge of the classics, Greek history in particular. Totally acceptable in amongst the landed gentry and well to do, but in the East End of London, he was considered several sandwiches short of a bucket and spade day out, not that any of his newly established cockney fellows had been to the seaside to need a bucket and spade, and most thought Cannes was what peas came in.

Snotty did, however, have a novel persona, a posh appearance which included a top hat, and as a consequence, and in this district in which he was compelled to live, the kids used to enjoy trying to knock his *titfer-tat* off and punch his goofy *Hampstead Heaths* straight, as is the way of many tooth fairy street bullies, whilst he haughtily allowed his eyes to be continually elevated, thus making his snooty fireman's hose, a sitting duck.

The D'Artagnan, to the three musketeers and older than the other kids in his street, his mum getting a tad carried away on VE day with a series of Yank sailors up from Portsmouth, was Flan Flummery, not that he truly realised the importance of his role or his destiny. As a schoolboy, Flan, when he was not in and out of the *homes for boys,* was a known dipstick, but lovable with it, and he had aspirations which impressed the muske-teers, especially Blossom, and from a suitably aromatic distance, Rinso.

Flan wanted to be a milkman, and his dad, before he was found upside down in the mud of the banks of the Thames, because he played with the naughty boys and had transgressed the unwritten law, had taught Flan how to whistle. It should be noted that it is widely thought that it was Flan's mum, *what did 'im in*, though the police considered this was another act by the White Tide man. Whatever the case, whistling was an art Flan practiced, even when he was suffering in the care homes. It was a form of discordant musical denial. He would whistle and juggle empty milk bottles whenever he could, suffering painful punishments when he smashed them. Whistling kept Flan sane if he couldn't have a go of Mickey's eye, that is.

Everybody, whoever they were or whatever they wanted to be, thug, docker, bishop, milkman, gangster, at that young age, or any age in the Church if it involved getting on your hands and knees to be with the little boys, wanted a go of Mickey's eye. Except for Blossom, she didn't play marbles but she often would say to Mickey, "Give us a lick of yer eye, Mickey, go on, just a little lick." Mickey was reluctant, as Blossom was want to take the eyeball into her mouth like a gobstopper and he would have to chase her to get it back, which, with only one eye, drainpipe ricket-ridden legs that bowed and went in different directions, and flat feet, proved a difficult task. One time he had caught her, and as he grabbed and pulled her back by the collar of her liberty bodice, she swallowed it. He had to call at Blos-som's *Home for Wayward Girls* and ask matron to wait for it to *show*, preferably give it a wash in *Dettol* and, by and by, after a big bowl of rhubarb, prunes, and an efficacious laxative custard, Mickey got his eye back, and for a time the left side of his head had a distinct aroma, not unlike the Rinso Kid.

What all of these Myrmidons had in common was they had

been used and abused in the system. They each dealt with it in their own way, but some were more damaged than others, possibly because they had not the nous or wherewithal to find an outlet for their emotional baggage, but it was there, simmering.

However, along with Blossom's baby, the result of a rape by a local priest and not a by-blow of Tanner, Tommy was born with stunted legs as a result of the *Thalidomide* drug, and these kids and Flan shared a destiny, along with the crippled runt Chas Larkin, who apart from the little gang of outsiders, nobody associated with and with whom he had never played marbles. Because, together, with the help of a few other well-placed police and spies, they would deal a blow on the *establishment* of London, a wake-up call at the very least.

5

Thursday, 12th June 1969

BEN DOONE WAS A NIGHT WATCHMAN ON A BUILDING SITE IN THE City of London. When his shift finished in the early hours of the morning, he liked to walk to his home in Wapping along the north bank of the Thames, a small detour to round the Tower of London, to appreciate the ancient massive structure and the history attached. He had lived all his life in this part of London and appreciated the view of *his* river through the seasons. He loved the early morning summer mist magically hovering the still water of the Thames. This was a treacherous river, its current lay underneath, and if anything was dumped, bodies for instance, as the tide turned out it would likely take them out to sea, never to be seen again.

In this early summer morning, already the heat was building, burning off the shimmering haze, and as he passed a little tributary to the Thames he saw something that grabbed his attention. When he peered more closely, leaning upon a hefty greenheart timber post that formed a part of a jetty, he saw three naked bodies, children, tangled together and caught up in the mud and piled maze. Someone had tried to dispose of the bodies, this he intuitively knew, but clearly they had not understood the tidal patterns. Was this ignorance or hubris? Would it come back to haunt those despicable people?

Yes, it would.

Would the police react to find out what happened? No, they wouldn't, and Ben, after spending two hours in the police station in Wapping, had agreed that due to the morning mist, he had likely seen dead seals, not children.

Maude and Bess.

Bess struggled to wake Maude. She demonstrably looked at her watch; they had a meet planned with Chas and here was the woman she loved, flat out, almost comatose. Jeez, how much had she had to drink last night, Bess thought to herself as she blew a gentle breath into Maude's ear. This she knew always tantalised her wife. It did and Maude revealed that she had only been playing, luring Bess into a clinch and planting a booze-drenched kiss upon her wife's lips. Far from being revolted, Bess returned the embrace of her lover. She considered, as she always did the thinking for Maude, yes, they may have time. She was in Maude's hands as she was always. Bess was submissive, in the bedroom at least, and enjoyed the dominance of her hot-headed gorgeous lover.

Outside the bedroom, Bess provided the clarity of intelligent thought for the Saint Larkin family, and it was upon this reasoning that the local people depended because everyone knew that unchecked, Maude Larkin was dangerous to anyone who crossed her path; she was even known to go out of her way to wreak perceived retribution. Bess was entering the third trimester of her pregnancy, and in this building hot summer she was regularly discomforted, but she could never resist the attentions of her sometimes severe and dominant partner. She loved Maude and always had since their school days together; they ran Incubator school, and Maude reciprocated that love in equal measure.

'My love, can you tell me, please, what have you planned?' Bess whispered into Maude's ear. This was important to her and had felt out of the loop, weighed down with her distended belly.

Maude flipped to *red alert*. She may be dominant in a shared and accepting way in their sexual union, and Maude truly loved Bess; however, outside of their sex games, it was Bess who ruled the nest. 'Planned, darlin'?'

Bess demurred, her peaches-and-cream face with rose-tipped blushes and strawberry lips pouting. 'Yes, sweet'ums'

Fuck, Maude thought, "sweet'ums". This did not bode well. She had to admit that she sometimes struggled to keep up with Bess and rarely if ever could discern her thinking, especially within the domestic scene. In the villainous machinations, Bess always explained in simple terms what was what, so there could be no mistake, but here, in the bedroom and their family life, Bess seemed to take pleasure in torturing Maude psychologically. 'Planned? I have no idea what you're talking about, sweet love?' and she drew Bess into an embrace that her beautiful partner resisted.

Pushing Maude's lean and athletic body away from her own, more fulsome frame, but taking time to show how much she admired the look of her lover. 'It's just that in my condition...' and she took Maude's hands and smoothed them over her swollen belly, '... I need time to prepare, you know?' Maude didn't, and worried her face displayed confusion. 'Oh, my darlin' Maude, I do love the way you tease me...' Maude leaned in and kissed Bess, which she hoped concealed a tight grin, knowing Bess was all seeing in matters of intimate exchanges, all of which Maude struggled with. 'Maude...?' The kiss exchanged, Bess could tell by the stiffness of Maude's lips that her lover hadn't a clue as to what she talked about. '... I suppose... yes, it's a surprise, eh?' and Bess offered her lover a coquettish sloping head.

Maude thought to herself, Gawd blimey, she loved this woman and wanted to ravish her, maybe even a little spanking as retribution for teasing her, but settled on a safe answer knowing the Chas meeting and the timing of this meet was critical, *life and death* important. Allowing her straightened lips to curve into a smile. 'Sweet'art, please don't spoil the surprise. Now, get dressed, we don't want to be late for Chas, and tonight, maybe I will have to give you a seeing to...?'

'Oh, my lovely, I hope you will because I intend to be naughty today...' and Bess winked, and despite her condition, she leapt spryly from the bed and raced to the bathroom. She knew Maude would let her win, and she felt excited for their anniversary surprise on Midsummer's night, the anniversary of when they consummated their *marriage* back in 1966.

Maude watched her beautiful wife disappear into the bathroom and thought she would redden that glorious bottom tonight, but what the fuck was she going on about? More subtle probing may be needed. Can Maude do subtle?

6

The melting pot - early summer 1969:

THE IRISH TROUBLES WERE ACRIMONIOUS BUT DISTANT TO A British populace who were, on the whole, politically unengaged. *The Irish troubles?* A decorous and British nomenclature that served to play down the reality of a situation; the people need not be disturbed with thoughts of political revolution or resistance, lest they get ideas? And in this, the news media complied. In London, the early summer temperatures built, close to boiling. There was nothing to worry about, was there?

There was at least no rioting on the streets, but in Northern Ireland, the campaign to end discrimination against the minority Catholic population, whose polarised thoughts were often inaccurately ascribed as wanting unity with the Republic of Ireland, was certainly an aphorism promulgated by the press and the protestant majority. However, first and foremost, the Catholics wanted fair rights, but this was resisted violently by the Protestant majority whose mainstay and justification seemed to be for maintaining the status quo, Unity with the

34

United Kingdom, and with that came their control of the province of the six counties.

A pogrom it wasn't, at first. It was about political dominance, but the fanning of the flames of discontent had the makings of it becoming fratricidal. The mutual arrogance of the political leaders risked precipitating the destruction of both communities in a bloodbath, a war that could easily be hijacked for more obvious underlying reasons, depending upon your denomination, religion: unity of all Ireland or to maintain the union with the UK, and no longer about *Human Rights*.

Things had become a tinderbox since the civil rights marches in October of the previous year, but it had been brewing long before this, and undercover of this unrest it was widely held that the IRA would take a campaign to the mainland of the UK, in particular London. However, the initiative in Britain, in its infancy, had been snuffed out in 1966 when sources of finance and supply of arms and materiel, by unscrupulous manufacturers and bankers, was violently closed down. Despite this, it was only a matter of time before other means of supply would take over, it being the nature of the game, namely money and the ability to make lots of it off the backs of the suffering of ordinary people as they react to the increasingly jingoistic claims.

In London, the East End had the docks, for import and export. It also had immediate proximity to the City of London and the financial Institutions of Great Britain, wherein the money men rarely had the greater good at heart, and it was known that there would be no compunction in funding both sides of any conflict. It was again the way of things and always had been. With conflict came opportunities.

Thus the irony, whatever side you were on in Ireland, you had an incentive to close down the money sources, and this was thought to be a principal preoccupation of the IRA, in that they were thought to have secured funding from America; the descendants of Irish exiles saw something romantic in funding death and destruction in the name of freedom, insurrection in the *Auld Country*. Maybe they had a point, but at what cost? And, they were far away from any consequences, but still they sang the songs in the safety of their American *Irish* bars.

There were, however, two sides of the coin of patriotism, profit and deadly romance, and both were already crushing the ordinary peace-loving people of Ireland. But it was happening a long way away, such was the perception of the people of England, and in particular, Londoners, who could not comprehend the enmity felt. The republican resistance to their former *oppressive rulers*, and all of the hurt that had historically become an assiduous bile that still etched the lining of an Irishman's stomach, which ironically, was grist to the mill for the power brokers. Especially so as their battle for Independence had been only partially successful, thwarted in the North, the Six Counties annexed by the British as Independence was reluctantly ceded to Eire.

Although the vast majority of the Irish people wanted peace, the British government chose not to see this, and in April 1969 troops arrived in Northern Ireland to reinforce the police. In some circles, it could be seen that quelling an uprising in Northern Ireland would be a lesson to the working man and woman in the United Kingdom, who had always been repressed. It would not do for the British people to take a leaf from the Irish book and rise up and take back the country from the establishment. The troops were there to *enforce* the status quo, not to resolve any differences. No political solution was *openly* sought.

There were, though, politicians, individuals, Irish and British, forever looking for a peaceful solution, the hurt to the innocent being unacceptable. Except that would not be good business, so the fires needed to be stoked to balance the peace movement and peace-mongers. While accord was being violently fought for in the Northern Ireland streets, the campaign for negotiation continued, and it was a dangerous business; the green of old Ireland separated from the William of Orange by the white of truce and a desire to live in *unified* peace; this was the republican flag.

Yet it is an unavoidable reality that dystopia offers so much for the unscrupulous and the fires of jingoism, on both sides, can be easily aroused by those wishing to profit, and never more so if the fight came to mainland England; it was expected. Patriotic songs were sung in the London pubs, and *patriots* were recruited.

And the Churches? Because this was seen by many to be a religious conflict as much as anything: Catholic versus Protestant. The Churchmen had peace as a priority, surely? You would think so, but that would be to underestimate the nature of man, whether dressed in a frock or a dog collar, power was power, mammon was ungodly but lucrative, and eschewing vows offered up more power, albeit veiled.

———

While the factions squabbled, a reality dawned. There was to be a dire consequent fall-out for the ordinary person on the Clapham Omnibus, who were now vulnerable. Who would fight the good fight in Britain? Troops were deployed in Northern Ireland, another Imperialist hammer to crash down on a political anvil, and the resounding clanging clamber will this time be heard in Britain; it was just a matter of time.

And what of MI5? Yes, of course, and anti-terrorist units in the Metropolitan Police were aware, intelligencers learning on the job of the new threat, and this time it was domestic and artfully Machiavellian. Special Branch was originally called the *Special Irish Branch* and was formed in 1883 to combat what was then known as the *Irish Brotherhood*; in all but name, counter espionage. Even so, all of these organisations were about dealing with the fall-out and not particularly effectively putting out fires, and never looking to solve a chronic problem, or at least ameliorate the consequences until a political solution could be secured.

The answer has always to be political, but those brave people prepared to talk had not only the radical forces of alternate violent factions to deal with, they had a greater enemy: The Establishment, and that included the Church. The voice of reason, though, always came from women, but their voices, apart from one or two, were suffocated. One day, women would rise to the power positions and not because they acted like men, but because they acted like empathetic and caring women – the true *Mothers of the Nation*.

7

The Royal London Hospital – Whitechapel – the mortuary:

PROFESSOR BRIAN CHARNEL LEANED INTO THE CHINA-WHITE mortuary table, the spidery threads of blood still evident after he had completed the autopsies on the three dead children. It sickened him and not just the waste of life, he dealt with that daily, it was what had been done to them. His guess, the children were no more than eight years old, it was almost always difficult to say: malnourished, used and abused, evidence of regular beatings. He buried, as he always did, any self-recrimination into his burgeoning and secret conscience because he knew his report would be lost and the children's bodies disposed of, never to be seen again. They were orphans and had no family, at least none that knew of their whereabouts, no longer able to protect their children and nobody to mourn them. They were the disappeared. He should be their representative in death, but he couldn't be. He was afraid to be. He knew only too well that he could not fight the establishment, and in his mind, this was an even bigger crime than his cooperation in the never-ending and long-running cover-up.

As he stared into nothingness, he waited, expecting a visit. Goons sent to take the bodies and to ensure that there was only one copy of his minimal report, and they would take that after which the children no longer existed or had ever existed. His only sense of righteous salvation was that he did do two copies, every time, and the second one was in more detail, and these he hid at his home. Not in his study because this would be where, after his death, people would look. He hid them in the airing cupboard, a secreted panel behind the immersion heater. His dilemma? Who could he tell? Who could he trust to collect the papers and to broadcast what had been happening and enforce the changes that were needed? To make the arrests? To break up the syndicated diabolical secret organisations? Who would stop these terrible crimes against children that were so insidiously a part of a corrupt establishment culture in the East End of London? And who would protect his family when or if his revelations were made public?

Brian Charnel glanced up from the blood of the children, his unholy stare of shame, and looked into the cream and bottle green glazed tiles of this old mortuary. He had worked virtually all of his professional life, some forty years, in these cold rooms. He should be able to reflect with pride, but he couldn't. He looked down at the black quarry tile floor and this to him seemed to represent the depth of his mortification and self-hatred. He heard the familiar squeak of the double doors and his heartrate dropped several beats. He coughed his heart back into action, at least for the time being; how much longer did he have? His hacking, cancer-ridden lungs provided him with a moment of respite, not for life, but from facing up the *collection team,* and he was surprised to hear a female voice, delicate and with a hint of an accent, and if he had to guess, it would be Middle Eastern?

'Professor Charnel...?'

Charnel could not resist turning, and he was faced with a

tall and stunningly beautiful woman with a clearly defined caste that had his guess of accent proven. 'Yes?' he answered, questioning, checking his coughing fit, temporarily sucking in the disinfectant-deodorised air, a smell so familiar to him. The woman wore a white coat; she was a doctor. He relaxed. This was safe and familiar territory, surely? 'You are?'

'Dr Naadhira Khalidi, Professor, though people call me Dr Nadia.' She was matter of fact, which defied the softness in her voice. 'Are you still smoking?'

A medical question, and Brian Charnel knew that this intelligent-looking woman had heard his coughing fit, taken in the yellowing pallor of his prematurely aged, paper-thin skin, appearing older even than his sixty odd years, and worked out that he was not long for this world. 'Not much point now...' he drawled out with his precious breath.

'Hmmm...' Dr Nadia responded whilst turning her head to take in the look of the bodies of the three children and sighing, '... I presume they are to be collected soon?' Professor Charnel nodded and hung his head once again in remorse that he sensed Dr Nadia could see. 'And your reports?' Charnel waved a sheaf of three foolscap papers, dreadfully light for such a heavy event. 'Just the one copy?' Charnel again lifted his gaze to really take a look at this woman, to look into her penetrating dark brown eyes. Was she sent to see if she could smoke out of him if he did keep other records? 'Professor, you can trust me,' she added, but knew he lived in fear, and for the sake of his family after he died, he would need to be circumspect.

'Yes, just the one copy,' he confirmed, for the sake of his family.

'Okay, I understand, but I hope to be able to prove to you that you can trust me, and that I can introduce you to police officers you can rely upon, but in the meantime, I understand you would want to maintain a facade of cooperation, okay?' she said. Charnel had no choice but to insist he had only one copy, and he offered it to Dr Nadia. She took the papers, flicked through them before returning them to the professor; one page for each child and woefully inadequate. 'Thank you, but you will need these for when they come to take the bodies, I presume?'

Again the professor read this as a subtle ruse, an attractive lady looking to entrap him. 'You are not here to take the bodies then?'

'No, professor. I am here to build a relationship of trust because I have seen maltreated children regularly in casualty and could not fail to notice that my reports of abuse to the police are never taken up, after which the paperwork conveniently disappears. I heard of the three bodies you have...' and she glanced to the children, '... I see all, and when you are ready, come to me. Nobody else, please. And there is no need to acknowledge, except knowing your reputation as I do, I suspect your duplicate reports contain more information as to your conclusions and possibly as to who might be responsible, but one step at a time.' And at this, Dr Nadia turned on her toes and left, the familiar squeak of the doors this time offering the professor a little comfort. He needed to do some thinking, but first of all, he should make discreet enquiries as to who this Doctor Naadhira Khalidi is.

———

Wendy Richards – consultant psychiatrist – The Royal London Hospital – Whitechapel

After leaving the mortuary, Nadia headed to see her friend and colleague, Wendy Richards. She climbed the stairs from the basement to the second floor and walked the maze of corridors in the old building, collecting her thoughts; she had many, and none were comforting. She had counselled that she would talk them all through with Wendy, not just because they were friends and shared innermost thoughts, but because Wendy's partner, Detective Sergeant Flora Wade, was the working partner of her man, Detective Inspector Padraig Casey.

It was not exactly an incestuous relationship, the four of them, but the friendship had created a formidably expert team: Wendy, a psychiatrist, was developing research into the underworld of the East End of London, especially the relationship of the poor people with the gangs and how they relate to the authorities. A lot of Wendy's research was based initially around Chas Larkin as she had been involved by Nadia to help Chas as a young lad out of a life of serial abuse and violence.

Wendy stayed in the East End, she said, to be with her lover, DS Flora Wade, a born-and-bred cockney, her father an impressive and hefty East End docker and her mother, a more delicate Maltese woman. This made for an odd couple, Flora, a dusky robust beauty, a woman who had made her way in the misogynist police force, now into CID and eventually incorporated into MI5, whereas Wendy had the appearance of a flaky and flouncing ditsy blonde. However, this façade of flightiness disguised a powerful intellect, and she was more than a match for Flora Wade when it was required.

Dr Nadia was a trauma doctor and a surgeon, with more than enough experience of prejudice and violence, her family having been driven from their home in Palestine by the Israeli government. She and her parents had found a new home in Britain, and she had repaid that kindness by qualifying as a doctor and dedicating her resourcefulness to the poor people of the East End, paying back a debt of honour. Nadia had been on casualty duty when Chas Larkin, a boy presumed to be fourteen or fifteen at the time, had been brought in after a particularly brutal assault on him by his mother. Chas had been the runt of a litter of six children and suffered bullying from both the rival gang of the Saints as well as his own family.

Nadia operated to save his eyesight and eventually had corrected his club foot but was insistent Wendy Richards counsel the lad as he had lived a life of almost continual abuse and trauma, physically and mentally. Slowly, after three years, Wendy had worked wonders with the now debonair, in a dangerous way, young man. Chas was beginning to open up and, as a consequence of growth and trust, was becoming a mine of information that convinced the psychiatrist that there was valuable research data to be had by staying in this deprived part of London, as well as Flora, naturally.

However, the building of the relationship of Chas Larkin with the enigmatic Irish detective, Padraig Casey, had helped Chas gain not only some self-esteem, but most importantly, violent vengeance on not only the Saints, but also many of his own Larkin family. *See, Black Rose – A Midsummer Night's Chutzpah*

Chas Larkin, with the assistance of Casey and MI5, had not only exacted his vengeance, he had formed a new family, visibly led by his cousin Maude Larkin and her lover, Bess Saint. This established not a new gangland presence, but a modified one, and one that provided not only a service to MI5 and Scotland Yard but also, for form, a *benign* gang, a *controlling* presence. Obviously, there had to be regular villainy to keep up appearances, but essentially the Larkin Saint family worked for the good of the people, and Chas Larkin was the discreet head of the organisation.

At the same time, Padraig Brendan Casey, known as Paddy to those few he allowed this intimacy, had fallen head over heels in love with Dr Nadia; not an easy relationship, although the love was reciprocated by Nadia. The expected tensions of a Muslim woman and a Roman Catholic copper / spook, notwithstanding, it was for Nadia, the dark deeds that Paddy involved himself in, not least of which he was not a Casey, but an O'Neill, that she steadfastly refused to marry this will-of-the-wisp Irishman whom she more than half thought was an IRA operative. However, they did live as man and wife, except when Nadia kicked him out to sleep on Flora and Wendy's couch, always to take him back when he had learned his lesson and revealed a little more of himself.

And this was the powerful composite and unlikely quartet, with Chas Larkin as the sore thumb of unknown quantity. A force for good or evil? Or just out for himself? However, there was no doubt his love of Blossom Temple moderated the underlying malevolent personality that was Chas Larkin.

And then there was Roisin Dubh (pronounced Rosheen Dove), the Black Rose. A mythical Irish Valkyrie or an O'Neill? Another force for good, or was it evil? Whatever, Roisin was a force, and that of a guardian angel for Chas Larkin.

8

GANGLAND LONDON – WHO RULES?

DYSTOPIA RULED UNDER THE GUISE OF PEACE. BUT HOW? To understand this you need to understand the underlying structure of the London gangland underworld and the power struggles therein:

The Queens:

Four Queens, four territories, one true crown. Four Queens, four missions: peace, power, territory and, love, or was it empathy? Each had a crown, only one had *the jewel in the crown*: the East End of London. Why was this arguably the poorest quarter of London so important, so desired? To understand this, you also have to understand the motives for wanting to keep or take the East End crown, and the interested power brokers.

The Queenmakers:

There is always someone or some organisation behind any powerful public figure. In the past they were called the King-makers. In London, at this time, they were known as Queenmakers, the matriarchal lines all-powerful in London families. So, what was the motivation? Power? Obviously, but some saw their position as a perceived right, by dint of inheritance that the family had ruled in, for instance, the East End, for so many years that it became more than just folklore; it was a reality.

Or because *Pretenders* to a cherished throne could muster gangland muscle to assert a perceived right to install their own Queen, or King, but gangs such as these always needed funding.

Or, in an existential way, a *Pretender* had backing offshore and needed the East End docks with the proximity to the City of London, the country's commercial heart, in order to launch attacks on Britain. They could fund a family and install their own compliant Leader; the docks would be theirs.

Or the *Pretender* could just want to make things better for the poor, the disenfranchised and, in one particular case, the orphaned and abused girls. To make their lives better with an agenda to slowly, inexorably, produce natural female heirs, *Queens*, to overtake the male-dominated Establishment. The irony in this case was that this particular Queen, *the head*, was the very essence of the establishment, an aristocrat, and she ruled immune from prosecution from within a Royal Peculiar.

Who would win would likely depend on allies or pacts, but trust was ephemeral and could prove deadly if relied upon, and there were some men who aspired to be Kings. Would that be possible? Acceptable?

———

The players.

Mother:

A new mother Superior was appointed to the Convent of the Sisters of Clemence, in the City of London, not far from London Bridge. The Mother was Lady Adelaide Pimple. Always, the Mother Superior was taken from the ancient aristocratic *Famille Pimple*. It was their birthright, and always a daughter would be provided. Adelaide, the name came from German roots and meant the Noble One, and she was all of that, a strong woman on a mission to set her Convent on course to educate young women and seed them into the establishment power base.

Secret Squirrel:

Detective Inspector Padraig Brendon Casey (*aka* Paddy O'Neill, *but that was a secret*) and his Bagman, Detective Sergeant Flora Wade, worked out of Arbour Square police station, Stepney. On the door of their broom cupboard office, just off the main CID hall, was the title, *Aunty Terrorist Unit*. The famed East End cockney wit? Yes, though more often than not, Casey and Wade were elsewhere in the city; *ours not to reason why*, the CID motto? It could be because Casey and Wade had not only been complicit in the destruction of the powerbase of the Saint and Larkin gangland families on their manor, they had also destroyed the O'Rierdon gang out of the West of London and, in the interim three years, sent packing, Tanner, the would be Pretender to the crown of the East End: a *King*.

Tanner and the West:

Tanner licked his wounds, and with his tail between his legs, he took up residence in Kilburn in the West of London, where he began to fill the vacuum left by the O'Rierdon family. He nursed his pride, nurtured his anger and desire for vengeance. He would have a war and he considered his chances were best served in an alliance, an enjoined rivalry with the George family, relatively newly established in Tottenham, North London. Tanner saw the George family's ambitions to increase their manor to incorporate the East End as his *subtle* key to opening the door to the East End for himself.

The Georges:

The George family, it seemed, wanted total control, but that was not possible. Tanner saw this, knew it would be too big a territory for one family, especially a new-kid-on-the-block gang. However, he considered he would allow these aspirations, and even support the proposed coup as it suited his own ambitions. He had no interest in the West, except it provided him contact with the Irish populace, and in particular the IRA. For Tanner, the West and the North mattered only as a bridgehead for his own aspirations, to regain first and foremost, a particular cockney sparrow woman, the love of his life, and to wreak vengeance on the newly formed alliance of the Larkins and Saints and in particular, Chas Larkin.

A Deadly Alliance:

So you could say there were two wars coming: The Georges from the North and Tanner from the West, but there was a third and more deadly risk coming from the IRA, and they also saw an opportunity by encouraging a fratricidal conflict between the three territories. To encourage this they funded Tanner with an acceptance that he pass funds onto the George family. The IRA needed the East End under their control, whoever won the gangland battle, knowing they would never have the support from the current East End family, run by Bess Saint and Maude Larkin, because the head of the organisation, though discreet in his presence, was Chas Larkin, and he had the even more discreet help from MI5.

A power conundrum:

A conundrum, the O'Neill family. Not much was known of them except they exerted a malevolent and Irish presence, and most of all, it was thought that the Black Rose, a mythical Irish Valkyrie, supported the O'Neills. The IRA, although comfortable in their innate support in the West, Kilburn in particular being the home of Irish exiles, whichever family ruled, they knew it was the East End that would be the jewel in the crown for whoever won the war. The IRA needed safe access to the docks for importing and warehousing their weaponry, and as a secure base for the attacking proximity of the City of London, the business heart of Britain. However, it was in the East End that the O'Neills asserted their ethereal presence, supported, or so it is now openly remarked, by the Black Rose.

Religion:

And what of the Churches? Catholic? Church of England? Was this a more subtle war for the *hearts and minds* of the *People*? Or *Avarice and enrichment*? Another power struggle, another war? And who funded them?

Four wars, forewarned:

It was a prophecy oft talked about, but most could only see three, but there was a fourth and it was a war of kindness, although a little ruthless streak never hurt to move things along a bit, at least Mother Adelaide, of the Convent of the Sisters of Clemence, thought so.

———

Wars, what are they good for? 1969:

Pax Vivendum – we must live in peace. If only, but then power mongers ruthlessly ignore the peoples' desire to live a peaceful tranquil life. Ironically, in the East End, peace did reign, although currently the Queen was a *tad* volatile. A tad? Maybe the maintenance of peace wore heavily on the crowned head of Queen Maude, an instinctively violent gangster. It certainly seemed that way now, and this perceived implosion was observed with relish by Tanner and the Georges. Could this be their chance? To capitalise on confusion?

The alliance of the Larkin and Saint gangland families, formed back in 1966, held in check this notoriously violent area of East London. People during this period now lived their lives relatively unmolested, at least not in so much fear as they were historically accustomed to. The area prospered. The people prospered. Sadly, by some this was seen as a weakness, making it a vulnerable target, for *nature abhors a violent vacuum* and attracts the crazy mixed-up thinking of prospective Kings and Kingmakers. The prime territory, it seemed, was ripe for the taking, but what of the authorities? Well, they had their hands full with the threat from the IRA that had been shown to be real in 1966, snuffed out, ironically, with the help of the Larkin Saint alliance with the strangest of bedfellows, MI5.

The East was a controlled peace, unlike that which reigned in the North and West of the city wherein the powerbase was unclear; challengers surfaced, needing to be beaten down, but for the time being Tanner ran the West and the George family, the North. The South was never thought to represent a threat; it was separated by the River Thames and they had their own issues that never threatened the turf of East, North and West. Maybe this was changing? Tanner, the closest challenger was about forming a southern defensive bridgehead that could at any time become a springboard to attack the East. And now, Maude Larkin was showing that she had gone bonkers; to all who observed, she definitely had her eye off the ball. The way was open sooner than most felt possible.

War was expected:

It would not be a war like the one that decimated the East End and the boroughs south of the river, areas that still bore the scars of the blitz. Recovery was slow, but then it would be; there was money to be made renting out bomb-damaged hovels by unscrupulous landlords who had acquired properties from families who were either killed in the bombing or finished off if they resisted. Areas were slowly being cleared with new homes and business premises constructed, but still, the poorer neighbourhoods of London remained a tableau of devastation and a nest of racketeer vipers.

Terrorism was expected:

To be played out on the streets of London in a more artful and specifically targeted way, what form would the terrorism take? If you lived in the capital city, it seemed that the threat of the IRA was chicken feed compared to the rise of the gangs in West London with tentacles spreading south of the river. Perhaps even more worrying was the threat from North London where the *upstart* George family were beginning to become entrenched, all *pretenders* dispensed with, and they made no secret of their aspirations for the East End. They posed a real threat to the stability of the East End and possibly the recently *cleansed* West.

War had always been expected:

It was the way of life for street gangs and those gangs who had built empires in amongst the blitzkrieg territories they had claimed. Always there would be a *Pretender* to the throne and those people, behind the scenes, who saw themselves as *King or Queenmaker*. It meant that intelligence was key in survival and the Larkin and Saint families, who had been controllers of the East End for more than fifty years, had a network of sources that had always enabled them to be one step ahead of any threat, even more so since Chas Larkin, Maude and Bess, had cleared the families of, for want of a better expression, dead wood; at any rate, they were now dead.

Rationally thinking, it was the other quarters of London that had the instability. These quarters not having had a ruling presence for any extended amount of time, but when has that ever stood in the way of violent ambition? And now, it looked like the East End was being disrupted by the chaotic and violent behaviour of the Queen herself, Maude Larkin. Off the rails? It certainly looked that way.

Intelligence is key:

The State had a structure of covert Intelligencers to source threats, along with experienced operatives to build strategies to deal with those threats. MI6 for foreign intelligence and MI5 for domestic intelligence; spies, honed in skills to deal with any perceived peril, to sense the auguries.

The Catholic Church also had a hush-hush structure known as VI6 (Vatican Foreign Intelligence*) and they shared information with the domestic spooks.

Scotland Yard had their own specialist officers that grew in

---

* *See Dead No More*

strength and influence, known simply as Special Branch. This acted for the police force as an anti-terrorist unit and they had seen over the past few years how the street tensions in London had been subtly manipulated to provide a position stable enough and well-resourced enough, to launch attacks at the Establishment.

Even the thought that these interloping forces would use the street gangs as their allies was something that had been considered and *handled*, (*see book 1 – Black Rose*). It was something that MI5 and Special Branch monitored and in a roundabout way, controlled. Controlled because *their* discreet officer, Chas Larkin, the de facto head of the Larkin Saints, controlled the most strategically important area of London. If an attack was coming, it would come from the East End, and so any threat to the Larkin Saints was viewed as critical. The powers that be were always alert, because an assault was imminent. To take the East End, Chas Larkin had to be your number one target. However, there was more to Chas Larkin than was immediately evident.

There was also the O'Neill family who were reputed to have spurned power but enabled the devastation of the separate Saints and Larkin families, paving the way to establish the *New Order*, Bess and Maude. A *benign* gang? Did the O'Neills and, inter alia, the Black Rose support the Larkin Saint gang? This was another option the IRA would have to subtly investigate; a trickier strategy, but sometimes the best plans are those less obvious, and they could always drop any alliance at any time, couldn't they?

Maude and Bess were always alert. Chas, in his newly adopted role within MI5, worked closely with the Irish Officer seconded to Arbour Square police station, Padraig Brendan Casey, and with DS Flora Wade, now also incorporated into the secret services, and movement in the West had been flagged.

Sources reported that Arthur Schilling, AKA Tanner, was making moves, so he was closely watched. The North was considered to be relatively quiet, but things were brewing there also.

9

WENDY RICHARDS AND DR NADIA

NADIA REACHED THE SUITE OF ROOMS OF THE PSYCHIATRY department. No receptionist, it was early. It was no surprise either to see the messy array of magazines and publications on the waiting room table. This was the receptionist's continual battle with Wendy's desire for order. You only have to witness the battles between Wendy and Flora about the washing up and the state of their kitchen, but in the reception area of her office, Wendy allowed Muriel her way; it was her territory.

Nadia stepped through the battle zone of periodicals and reached Wendy's office. No illuminated red light; Wendy was not engaged. Nadia knocked and entered straight away. The office reflected Wendy's personality, neat as a pin, and the lovely lady bounced up in evident pleasure at seeing her friend and colleague.

'Nadia, so lovely to see you,' Wendy remarked as she stepped into an embrace with the Palestinian woman, with whom she never disguised she considered a most attractive woman.

At first, Nadia had felt Wendy's intimate hugs and often leering looks discomforted her, but nowadays she played along, enjoying Wendy's sport and reciprocating with one or two weapons of her own. This morning, a deep-cut blouse. Nadia was aware of Wendy's admiring gaze as the psychiatrist held Nadia's shoulders, stepping back and not disguising her line of sight. 'Pleased to see, me...?' Nadia said, offering a smoking smile, a reciprocated pleasure seeing Wendy blush, and so she should, Nadia thought.

'I wasn't expecting to see you this morning, although having said that, Flora has hinted at something that I am not at all comfortable with. Is this why you're here?'

'If it involves someone getting shot, me having to treat the wound and report it to the police? Then, yes.' Wendy's face said all that was needed as she returned to her swivel seat behind her desk and slowly lowered herself, sighing as she did so. 'Extraordinary, isn't it?'

Wendy nodded. 'Yes, but what I find most disconcerting is that I seem to take this sort of thing in my stride lately.'

'Well, I'm not sure I am that comfortable with it, and if it involves Maude Larkin, I am doubly...' Nadia responded but was cut off by Wendy.

'Maude does seem to have gone, as my Flora would say, Radio Rental, as mad as a box of well-armed frogs. When I try to raise this with Flora, all she says is that maybe she should have a dickey bird in Maude's shell-like, and get this, tell her to get anger management counselling, from me...!' Wendy had milky white skin that suited her blonde hair and tight curls, but Nadia thought the psychiatrist blanched even more; most people did at the mention of Maude Larkin.

'What if Maude did come to see you...?' Nadia asked, musing at the same time, likely picturing the event with a suggestion of playful malevolence.

'Fuck that for a game of bleedin' soldiers, as my dearest lovely and scary Flora would also say.' Nadia chuckled. Rarely did Wendy swear, although Flora she knew was the relative foul-mouthed trooper. 'It's not funny. I know Flora regularly meets Maude and Bess, but I would not want to encounter the woman myself, she scares the bajeezers out of me, as your equally scary, Irish scoundrel, Paddy would say,' and Wendy could not resist a chuckle, enjoined by Nadia. 'Though at the same time, she intrigues me, and more so, if I'm honest, than Chas and Bess Saint...' and she hemmed in thought, a sloping head and bemused grin that fascinated Nadia, which prompted a cautionary thought; maybe she should mention this to Paddy?

Nadia glanced down at her watch. 'What time do they let people out of prison?'

'How the jeffing 'ell would I know? Early I suppose, so maybe you had better get down to casualty and await the victim of the Okay corral?'

Both women laughed and both wondered why they were laughing. Were they now players in the start of what could be a new gang war? Wendy was scared. Nadia, not so much.

———

Just off the Mile End Road, Stepney, and 'Opalong Saint.

'Allo Chas,' a mendacious welcome, polite but threatening. A menace to scare the living daylights out of anyone, even if you ignored the straight arm pointing a gun. However, Chas Larkin was barkin', wasn't he? Was this why he was disturbingly relaxed?

"Opalong, 'eard you were being released today. Early. Good behaviour wasn't it, or was it a nine-bob note, Guvnor?' Chas replied, cool as a cucumber especially as he, via the good offices of MI5 and Scotland Yard, had arranged for Brian ('Opalong) Saint's release. A ten-year stretch for attempted murder of

Chas, when he was a young lad*. Released after only three years. Quite remarkable, people had said. A bit dodgy, people in the know had countered, not wanting to be in 'Opalong's shoes, even more so as he only had one foot.

'Opalong had a steady hand, the gun pointed at the forehead of Chas, not wavering. He could hardly miss at this distance. He had dreamt of revenge on Chas Larkin for his part in the demise of so many of his family, the Saints, and even some of the Larkins killed in the shootout in the East India docks, midsummer's night in 1966. For 'Opalong, his desire for personal revenge drove him. He had stewed in his prison cell, had weathered all the smart-arse comments about his missing foot, "Best foot forward eh, 'Opalong", "You'll 'ave to play in goal, 'Opalong," and all of this contributed to a head of violent steam.

Resisting the urge to shoot straight away, 'Opalong took this moment of control to release his pent-up invective. 'Good behaviour. I kept me 'ead down so I could the sooner get out and stick a bullet into your loaf of bread. I've dreamt of this...'

Chas interrupted, 'I know. I 'eard about you telling other prisoners what you intended to do, so I thought I might meet you. I was particularly interested to learn about you paling up wiv the George boys. Not particularly loyal that?'

'What? Why? How'd yer 'ear about that?'

Chas noticed a nervy reaction from his would-be assassin, clearly unaware that Chas had his informers in the Scrubs prison. Brian Saint was never the sharpest knife in the Saint family drawer, just a particularly nasty and violent soldier. It was in an attempt to kill Chas, when just a young lad who had been brought into casualty to be treated by Dr Nadia that three of the Saint Brothers, tooled up with sawn-off shotguns, intent on doing the biz on the boy, when they inadvertently shot each

---

* See Black Rose – A Midsummer Night's Chutzpah.

other, thanks to Roisin Dubh's intervention; three nil to the Black Rose. One boy died to commence singing in the choir not so celestial, one had his wedding tackle shot off to sing treble, and Brian Saint inadvertently blasted his own foot, henceforth becoming known as Hopalong Saint.

'Opalong gave the impression he had had enough and just before he was able to squeeze the trigger, he felt cold steel against his neck. 'Allo 'Opalong, 'ow's yer belly off for spots?'

'Opalong detected the menace in the female voice. Well, he would because it was Maude who now controlled the situation, at least the menacing side of it, but more dreadful than the feel of Maude's words and gun muzzle pressing into his neck, was the warm moist breath in his ear. 'You been a naughty boy, 'Opalong.' Bess Saint's voice detached of emotion, especially considering 'Opalong was a brother, not liked, but still kin. 'Opalong wanted to turn his head but couldn't, and fixed to the spot he was obliged to allow Chas to relieve him of his gun. Chas said nothing. In the exchanges, he had not moved a muscle and to 'Opalong this was almost as scary as having Maude and Bess behind him. 'Nuffink to say then?' Bess, whispered as Maude screwed the gun further into 'Opalong's neck.

'Opalong oomphed. ''Bout what?'

'Well, we could start with the George cronies in stir? Right friendly is wot I 'eard.' Bess still controlling the conversation, her hot breath causing a cold tingle down 'Opalong's spine.

'Opalong had thought this morning that it had been fortuitous the street being deserted. He now realised this was all manufactured. He knew also that he could be shot, killed, and his body taken away without a murmur from anybody. Any witnesses would know better than to say anything, and the police? Well, they were likely staying well clear, warned off. He had to answer Bess. 'What could I do, the Georges ran the block...'

Interrupting his pathetic excuses, Maude clarified a few

points for the gangster. 'So, you bigged yerself up, eh?' This time Maude did not disguise any underlying violence with sweet nothings. She had an obvious excitable tremor in her voice. A prelude to execution? 'Opalong could smell a womanly scent off Bess, a sweet-smelling pungency, but with Maude, it was perfumed violence.

Choking on the ambrosial scent of the two strong women, he answered with all he could think of as an answer, aware through his peripheral vision that a black van had silently pulled up alongside the kerb. Thinking this was it, so in for a penny. 'Wot the fuck else could I do?' A bravado he didn't feel. He knew now how many of his victims must have felt just before he had despatched them.

As the rear doors of the van opened, Bess stepped away, and flipping her head to one side, in an understanding manner, 'A fair point, 'Opalong,' she said, confusing the cowardy custard gangster, close to soiling his nice clean, going home prison underwear.

'Opalong also became aware of a strange look on the face of Bess as she casually strolled to stand beside Chas. She flicked her head.

'Wot?' he asked.

'In the fucking van, you prairie 'at...' Bess answered, still with her butter-wouldn't-melt voice through sweet rouged lips on her chubby but beautiful face. Rose tips on top of china-white cheeks should have told 'Opalong that Bess was a tad irritated, but 'Opalong had no experience of feminine signs.

Well, this is it, 'Opalong thought to himself. In the back of the van, shot dead, the doors closed, and off to be dropped into the Thames. He had a sense of the inevitable but thought he could at least go out with some clever remarks that would show to those left in his family and still on his side that he went out like a man. He clambered awkwardly into the back of the van, turned and faced the cold staring eyes of Chas Larkin. 'Fuck you, you crippled runt of a cunt,' he thought that was quite good, but clearly Chas disagreed as he shot Opalong in his thigh. 'Fuck. Wot the bleedin' 'ell. That 'urts.'

'Does it, 'Opalong?' Maude asked, looking like she would have liked to have pulled the trigger and was pissed off she had been deprived of her early morning violence. She loved early morning violence, a bit like morning sex for her, it set her up for the day, and Bess knew this.

Now on his knees, his one-and-a-half legs folded under him, he faced Chas, the pistol levelled still, and this time Chas spoke. 'I personally would like to finish you 'orf, but Bess and I fink we could use you.'

'Wot?' A ray of hope crossed 'Opalong's face, desperately trying not to cry. 'Wot d'yer want me to do?'

'We want you to use your friendship with the Georges and go over to their dark side,' Chas said slowly, without emotion. 'You've already laid the ground in prison that you hate me, and by extension, Maude and Bess.' 'Opalong looked into the cold stare of Maude Larkin, her hand with the pistol stayed by the steadying influence of Bess, otherwise 'Opalong was pretty sure he would be brown bread by now.

'I bloody do...' 'Opalong responded, seeing a possible way out for him.

'I know,' Chas answered sensitively as if he cared, 'so we want you to go to the George family and ingratiate yourself. And then, marry Queenie.'

'Wot? Marry Queenie?' 'Opalong thought this day could not get any stranger.

'Correct,' Bess answered.

'Opalong managed a muted chuckle. 'You gotta be fuckin' kiddin', ain't yer,' but already he could see Chas was deadly serious. 'She's a bleedin' *Denis the Menace* and not at all friendly like...' he paused, thought, then carried on, '... she's a violent...' thought for a moment more, '... fat cow.' And there it was, Chas,

Maude and Bess knew, and chuckled at the thought; the violence 'Opalong could handle, but marrying a steam roller, well, that could be a bridge too far.

'Yes,' Bess said, sighing, 'I'm afraid she is, but we have already heard that she was interested in you from her prison visits. So, fat and blind... as well as radio rental,' and Bess tittered, looked to Maude and saw a wonderful smile from her lover; that was a good joke.

'Oh, no...' 'Opalong was already resigned to what could be a fate worse than death, fucked to death by a hippo who had serious problems with personal hygiene.

Chas took over the conversation. 'This is what will happen. You will be taken to the hospital, having been shot twice. The doctors are obliged to report gunshot wounds to the police and you will be taken in. You will be questioned but all the time in hospital and with the filf, you will be screaming that you had been shot by the Larkin Saints, obviously refusing to mention specifically by whom. The Georges will hear of this, and if I know them, and I do, they will collect you after you're released and take you for their own. Then all you have to do is... woo Queenie...' he offered a muted laugh, disguising his real enjoyment of the situation, '... without being sick that is.'

'Yeah, that would give the game away 'Opalong,' Maude said, enjoying herself.

'Opalong looked like he was considering his lack of options and then Chas saw the light bulb moment. 'Shot. Twice?'

Chas shot again, grazing 'Opalong's shoulder. 'Yes,' he said, and the van doors closed on a screaming 'Opalong, and it headed to the hospital.

10

THINGS ARE AFOOT (NO, NOT 'OPALONG, WELL, JUST A LITTLE BIT)

The Georges - North London:

GEORGE GEORGE'S DAD HAD A SENSE OF HUMOUR, LIKE CALLING his first-born George when his surname was George. Some felt it was this turn of events, whilst amusing when the family George gathered around the font back in the day, may have had an effect on how George George turned out; he was a ruthless, violent bastard. Dad George bred children of the same ilk, none more so than his daughter, Queenie. His sons were good for violence when needed, even the son who became a priest. Mild-mannered Steve was the exception in just about everything and tipped for University, but none had the wherewithal that Queenie had, or at least she thought she had, and told people she had.

If you asked her, Queenie would say she helped her dad run his gangster firm in Tottenham, North London. He had started with a series of betting offices called after his eldest son, George George, and this had become GG's. His first shop was in The Seven Sisters Road and this building remained as their, headquarters. It is from this office that Lavinia, the wife of Dad

George, allowed her husband and Queenie to think they ran the now expanded operation, drugs, prostitution, protection, and all sorts of knavery, until she had her husband killed, a necessity she explained to her children and they understood, all with an eye now for the main chance.

Gwen George was no oil painting and no angel either, butter wouldn't melt in her mouth because she "'ated fuckin' butta'". Brown sauce, however, she did like and she had lashings of it on her bacon sandwiches for breakfast and similarly on her sausage sandwiches for lunch. Dinner was more often than not a pint of ale with her saveloy and chips, no brown sauce (she had her standards), down at the family rubbadub. This pub was formerly known as the Crown and Anchor, but when Gwen's dad bought, or at least acquired, the premises in Tottenham, North London, he changed the name for his princess, Gwen, calling the pub, *The Royal*.

Gwen immediately threw a violent tantrum. She hated being called her dad's Princess. She considered it demeaning and presented her dad with an academic solution that nobody could deny, and nobody was brave enough to deny this young lady anything. She argued that her name came from the ancient *Cwem,* meaning woman, but in the context of a *Queen*, and henceforth she was known as Queenie, and the pub, with the big sign swinging on a gallows bracket, had a painting of Queenie seated on a massive throne, eating saveloy and chips: The Queen's Head. The sign needed to be large to accommodate the expansive body mass of Queenie, and many, behind her ample back, suggested the pub should have been called, and was known colloquially as, *The Fat Cow.*

However, since her heart attack at the age of twenty-two, Queenie had shed her weight, at least this is what she told everybody, and changed the picture on the gallows sign above the pub to show a lithe portrayal of the still fat cow. The Queen's Head was no longer nicknamed *The Fat Cow*; she thought, because Queenie George was a *stunner*, because she said she was. She did, however, still have a temper that you had to look out for, as she retained the body mass to back up her menace.

This was her rep, and it was well known because Queenie encouraged that also. To survive in the gangster world of her family you needed to be violent. You needed to have the reputation that you took no prisoners, even after a *heart-felt* heart attack epiphany and you saw the *Road to Damascus*. At least this is what Queenie's priest brother had said it was, but he was a wanker and a nonce, though it was again wise counsel to not broadcast this fact, though everyone knew that the priest brother was a molesting paedophile bastard. But, of course, he had back-up to protect him: the Church, and the George family. It was fair to say that Queenie's propensity for violence to get her way reduced along with her *body mass*, in other words, not much, although her street smarts grew because she had a good teacher, her mother, Lavinia George. Vinnie knew how to delude her daughter and all around her, not least the thicko men, good only for the violent tasks she subtly gave them. If it was wrong to love one child over another, it did not bother Vinnie; she loved her youngest, Steve, he was bright because his *dad* had been.

It didn't matter that Queenie held greater aspirations outside the family *firm*; not that she told anyone except her mum. Queenie was low down the gangster family pecking order, and she was a woman, albeit she was well protected by brutal brothers; she was still *their little girl*... Aah... and, she hated being *their little girl* and Dad's, before he upped and died, *princess*. She was Queenie to her brothers, Gwen to her mum, Vinnie, the slight and feminine, cockney sparrow powerhouse woman, who urged her girl to lose weight, doll herself up and to better herself, ideally outside the family firm. Queenie did, at least she thought she did, as people commented on the still fat cow as to how lovely she looked now she had lost the weight. However, Queenie maintained an open eye for the big opportunity.

The George family had always wanted to cast their net wider. They now had a prosperous manor, but always the *cream* was the East End. Whoever controlled the East End, controlled London.

Queenie had grown bored of the number of family meetings they held, where the men talked of a coup in the East End. However much Vinnie, and Queenie to a certain extent, following her mum, counselled that a violent assault would never work, it was the only way *they*, the men, could conceive a takeover. This prevailing and popular thought was considered as reckless by Vinnie, and as Queenie followed her mother's wise council, she shared these opinions; the men were violent thickos.

———

Father George gave absolution, he always did, especially for his family of notorious villains, so it would be considered unfair that he should have been shot. He was a priest after all, even though he was known to partake in the occasional knee capping and the odd murder, for which he rewarded himself with a choir boy or two, not unreasonably, he thought. However, to be bumped off in the confessional box, a priest, who was considered by everyone to be a decent man of the cloth because they were told this was the case, but this was sacrilege, wasn't it?

Father George preached from the Holy Spirit Church in Tottenham because he was surrounded by his family and they would protect him. It was at the centre of his family's manor. There were now no other turf accountants in the manor. The competition had either been taken over, encouraged to leave, or rubbed out, in the local parlance. People supported the expansion of the family firm; there were hardly any dissenters left alive, because if you didn't view the family as noble, the sons and the daughter would come down on you like a ton of bricks, maybe even with a ton of bricks. That was their style, construction being a sideline, a convenience really, to assist in the disposal of bodies into foundations and the like, as well as to build and expand their property empire.

Queenie George found her brother slumped in the central box of the confessional, a stream of blood pooling at the bottom of the step that she delicately stepped over after drawing the curtain to reveal the body of her holy ponce brother. She showed no surprise. There was always a resentment about kiddie fiddlers; even her mum disapproved, saying that it was this sort of thing that could turn around and bite you in the arse. People were funny about kids.

It had to be a gun with a silencer and also had to have been the nun she had seen leaving the church as she was entering; there was nobody else there. A close-range shot through the merciless heart of the holy gobshite priest, fired from the penitent shriving pew, because her brother was not just a ponce, he was a nonce. She looked at her brother with utter disdain. As much as she respected family, she knew her brother to be a paedophile, and despite her *unreformed* ruthless character, she drew the line at molestation of children, unless it suited the business that is, but with her brother, it was simply a preference for his perversions. The family made no money out of it, and she knew her mum detested his perversions. Had she arranged his assassination?

Her brother had it coming, so she didn't feel too bad and well, it would help her cause. Queenie leaned into the priest cubicle to read the note pinned to the bloodied cassock, careful not to stain her clothes; she was most particular in the matters of dress, fashion and decent clobber nowadays. The note read:

"Back the GGs and die – you have been warned – The
O'Neills say hi."

'Jesus,' Queenie said out loud to herself. The O'Neills, in their territory? Now this was a cause for concern and she hurried off to tell her mum.

11

TANNER IN THE WEST

WITH THE DEMISE OF THE O'RIERDONS, THE WEST LONDON boroughs, especially the Irish immigrant areas of Kilburn and environs, were a vacuum waiting to be filled, and it came with a built-in populace sympathetic to the *Cause*. The *Cause* was Irish Republicanism, and the O'Rierdons had the infrastructure of support already in place. The problem was Arthur Schilling was not Irish. He was the descendant of a German Jewish family who managed to escape Hitler just before the clamp down and they had settled in the East End of London.

He was Jewish, which was not a problem in the East End. There was a strong group living, trading, and prospering in and around Spitalfields. Arthur was a smart, good-looking lad with a likeable personality, and that was the rub. Just about everyone had problems, had some cross to bear, not that the Jews carried a cross, they just carried an historic burden. However, Arthur Schilling seemed, at least to outside observers, to be without burden. He had an air of confidence born out of a stable and well-off family of tailors with their own warehouses; he even lived comfortably with his nick-name, Tanner. He liked his nickname, he told people. It meant he belonged, was what they told him in return; he bided his time.

Tanner had an ease about him that continued into his young adult life as he grew into a tall, svelte, and swarthy young man, always tailored to the nines. That was until a traumatic pressure was brought to bear on the family business. The Larkin family wanted the warehouses. It was not so much the business, they had no interest in the manufacture of clothing, just the warehouses, for they were strategically located. The reasons for wanting them was never made known, and for some time, they remained vacant. The Schilling clothing company was forced to relocate. They moved west and had to pay dues to the O'Rierdons, and as a consequence, business became less comfortable and a lot more expensive. And thus was born a chip on Tanner's shoulder.

He eschewed the clothing business. He left that for his brothers to run in order for them to fund him directly and indirectly. With the income, he established a small chain of pubs and clubs as his *fortresses* until he could be set to sally forth and take over the East End of London, his home turf as he saw it. However, to do this required the elimination of the now Larkin Saints, and this required more than Tanner had.

He had the Irish community, not in his pocket, but at least supportive, and they were on his manor as he saw it, as it expanded, and *his* territory bordered on the wealthy Jewish areas of Golders Green for which he offered *protection*. He wanted the East End and with that, he wanted Blossom Temple; he loved her, and Tommy, Blossom's son by him, which Blossom vehemently denied; another chip on Tanner's increasingly chip-full shoulders; his male ego severely dented.

After he had provided Intelligence to the authorities about the O'Rierdons planning an assault on the Saint warehouse of IRA munitions in the East India dock, and after they had been eliminated, ironically by the newly merged Saint and Larkin family, Tanner was now the de facto master of the West and part of the South, but Tanner wanted more. Arthur Schilling was no longer a tailor's son. He was a villain, his necessary aggression, as he saw it, exacerbated as he nurtured the grudge that he had been run out of the East End of London, and although he had made himself a lucrative living in the West, and investing, as he saw it, south of the river, he wanted to go home. However, he wanted to return as the all-conquering hero; this was his dream.

Tanner was proud of his heritage, his refugee German / Austrian family arriving in 1935 and being welcomed. He was not too pleased with the cockney wit, in that they called him from an early age when he attended Incubator Street School, *Tanner*. His mum had told him it was a way of being accepted and he should see his nickname as a good thing. But he didn't, just pretended he did. He couldn't see the funny side that Schilling was like a *shilling* in the currency, and that Arthur Schilling was like half a shilling, which was sixpence, known locally as a *tanner*. The nickname festered within him. He blamed the cockneys as the epithet had followed him to his West and growing South of London Empire. Feigning acceptance, he named his chain of betting shops Bet *Tanner*, his pubs and clubs, all derivatives of the name, such as The Half a Sixpence, The Tannery, Tanner's, and in Golders Green, Shekel's and Hide, and many more diverse adaptations. His determined aim was to make the Cockneys eat the name.

It was no secret he had a hankering to be home, and when he did make his return, he intended to be *King*. He had made attempts before, subtle but deadly forays into the territory of the Larkins, the houses of prostitution, racketeering and drugs, all to no avail. He did not even attempt to take over the Docks, the territory of the Saint family; he was not strong enough in the East End and had little support from those he considered childhood friends. His curiosity though had been piqued back in 1966 when reports (made by him to the authorities) of a direct assault by the O'Rierdon family from the West of London on the Saint warehouse of arms and explosives had been brutally snuffed out in a pitch battle in the Docks.

You would think that this would be warning enough, but Tanner, in delusion, saw this as *his* plan that had been more successful than he could ever have imagined. It puffed his ego and provided him with an enhanced incentive because many of the Saint family, formerly the highest ranking and long-lasting gang in all of London, had been killed in the battle, as well as some major soldiers in the Larkins, caught up in the crossfire. In order to survive, the extant families, the Saints and Larkins, had formed an alliance, although it was being reported as more than a coalition of villainy, it was a marriage between the lesbian leaders, Bess Saint and Maude Larkin. A good reason to be cautious as these women were not to be underestimated, but that never stopped Tanner. To Arthur Schilling, these were, first and foremost, women and not to be taken seriously, another part of his heritage that might be his downfall. He had not learned that in the East End fold, homosexuality was seen as a part of life and accepted. Tanner never grasped this, nor that it was a long-established matriarchal society.

It was also rumoured that the demise of so many Saints, and the serious weakening of the Larkin family, was brought about by a mysterious Irish family, the O'Neills. It was at first thought that the O'Neills were, in all but name, the O'Rierdons, but clearly this was not the case; Tanner now knew that. However, if the O'Neills existed, why had they not asserted their superiority and taken over from the Saints and Larkins? And this was where Tanner stepped into the world of incredulity, for it was further reported that the person now in full control of the East End was none other than the cripple runt whom he and young Mickey Saint famously bullied at school and on the street, Chas Larkin.

All of Tanner's instincts were to charge into the East End and take control by brute force and intimidation, but he had wise counsel from Ruth Golding. Ruth was a tour-de-force in her own right, even if Tanner disparaged her as a woman. Ruth, however, held a powerful position in the Tanner network, even if he could not see it. She stood as a functionary accountant, *The Bookkeeper* for all of the Tanner Empire. It had been Ruth, out of Golders Green and also of Jewish stock, who had advised caution first, and maybe send a message to the IRA in Ireland via the Irish community because it was well known the Saints supplied weaponry to the Republican Army, but also to the Ulster Defence Force, the opposition protestant terrorist force in the separated Northern Ireland Counties. And this was when things got really interesting, but the complexity of it all gave Tanner a headache. However, he had Ruth, and she had a handle on things.

———

Ruth Golding wanted Tanner, but she knew Tanner wanted Blossom Temple. Tanner thought he was strong. Ruth knew better. The ground was clear but was based on pipe dreams, and those pipes conveyed muddy and shit-strewn waters in the sewers of Tanner's mind. When Ruth became Queen she would decide what to do with Tanner, consort or *dead* weight; this always amused Ruth.

12

WATT WHAT

THE UNEASY PEACE IN THE EAST END WAS HELD TOGETHER BY THE combined strength of Maude and Bess and the elusive and volatile threat from Chas Larkin, still very much an enigma. However, the East End, with its Docks and supporting underbelly of profit and malevolence, represented a tempting target for any ambitious gangster anxious to make a name for him or herself, along with a perceived commensurate wealth. What these Pretenders to this perfidious throne, fraught with sycophantic traitors, did not realise was that the taking actually might be harder than they thought. The Saints and Larkin families had controlled the East End for more than fifty years and although seriously thinned out, it could be argued this new, lean and mean, reborn and combined family was more potent than anyone imagined possible.

Maude and Bess had learned at the knee of their grandparents and parents how to maintain the dominion, now their fiefdom; they were a constituent part of the powerful *Matriarchy* from the two dominant gangs for as long as anyone could remember. With these two women came more than just street cunning and a willingness to use violence to reinforce their dominance, they had experience and guile born out of observing how things had been run over time, and the unique edge they offered the people of the East End was *peace*. For the first time, the residents had a *safe* place to live. The *rules* were exacting but clear, though inviolable. They brought a rare *serenity* and an ability to safely bring up your family.

There would, however, always be the odd person who wanted to feather their own nest, to spread wings, to take what was not theirs. They could see that a path of greater prosperity might be possible by helping, say, a new kid on the block to take over the territory and share in the spoils from the territory, never realising that their act of treachery would mark them out as unreliable, and therefore, dispensable, and as soon as maybe following any coup.

One such snake-in-the-grass character was Walter Byng, his name shortened to Watt and much to his continued annoyance, he was referred to as *What?* The questioning inflection emphasised, and this would be followed up with a joke poke to his paunchy stomach accompanied by a high-pitched chorus of, "Bing".

What Watt didn't realise was that his entrenched resentment of his appellation left him with no allies in the dominant camp or the camaraderie of the downtrodden. He was friendless, but still he had a role in the Larkin Saint gang, albeit a low-ranking one, and this rankled even more. In short, and Watt was short, which exacerbated his feelings of being dealt a bad hand in life, he harboured a growing resentment, and this made him an ideal target for *weasel-in-chief* within the Larkin Saint Camp. As a consequence, Watt had been approached by Tanner's agents and given a strategy to play out, which mainly was feeding back intelligence on what Maude and Bess were up to, and if possible, Chas Larkin, although his movements were often more covert and less easy to identify, even to Maude and Bess.

However, on this summer's day, a Saturday, the kids played in the street, and Chas Larkin was reported to be intending to spend the night with Blossom Temple and was expected to leave in the next day or two for a trip to the West End of London. This was a known fact, but nobody on the Weasel side had considered following Chas, and if they had, and survived the stratagem of obfuscation and the discreet minders, they would have seen that more often than not he would call in at Scotland Yard. And, if they had managed that extraordinary feat, and overcome their amazement that a notorious gang leader was casually walking into the Metropolitan Police head-quarters, albeit by the back door, they would never know that, via a tunnel passing under the River Thames, Chas Larkin would enter the discreet office building that housed the anti-terrorist unit of MI5, on the opposite South Bank.

None of this mattered as Watt had conspired with Tanner's gang to assassinate Chas Larkin that next morning as he set out, and they had set up at the end of Incubator Street, a striped red-and-white tent, familiar to all Londoners as the cover for road works. Nobody questioned the tent, presuming it was to complete the connections to the road services for the now completed development of the Church of England Youth Club and Orphanage. Within this tent, the gunmen lay in wait, a straightforward killing.

———

1969 – Stepney, East End of London – gangsters abhor a vacuum.

The ersatz peace that had existed in the East End of London since the summer of 1966 was about to be broken, the grip of the Larkin Saints perceived as now weak. Gangsters can be sensitive souls and can sniff out a fake where it has existed, even for three years; what took them so long? Some said it was the Authorities that preserved the peaceful coexistence, just token extortion, violence and robbery, for *effect*. The peace, however, was more than that, it was the Matriarchal alliance, a *marriage* between Bess Saint, the brains, and Maude Larkin, who was a natural enforcer. They loved each other, and the historic gangster families of the Saints and Larkins in partnership, were a force never to be underestimated.

Bess and Maude were aware of Tanner, of course they would be, and they monitored the growth of Tanner's Empire South of the river adding to his establishment in the West. His betting shops, slowly building territory as they moved inexorably close to the river, where it would be just a small leap into the East End. It was the boldness of the Tanner stratagem that truly alerted Maude and Bess. Tanner's method was to buy out chains of betting offices in the West and then into the South. Each betting shop, *castle,* came with its own fiefdom of attached mobsters, and those mobsters answered to a central local betting shop, and now all answering to the West. And in the centre of the spider's web of fortresses was Tanner Schilling, powerful, manipulative, strategically impressive and threatening, or was it Ruth Golding pulling strings behind Tanner, her puppet?

———

The growth and the aspirations of Tanner could not go unnoticed, and Bess and Maude considered it was time they prepared for a full-on assault of their own territory. Chas raised the issue when he met with his colleagues in MI5. This was not strictly anti-terrorist unit territory, but Detective Inspector Padraig Casey had had his own feelers out, not so much in his law enforcement role, but as an officer in MI5 with particular portfolio to monitor the anticipated threat from the IRA.

The MI5 Unit, headed up by the Major, a small cohort of intelligence officers, and Padraig was the key Irish contact. Casey had been posted to Arbour Square police station in Stepney in order to sniff out and snuff out the very real threat posed by an active IRA cell that were being supplied by the Saint family (*See – Larkin's barkin' – Black Rose – a Midsummer's Night Chutzpah*). It was in this posting that Casey formed a sound working relationship with his allocated, for a laugh, *bagman,* DS Flora Wade; a major breakthrough, a woman detective taking such a senior role, but then she was the only one prepared to work with this Irish interloper. Pretty soon Wade proved her stripes and was indoctrinated into MI5. It was indeed a small band, just four people at the top and in the *know*. The fourth member was Hemmings, head of the MI5 Irish desk, intelligence filter, and together they were this tight team charged with defending the City of London from the inevitable threat from the IRA.

After they had closed down the Saint's network of support for the IRA it was thought Casey would return home to the Emerald Isle, but he had fallen in love with the tenacious Palestinian doctor, Nadia. Casey wanted to marry Nadia. Nadia wanted to marry Casey, but she insisted he would have to stop his dangerous work, become a normal policeman, before she would contemplate this. They lived together, but she would never tie the knot and she would never allow herself to fall for a baby; she already had one of them with the immature, Padraig Casey. By way of additional coincidence, Flora Wade's partner was Wendy Richards. A team that over time grew in strength, DI Casey and Nadia, DS Wade and Wendy, and a formidable partnership they were too, and they would need to be. Casey had learned from Hemmings that Tanner Schilling was able to buy into his Empire with funds sourced, allegedly, from the IRA, and he had possibly made dubious investments in the East End and even into the George family in the north. This was good enough for Casey to instigate his operation to monitor Tanner Schilling, and of course, Chas Larkin had been briefed by Maude and Bess to expect an attempted coup sometime soon; Tanner and his allies were gearing up.

Maude had been all for a big attack on Tanner, and then the Georges, but Bess, supported by Chas, urged caution and presented a deft plan. Bess, because she saw this as a route to neutralise the Tanner Empire or install their puppet controller, and Chas with Casey, as a way to track the source of the IRA funding and the IRA cell already in London. You do not enter the East End of London with a view to taking over the manor without serious back-up for the attack, and then to consolidate your victory; if you won that was.

The threat was known, Tanner Schilling, but he must have insider help for his plan to have any chance of working. The troubled souls of potential interloping gangsters can have one or two defects in their excitable vision of a usurped utopia, and that would be the mistake of most who had tried to muscle in where they saw a perceived weakness. Bess and Maude were not weak, far from it, and they had their own backup if necessary, and this time it was looking as though they would need to call in the Big Guns. Padraig had already arranged the antiterrorist unit in Arbour Square police station, who were primed and already acting.

Padraig had his Irish contacts. Nadia was always suspicious of her Irish enigma bedfellow; was he IRA, a duplicitous, but irresistible, bastard?

13

THE ARRIVAL OF 'OPALONG

DR NADIA MET THE BLACK VAN IN THE ACCIDENT AND EMERGENCY porte-cochere. Her feelings of trepidation she knew were natural, but her fear compounded when Maude Larkin exited the passenger seat and casually walked around to the rear of the van. She was a striking woman.

'Doctor Naadhira, yes?' Maude acknowledged Nadia using her Palestinian name as she opened the backdoors, and this increased Nadia's emotional tailspin. Maude sensed the doctor's nerves, and taking her pistol from a concealed shoulder holster under her suit jacket, she wrapped the gun and her arm around Nadia's neck, the muzzle of the pistol brushing the doctor's breasts via the plunging neckline of her silky blouse. It was cold. She shivered, the feel of the metal and the close proximity of this dangerous woman, and marked to herself never to wear a revealing garment to work again in order to tease Wendy. 'So, you're Paddy's twist and twirl, eh?' Maude said directly into Nadia's ear, as friendly as you like, apart from the gun barrel that nestled in her cleavage.

Nadia was rigid with anxiety and a sense of despair; what could she do? What could she say? She had faced people holding a gun before in Palestine, her aggressors Israeli, but never expected it here in England. Her fear was exacerbated because she was aware that Maude, this tall and sinewy woman with cropped black hair and dark glasses, suited and booted in all-black, had reputedly gone off the reservation, a loose cannon. Nadia knew what Maude was capable of, but not what she would do. It was all that everyone was talking about, how she had gone, in the parlance, radio rental, and she had even discussed this with Paddy.

'I take it you are then...?' Maude pressed verbally and physically with the dangerous end of her weapon, clearly taking great pleasure in the sight of a beautiful woman with glorious breasts, so openly available; stunning and stunned, like a gorgeous rabbit in headlights.

Nadia found some inner strength, and palming away the gun, she twisted out of the gangster's unwelcome embrace. 'I am Paddy's woman, his squeeze, his mother of pearl, and I ask you to respect that, please.'

Maude smiled and Nadia trembled; there was such malevolence in that grin as she removed her shades and spun the sunglasses through her fingers, again the smile, menacing. Or was this in Nadia's mind, driven by a pulsating heart rate? Nadia looked directly into Maude's dark brown, almost-black eyes that showed just the hint of respect for the Palestinian doctor. The tight lip grin curved up, and Nadia thought she was a handsome woman, fucking dangerous, but a beauty, in her way. 'A Mick and a Darkie...' Maude said like it was a natural observation, no offence meant.

'Yes, and I am pleased to meet you, Maude, dyke gangster...' and Nadia reciprocated the fixed stare whilst offering a *warm* smile, conveying a confidence she did not have. Maude laughed; the tension defused? Maude's laugh, however, was manic, Nadia aware the local stories that if Maude removed her sunglasses you needed to be careful; this villainous woman had not finished toying with her.

Maude leaned in, circling her arm around the doctor's waist. Nadia fixated on the gun as the gangster pulled her into a tight embrace and violently kissed her. 'Fuck me sideways, you're a gorgeous bird, so you are. If Paddy can't do the biz, let me know and I'll give you a good seeing-to. Now, shall we get 'Opalong out of the van before he bleeds out?' and Maude left Nadia shocked through to her core as Maude swung her gun up and ordered a sturdy soldier, who had been enjoying the spectacle, to give the shit scared staff a hand.

The orderlies wheeled the trolley up to the back of the van as Maude stepped aside allowing Nadia to examine 'Opalong. She addressed the goon guarding the wounded Saint man. 'Get your foot off his head. NOW...!'

The goon stepped back, trained to take orders from strong women, but offered up an explanation, 'I didn't want him escaping...'

Nadia interrupted him, 'Escape? You fucking clown. He has two bullet wounds and you have a gun. So, why stand on his head?'

The thicko soldier looked confused but again offered up an explanation. 'It's what I do. I stand on 'eads.'

Nadia glanced at Maude, now completely relaxed and enjoying herself. Totally bonkers, Nadia thought. 'Yeah, it's wot he does...' a casual flick of her head, '... and, he's good at it,' and Maude leaned into the side of 'Opalong's head, looked up to the thicko goon, '... nice one 'Arry. Not too 'ard and not too soft.'

'Arry smiled. 'Fanks, boss.'

Nadia muscled in. 'Get out of the way and let us get this man into casualty, please.' And the orderlies manhandled a screaming 'Opalong onto the trolley, and not for the first time she thought that maybe these orderlies needed a bit of training in the arts of caring, but then, this was a vicious gangster, so, what the hell, and she joined Maude and laughed, recalling the last time she had seen 'Opalong, he had just shot his own foot off.

Maude seemed to approve. 'Lubbly jubbly, sweet'art. Now, you know what you 'ave to do?'

Nadia sighed and answered, 'Yes,' on an exasperated exhaling of breath. 'First phone the police and then look after my patient.'

'In one, babes,' and it looked like Maude was moving in for another kiss, so Nadia side-stepped and moved to look at 'Opalong's wounds.

'Only surface wounds, no real damage...' Nadia observed

'Surface? It fuckin' 'urts,' 'Opalong squealed. Whether it was the wounds or one last squash of a goon's boot to his head, Nadia was not sure.

'Shut yer norf and souf, yer fucking pansy...' and Nadia looked to Maude, '... did I just say that?'

Maude grinned, and Nadia noticed a lasciviousness behind the warmth. 'Gawd bless you babes, yer gorgeous, so you are. Now, you should be able to patch 'Opalong up and the filf can take him to a lovely cell in the police station. That sound nice eh, 'Opalong?'

'Opalong looked like a wounded smoked kipper. 'Yes, Maude...'

Maude stepped in and slapped him, and Nadia noticed the blossoming red hand mark immediately below the boot tread. 'Mrs Larkin, to you.'

'Sorry, Mrs Larkin.'

Satisfied with the answer and seeing 'Opalong being wheeled into casualty whilst crying, Maude turned to Nadia. 'Chas is a fucking good shot. If it had been me he would be brown bread by now. Still, that would fuck up Chas's plans, wouldn't it?'

'It would?' Nadia asked, unable to stop herself. This was the first time she had direct evidence that Chas had shot anybody, although Paddy had more than suggested that Chas Larkin was building a rep.

Taking advantage of an overwhelmed Nadia, Maude pulled her into another clinching snog. Nadia did not resist and could not answer why. 'Definitely fancy you, darlin'. I might be back later, so keep it warm for me, there's a good girl,' and as Maude sashayed away, she slapped Nadia's bottom, hard. 'I'm off for a bit of anger management counselling. Ta-ta for now,' and off the gangster went.

Flan – Milk Man

Flan Flummery tucked into his baked beans on toast. He loved baked beans on toast, it was all he ever had for dinner, mostly for lunch, and if he had no *Wheatybangs*, he would have beans on toast for breakfast as well. He liked beans, and often carried a tin with him, like *Popeye* had his can of Spinach. He sometimes liked a peanut butter and beetroot sandwich, whereupon he would first eat the beetroot, lick clean the peanut butter, before toasting the bread to have beans on top – this would be on Sunday, he never worked Sunday, so it was a special day for him.

Flan hated Church. Well, he would, wouldn't he, following his experience in the *homes*. He'd told his mum all about it but she just shrugged her shoulders and brushed his complaints under the carpet; the priests were her bread and butter. The fact Flan avoided church originally upset her, but her son had outgrown his attractiveness, his cherubic good looks now matured into a handsome, if seriously damaged man; not that she noticed, or cared.

Lil Flummery was devout, attending to all the needs of the

priests. Lil was her name, although not christened Lillian, she was called Lil as a titular diminutive of *little*, ironically, because she was colossally fat as a consequence of eating all the food that Flan wouldn't eat because he only liked beans. On Sunday, she would also eat the body of Christ, generally with strawberry jam before getting plastered finishing the wine with the priests in the refectory whilst assisting them off with their robes and sanctified Y-fronts in order to be blessedly anointed with Priestly seminary seminal fluid. It was a beneficial relationship that suited Lil, work not being a favourite pastime, but she was not overly keen on her religious East End counterpart, Lady Owseyfather. Lil resented having to bow to her erstwhile boss in a similar priestly manner, but needs must she always thought, and this was her lot, for the time being.

The best way to describe Lil would be the archetypal, seaside postcard, rosy-cheeked buxom housewife, wielding a rolling pin, waiting for her errant husband to return from the pub. But alas, Lil's husband would never return because he had had his brains bashed in by a blunt object and then stuck upside down in the mud flats of the Thames when the tide was out. It was rumoured that Lil had done for her wayward, dipsomaniac husband, but it was the eventual resting place of Albert Flummery, head down in the mud that had the police convinced it was *The White Tide Man*, but they could prove nothing. Albert Flummery was a small part player in the street scene, but another thorn in the police side had been removed, and by whom didn't worry them so much.

Nothing ever happened in Flan's life, if you excluded his dad being beaten to death, very likely with a rolling pin by his mum, and the police scared stiff of arresting her, focusing their attention on the enigmatic and most elusive White Tide Man, as a convenience. However, the demise of his dad meant he was taken into care more often, where he was used and abused, and it scared the living daylights out of him; he was damaged but didn't know it, people thought. Flan was dismissed as a loony, useful as a milkman but would never make it onto The Brains Trust panel. He wished he could contact the White Tide Man and ask him to do the biz on his abusers in the church home but knew instinctively that more would come along and this was just his rotten lot, and who knew, the assassin could actually be a Church man.

Flan, through no help of either parent, if you exclude whistling lessons from his dad before nose-diving into the Thames embankment, had achieved his lifelong ambition and was now a milkman in Stepney, and he loved it. A trick cyclist would probably call this *denial.* Flan didn't know about that, but he was able to throw his life into being a milkman, not realising it was his old school chum, Chas, who had got him out of his circle-of-hell life. Flan loved his milk float, had even tuned it so that it increased its speed from the regulation ten miles per hour to fifteen; faster downhill, not that there were any hills to speak of on his round, and even if there had been, the milk float would struggle to motor up, in order to speed down. He dreamed of *Ally Pally*, Alexandra Palace, the People's Palace on the hill, now the BBC broadcasting building, what a hill that was, and in his dreams he whizzed down it, whistling a tuneless accompaniment to the cacophony of milk bottles rattling in their crates.

Nothing ever happened in Flan's life until Monday, a sad day which led on to a day that became etched into memory of all Eastenders, and it turned out Flan would sacrifice his cherished float and more, for the greater good.

14

CHAS LARKIN HAD A TERRACED HOUSE IN INCUBATOR STREET. IT was a step up from his former family hovel, but his life had taken a turn for the better. He could afford to have a larger house if he wanted, but he didn't. He wanted to live near his childhood friends and allies, all of whom he had set up in the terrace of this street, his former school and the new Orphanage and Youth Club taking up the opposite side of the road.

His success did not go to his head. He had his mended feet firmly on the ground. As a child he had what was termed as a *club foot*, and this along with many other bodily and mental afflictions, a squinting lazy eye and an oppressive mother who chained him to her brutal apron, and suffering constant bullying from Little Mickey Saint, all combined to make his life a misery. Following a serious altercation in which his mother had viciously attacked Chas, her youngest son, she had subsequently been beaten to death by an unknown assailant. Chas had fortunately been admitted into casualty by Dr Nadia and she carried out emergency surgery that saved both of his eyes. Later, after his fortunes had changed for the better, the Palestinian surgeon corrected the foot, and to all intents Chas walked normally, carrying his well-concealed emotional baggage, revealing only titbits of pain to the psychiatrist Wendy Richards. Bit by bit, he bared his soul, and only every now and then the firebrand temper was let out of the bag to be tucked back in again after the police had been settled.

Settling the police was not that difficult a task as Chas Larkin had, over a short period of time following the self-discovery of his chutzpah, become not so much a selective police informer, but more a successful MI5 operative. It was in his position as apocryphal head of the Larkin Saint Families and enigmatic street operator, Chas was able to control things in the East End and areas close to the City of London, which it was anticipated the Irish Republican Army would target.

So it was, the Larkin Saints and Chas, ruled the underworld roost in the East End, albeit with the purview and support in both intelligence and physical assistance, where needed, of MI5, Special Branch and The Sweeney Todd (Flying Squad). Of course, the nefarious members of the gang, the rotten to the core foot soldiers, a necessity in this game of cat and mouse espionage, had to be allowed to rule the manor in an appropriate manner; robbery, violence, intimidation and the rest, so long as it was steered in the right direction and all for the *greater good*, the pretence controlled as best as could be by Maude Larkin and Bess Saint. If this were not the case, then there were other villains ready; nature and gangsters abhor a vacuum.

And who determined what was for the *greater good*? Chas Larkin? Yes, to a certain extent, as he had a real understanding of the life of his constituents, his friends, and the establishment and what they were doing. This was his main concern, the Irish troubles he cared about, sensitive to the struggles of the Irish people all of which he had learned through his connections with Roisin Dubh, the Black Rose. This was an intimate knowledge, but even Chas was nudged and steered by another person, a person who had the rights and needs of the Irish at heart, but no longer the stomach for the violence that the IRA felt necessary to achieve their ultimate aims. For it was the remit of Padraig (Paddy) Casey, to prevent the violence whilst allowing those few brave political activists to negotiate a peace settlement, behind the scenes.

The fact that Casey was not averse to a bit of violence himself, *for the greater good*, was not an irony that raised itself on the moral horizon for him; he had lost family to the IRA, even though his kith and kin supported the republican cause. It was after a lot of soul searching he had opted to eschew his IRA violent operational activities and to work on the side of peace and reconciliation, but in his own way. He knew that Nadia sensed this and that it was a stumbling block in their relationship, but what else could he do? Padraig Casey became an MI5 operative, albeit one who was viewed in a circumspect manner and maintained at a distance. It is a murky world in MI5, just ask Nadia. She was never sure if Paddy was IRA, and strangely, she wondered, would that matter? Apart from the hurt to innocents?

———

Chas's house was next door to the house he had secured for Blossom. He intended to knock them together, but Blossom resisted. Chas could not understand why. He was spending so much time he was almost living with Blossom now. However, she counselled that the house she had was enough for them both and Tommy, and therefore his house could become a home for another needy family. Of course Chas agreed, she was right. Blossom had always been very much a moral compass for Chas, even more so now he had the ability to improve the lives of *their* people; Blossom was on a mission and not a woman to be gainsaid.

So it was that Chas now, more or less, lived with Blossom Temple and her son, Tommy Little Legs; they were a family. Chas loved Tommy and now, Tommy had a dad and had learned to stand tall, even if he only had little legs.

People did laugh. Of course they did, but the *well-meant*, honest Guv, humorous asides, soon stopped as the lad was taken under the wing of *Mr* Larkin; why? Nobody knew, but Tommy did, it was because Chas Larkin had been bullied all of his childhood until he had met the Black Rose, when his life changed. He found his chutzpah and this he was about passing on to his stepson. It is fair to say that Chas Larkin had truly risen from his repressed hibernation hell and now, after a convoluted power struggle, a lot of death and destruction, he had become the head of the combined family firms of the Larkins and Saints; an invincible street force.

Chas was head of *the firm*, but the force behind the management were the two women heads of the confederated families, Maude Larkin and Bess Saint. Although the families had always been steered by a matriarch, these historic and powerful women had allowed a visible man at the helm. However, there now was a whole new code of respect and behaviour, but essentially, to the plebs and local hangers-on, it was pretty much business as usual; do as you are told and keep schtum, on pain of, well, lots of pain and possibly death. So, nothing much had changed, except the locals were *enjoined*, decreed to respect the relationship of Maude and Bess, now hand-fast; married. Bess, the brain box and intellectual strategist, domestically demurred to Maude, the enforcer, on the street and in their marital bed.

There was the Black Rose, but she was mainly seen as a myth, and an Irish myth at that. However, the ephemeral O'Neills were more than a mystical force, their potent presence manifesting itself violently, before disappearing. Who were they? They were thought to be a family from the west of Ireland, but stories grew from the imagination and the desire for one-upmanship; new intelligence being good currency and could get you free drinks for the night.

People were now slowly becoming aware of the *difficulties* in Northern Ireland, and also, myth or reality, the Black Rose was something to be taken seriously, especially as this virago of retribution was allied to Chas Larkin as was, it seemed, were the O'Neills. And all of this combined to reinforce the strength of the Larkin Saints and their grip on the valued territory of the East End.

In Incubator Street, Blossom Temple, known locally as 'Drop-em Blossom', for she had been, a *brass*, brass nail, a bit of tail, in reality a brass flute, a prostitute, but a step above the tarts who hung around the East India Dock gates. Now, she was the common law wife of Chas Larkin, and that gave her all the protection she needed. Chas loved the bones of Blossom and had embraced her child, Tommy. More often than not Chas stayed in what was becoming *their* family home, and in her counselling sessions with Wendy Richards, Blossom had expressed no doubts about their relationship, and this amazed Wendy. How could it be that a young man such as Chas with his history and tragic emotional baggage, build a tender phys-ical and emotional relationship with a woman? Up until that fateful Midsummer Day back in 1966, Chas had been relent-lessly bullied, used and abused, none more so than by his mother.

However, during her counselling sessions with both Blossom and Chas, the bond of love between them was evident, and Wendy had to admit it was heart-warming, and this was fast becoming a cornerstone of her academic study: *how do you survive in such a violent world.* But, realistically, she needed another cornerstone, and she dearly wished that could be an analysis and understanding of Maude Larkin, the enforcer, and Bess Saint, the cerebral partner, but that had danger written all over it. So, it would have to be second-hand interviews. Flora would never allow her near the gangsters, and that was something Wendy was willing to accept, at least for now, because the pull of the two women was almost irresistible.

Wendy would love to meet with the Black Rose and to make her that final cornerstone. She was convinced Paddy knew the hellfire Valkyrie, and she would get to him, via Nadia.

15

AN MP'S SURGERY

INCUBATOR STREET SCHOOL WAS THE HEART OF THE neighbourhood, so where else would Little Willie, MP, have his fortnightly surgery. It was in the school hall that he met and generally ignored his constituents, as they did him; it was an expected formality, after all what could he do for the people he represented? Nothing, because he would do nothing unless it was in his own interest. He was a busy and important man: Secretary of State for Northern Ireland, don't you know.

In the hall, at a table laid out with a green felt cloth cover, Willie sat in all his splendour, surrounded by lackey aides at his beck and call. Today there was just one caller and she stood at the entrance to the hall. A smart woman, tall and dressed in a cream trench mac with a knotted belt, a green silk neck blouse with a high collar and a black beret set at a jaunty angle on her long glossy red hair. Willie looked up, the clacking of stiletto heels drawing his attention from his reading material; *Playboy* – only not the one that most saw on the top shelf of the newsagents. This was about playing with little boys and was not readily available, unlike the boys he arranged for himself and his sponsors, and there were plenty in his bailiwick.

The woman, taller in the stilettos, handsome, young looking for what Willie assessed as her early middle age, approached, steely green eyes focused on the Member of Parliament; was this a constituent he had not met before, Willie wondered. The confident woman approached steadily, gradually untying the belt to her mac so that it flowed behind her as if she wore a cape. Like a wafting bird of prey swooping in for the kill, this woman did not falter, did not break eye contact. As she closed, Willie could see a creamy white face with a flourish of freckles atop the cheeks, a face set with no sign of emotion, anger or at peace. Willie's tummy churned; something was not right. She reached the table, looked at the toady aides, flicked her head, and the three sycophant men left the hall; she had that demeanour and presence that you naturally obeyed. The door clicked shut behind them. They knew the form, but not the woman; this was a private conversation and Willie was welcome to it.

In a lyrical and robust Irish accent, the woman spoke. 'Willie, Willie, still fiddling little boys are yer, so?' Willie had no answer. He knew this was what the IRA had on him. 'Will,' she paused for effect, '... have you done as we instructed?'

'I have... err, who are you? I mean, I know who you represent, but can I have a name?'

'All in good time, *Little Willie*.' She emphasised the name, intent on the MP getting the intimation he had a small cock.' The woman slipped her hand inside of her mac and Willie thought he was about to be gunned down, but the woman produced a wad of cash. 'Sausage and mash, I believe you cockneys call this...' and she laid it on the table, atop the filthy magazine, '... and here...' she removed a slip of paper from the money fold, '... is what we want you to arrange for us, now.' Willie didn't look, couldn't bring himself to. He just stared at this woman, subliminal beauty, a patent threat below the tracery layer of make-up emphasised by her crackerjack red lipstick. 'You will do as you are told, yes? Like a good little boy?' Her face fractured with a smile at that comment. Willie nodded. 'Good,' and the woman turned on her heel to leave, took two clacking steps then returned, leaned over to Willie's ear, he could smell her alien sweet breath, a hint of whisky and an intoxicating perfume blend. She lingered for effect, said nothing as she stood up, 'By the way, they call me Roisin Dubh in the Irish, you may know me as the Black Rose and... I have your number, Willie,' and she turned and paced strongly to the exit. She opened the door, rattling the latch deliberately so, before she called back to the MP, already shitting himself, 'Oh, and the O'Neills say hi,' and she slammed the large door behind her.

Willie's card had been well and truly marked and he knew it. He picked up the paper and read:

Arrange for all dignitaries, contributors and sponsors of the Orphanage and Youth Club to be at the formal opening on the 21st June, 2 pm – do not fail.

The Black Rose.

———

'Have the bodies been collected?'

Professor Brian Charnel rarely ventured above ground during the day. The mortuary was his domain, not that he truly ruled there nowadays. However, there was something about this Palestinian doctor that both unnerved him, and in an unusual contradiction, he felt he could trust her. 'Not yet,' the professor replied, his head bowed in shame in front of this beautiful and *proud* doctor, who was monitoring a patient being taken by the police. Was she shaken?

'Please don't worry about the police. The man you see...'

she pointed to the disappearing wheelchair, '... was shot. Not badly, but all gunshot wounds have to be reported to the police,' Dr Nadia explained, and this seemed to be enough of an explanation for the professor. Nadia noted this, aware that she could not explain that she had just witnessed, first hand, an encounter of the most extraordinary kind and with probably the most dangerous woman in London; she will need to talk this through with Paddy this evening. He had already suggested that Maude Larkin was behaving worse than ever, as if she didn't know. It was all people were talking about. Nadia was thoughtful, not giving the professor her attention, why single her out? Maude Larkin was specific, knew her, and even mentioned Paddy. Was it, because of Paddy?

It then dawned on Nadia that Professor Charnel was out of his territory and the fear she saw on the man's face was likely not because of the police. 'Brian. Can I call you Brian?' The professor nodded. 'I have a small office, maybe we could talk in there?' She pointed to a file the mortician carried. In case anyone was observing them, they would presume they were discussing a dead patient.

Nadia's office was no more than a large cubicle, glazed top half of the enclosing partition. Since they were in view, Nadia drew a chair around so the both of them had their backs to the casualty ward. She took the file and pretended to peruse the contents. 'Now, Brian, what do you wish to say?'

The Professor cleared his throat, which was more likely as not clearing his congested lungs, Nadia surmised. 'Nadia, you were right this morning...' He paused to see if Nadia would respond, but she didn't, she would let him say all in case he lost his courage, a ploy acknowledged with a face gesture by Professor Charnel. 'Right, about everything. The dead children you saw were by no means the first, and right, I have kept detailed files of all that I have seen. Children of all ages, boys and girls, used and abused, killed and discarded, but only arrive in my mortuary by coincidental circumstance, and so I believe what I have recorded is just the tip of the iceberg.'

Nadia nodded to indicate she had already worked that bit out for herself. 'Accidental circumstance being that the public were aware, so a show of a post-mortem would be needed; a coverup?'

'Yes, spot on, and you were right also, I am dying: lung cancer. I do not have long, and I fear for my family if I hand over the evidence I have.' Nadia acknowledged the troubled dying man with a sympathetic smile, her eyes watering slightly, sensing the pain this man was feeling and the burden he had carried for so long. He pointed to the buff-coloured file held by Nadia. 'In the pocket of this file is a letter to you and my authority to use my material if you can guarantee the safety of my family. It also says where the evidence is hidden. I also identify my opinion as to where the bodies have come from, what institution; an educated assumption, but I'm likely right. If this is followed up there may be records of the children kept in those institutions, but can only be identified by mortuary photos, I'm afraid. I trust you, and I don't know why or how I feel this, but I do.'

He was now bent over his knees, head hung low, and Nadia touched his hand. 'You can trust me, and you can trust the police officers I will give this to. I will also make it clear that their number one priority is to make your family safe. Is that okay?

'Yes, thank you.'

'I can see you do not have long to live. Have you had confirmation from an oncologist?'

'Yes, the consultant here...'

Nadia stopped him with her hand returning to hold his. 'Do you mean Mr Graham? I know him and have even worked some surgeries with him. He is a good man.'

'Yes, he is. We have been friends for some time and with his resident, Dr Green.'

'So, the prognosis, how long?' Nadia held both of his hands and was surprised that they were cold and dry. She expected them to be leaching sweat from fear.

'No more than two months, three at best but likely less; I can feel it. My wife wants me to stop work and spend my last days at home, with her and the children, but how? How can I leave?'

Nadia had to think on her feet. 'Brian, when you leave my office I want you to collapse as you enter the corridor. We will pick you up, take you back into casualty and I will summon Mr Graham or his resident. Together we will concoct a plan for you to be admitted to the cancer ward and from there, we will send you home. By that time, I will have worked out a plan for the safety of you and your family. Is that okay?'

Brian Charnel stood, he was shaky on his legs. He tapped the file with fingers and Nadia noticed again the paper-thin, yellowing skin. She watched him out of her office and he had barely reached the corridor before he collapsed. Nadia was of the opinion this was no act. Perhaps it was the relieving of his emotional burden that enabled him to *give in.*

16

ANGER MANAGEMENT?

MURIEL WAS IN, STATIONED AT HER DESK, GUARDING WHAT SHE considered her territory, the reception to Wendy Richards's office, and that included shuffling up the magazines, especially if Wendy had lined them all up, in order. She was a buxom woman and made up for her short stature with body weight and attitude, but she was no match for Maude Larkin, who made up for her comparative slight stature with patent aggression.

'Oi, short arse.'

Muriel was shocked. She knew who this was but had never been this close to rocket-fuelled danger before. 'Who, me?'

Maude looked around and then leaned over the reception desk and tapped her fingers to demonstrate a shortage of patience. 'Well, I don't see any other short fat people, do you?' And she made to look around the empty waiting room again, 'Nope, don't see any, but I do see a fine pair of Bristols,' and she leered into the receptionist's bosom. 'I'd say a front bigger than Brighton,' and the gangster took her weight on one hand whilst the other hand slipped into Muriel's knitted top, her action stretching the 'v' neckline. She forced the bra cup away and took a firm grip of Muriel's breast.

'Oh... I, err... please...' Muriel expressed shock but was careful not to remonstrate or show in any way the outrage she felt.

'It's okay, sweet'art, relax, I don't go for fat cows,' and Maude removed her hand, walloped Muriel on her face, several supposedly playful slaps. Muriel's already red cheeks now displayed the imprint of Maude's hand. The gangster raised herself up and looked around. 'That Wendy Richards's office? I'm here for some anger management counselling.'

'Yes, Miss Larkin.'

Maude went back down again and grabbed Muriel by her long dark hair, the receptionist squeaked. 'That would be Missus Larkin,' and she released her hair.

'Sorry, Mrs Larkin, and yes that is Miss Richards's office,' Muriel managed to say breathily.

'Good, next time remember, or I will bend you over your desk, pull up your skirt, pull down your knickers and give you a good hiding, you understand?'

'Yes, Mrs Larkin. I'm sorry,' Muriel answered as she watched Maude Larkin walk away and enter Wendy Richards's office without knocking. Muriel had no intention of risking this again. She packed up her things and left a brief note informing the doctor of her resignation, and she departed to spread the word that Maude Larkin was indeed stark raving mad and double, if not treble, dangerous.

———

Detective Inspector Paddy Casey and Detective Sergeant Flora Wade exited Scotland Yard, intent on making their way to Arbour Square police station, at least this is what Flora thought. They had just finished a meeting with the Major and

Hemmings. The gist being there was foment in all the quarters of London and this would likely facilitate a situation whereby the IRA could take advantage and get a toe hold. Paddy had said to the major that he had a plan and tapped his nose, and before he could be interrogated or Flora could insert her sticky cockney beak, he left at a pace.

Flora chased Paddy as he scooted along Whitehall, heading for Trafalgar Square, or so it appeared to Flora. Trying to insert her *sticky beak* into Paddy's face, she suggested it would be her boot up his Aristotle, bottle-and-glass arse if he didn't stop, turn, and face her. He stopped and Flora bumped into him. 'I suppose you fink that's funny,' she gasped, out of breath, and spoken as though her nose was broken; it was too good a joke not to be said, even if she was puffed.

Paddy tried to be serious but he had learned, as had Flora, that he could never resist the jokes of his *bagman.* They stood facing each other, Flora waited for the second laugh she knew she could elicit with a shrug of her shoulders, and chuckling, he asked, 'Okay, okay, what is it?'

'What is it?' she mimicked with her now accomplished west of Ireland accent blended into her rasping cockney. 'You daft bugger. 'Ow's about you tell me what the feckin' 'ell is 'appening, and you can start wiv, where the feck we are going now, you Irish ponce? I thought we were going back to the Nick?' Before she could continue her no doubt really long list and finish by booting him up his Irish arse, he raised his hand to indicate shut up; he knew this riled her, and walking on the wild side, he loved doing it.

'Don't you put your hand up to me, Paddy Casey, or...' She was halted because he left his hand up as though he was stopping the traffic, which she knew was for her motor mouth, as he had said many times before. Cooled and smothering a titter, she questioned her boss, 'Motor mouth...?'

'Motor gob, more like,' he answered, and she was smitten by

his Danny Boy grin. She had noticed he brought this out whenever he was in trouble. She fell for it every time, and she fucked women, well, just the one these days.

'Okay, Paddy. I'm totally calm.'

'I doubt that. Do you ever do calm?'

Flora offered him her own Maltese grin that she knew he liked and had even remarked before that she had the prettiest face he had ever seen on a chocolate-coated honeycomb ball. He melted, as she knew he would, when she deployed her less fattening centre. 'So, where are we going?'

'We are going to the rubbadub, as you would say. A little pub off the corner of Trafalgar Square, so small you would hardly notice it.'

She was in front of him. 'The Two Chairmen, I know it, a lubbly jubbly boozer, but don't we 'ave a lot on today and you, a lunchtime piss-up? Not like you? Or is it...?' She realised she had only been with Paddy at times of work or conflict and never relaxed with a drink, unless you counted the times when Paddy and Nadia had been to dinner at Wendy and her flat, but that of course was for the benefit of Nadia and Wendy to interrogate the two of them together, to play one against the other; expert interrogators were Wendy and Nadia, and Flora and Paddy were generally dead meat when they teamed up. 'Well?'

'Not a piss-up. I'm meeting my sister...' he glanced at his watch, '... and, we are late. You don't want to keep her waiting, she has a fearful temper,' and having dropped the bombshell, he recommended his brisk walk up Whitehall, crossing the busy thoroughfare by the Cenotaph, chuckling as Flora began chasing him down, calling out, "Your skin and blister?"

———

Wendy Richards looked up from her desk, surprised that someone had entered her office without knocking and also knowing she had no appointments that morning; even Muriel knocked. Upon recognising Maude Larkin, Wendy shot up from her seat, leaving it spinning as she backed herself to the wall.

'Miss Richards. I see you recognise me,' Maude said, offering the scaredy cat psychiatrist a menacing grin that Maude thought was a loving and warm smile. Mind you, she also thought, it is the exact same bedroom smile she used when she was telling Bess she had been a naughty girl. Bess liked it, it always made her wife come over all unnecessary, but it did not look like Wendy was quite so appreciative. Maude picked up a chair and manoeuvred herself around Wendy's desk, to place it, open to where Wendy would sit; she did not want any barriers between them during this consultation. 'You do know who I am, yes?' Maude asked again, this time leaving the chair where she wanted it, taking a step to invade Wendy's personal space, almost face to face. 'I'm Maude Larkin,' and the gangster stepped back and put out her hand. Wendy was frozen to the spot so Maude grabbed Wendy's wrist, pulled it out, inserted her own hand into Wendy's and shook. 'How do you do, shall we sit and start my anger management counselling?'

'Anger management...?' Wendy blurted out, trying hard not to cry as she looked to the door.

Maude noticed the glance, strode purposefully to the door, opened it, and leaned out, swinging her back leg like a ballerina at the bar, pulled herself back up and slammed the door shut. She enjoyed watching Wendy jump. 'Just as I thought, I may have intimidated that fat cow of a receptionist of yours. She's fucked off, so no help coming there then, eh? I did say she had nice tits, so why she would get the 'ump and run off like that, I don't know.' Maude was back at the desk and motioned with her hand to Wendy's office chair, 'Sit.' Wendy sat and Maude moved her own chair so she was close; knees to knees, not quite touching, but Wendy sensed the heat. Wendy was a most attractive blonde woman, Maude thought. 'You know you look like Shirley Temple, anyone ever tell you that?' Wendy managed a nod. 'Eminently fuckable, eh?' Wendy nodded again; she didn't know what else to do. 'Shall we get started?'

Wendy nodded like a nodding donkey, and she felt that all the blood had drained from her. 'Start?' She had at least spoken, but what else could she do, or say, she did not know. She could not recall any time in her life when she had been so terrified.

Maude chuckled. 'For a clever bonce trick cyclist, you are a bit dim. Still, I suppose that's what your Flora likes in you, eh?'

'My Flora? You know about her?' Wendy loosened her tongue.

'Of course I know about her. You are both dykes, like me and Bess, my wife. You know Bess Saint don't you?' Wendy nodded. 'Stone the bleedin' crows, keep nodding like that and yer bleedin' loaf of bread will fall off.' Wendy could only agree by nodding again. 'Okay, I'll start off,' and Maude edged her chair even closer to Wendy. Wendy pushed back on the wheels of her chair, and this clearly did not please Maude at all. 'Stay,' she commanded like she was chastising a dog. Wendy stopped her chair, and Maude scraped her chair closer and rested a hand on Wendy's knee.

Wendy did not know where her reserves of resilience came from, but her hackles rose. 'Please, take your hand off me.'

Maude half-lifted off her chair, leaned in and slapped Wendy on her cheek. 'Don't you talk to me like that, do you understand?'

All courage deserted Wendy as she responded, 'Sorry.'

'Sorry, what?'

'What?' and Maude half-stood again, and Wendy thought another slap was coming. 'Sorry Maude.'

'Mrs Larkin to you, Shirley.'

'I'm sorry, Mrs Larkin,' Wendy answered, hoping this was

what Maude wanted, and judging by the malevolent grin, it was.

Maude sat back down returning her hand to Wendy's knee and edged the psychiatrist's skirt up, slightly higher. Wendy did nothing other than hope Flora would walk in but recalled she had cautioned her lover not to visit her at work unless absolutely necessary. It distracted her. But now, she truly wished Flora, for once in her life, would not do as she was told and come to her rescue.

Maude guessed what Wendy was thinking. 'What? Hoping your tart copper will come and rescue you?'

'No, Mrs Larkin.' Maude lifted off her seat and threatened. 'Sorry, Mrs Larkin. Yes, I was. Please don't hurt me.'

'What on earth makes you think I am going to hurt you? You sweet thing...' and Wendy looked down as Maude's hand went higher and slipped to her stocking top and inner thigh. Wendy quaked but realisation dawned; she was excited. 'That bird of yours is in Trafalgar Square having a dink with Paddy and some other woman, and yes, we have her followed, mainly because Bess and I want no harm to come to her.'

This surprised Wendy, and with increasingly heavier breaths, she asked, 'You, err, you have her followed...? Please, what are you doing...?' Maude's fingers were sliding along the gusset of Wendy's knickers, making Queen Maude aware that Wendy wasn't just scared, and wondered if she was like her Bess? 'You are a naughty girl, aren't you?'

'What do you mean?' Maude looked up from spreading Wendy's legs and frowned. 'Sorry, Mrs Larkin.'

'That's better. You wouldn't want me to punish you, would you?' She looked intently into Wendy's startled azure-blue eyes and noticed they were beginning to glaze over as Maude pressed home her advantage. 'Would you?'

'No, Mrs Larkin.'

'No, what?'

'No, I do not want you to punish me,' and Wendy saw again the malicious smile.

Maude removed her fingers. After all, this was a professional appointment and she had learned all she needed to know about this psychiatrist, and whilst massaging Wendy's thigh, continued her anger management consultation. She never before had realised counselling could be so enjoyable. 'But, you see, my dear Wendy, I think you may need punishing, if only for allowing me to do this to you,' and her hand brushed Wendy's knickers again.

Wendy was scared but extraordinarily, sensually excited, the feeling of pleasure though was soon replaced with guilt. She had betrayed Flora. What would happen? What would she do?

'Wendy darlin', what do you know of my relationship with Bess?'

'You are married, Mrs Larkin.'

Maude was pleased Wendy had remembered to call her Mrs Larkin. She was such a lovely submissive, much like her Bess. 'That is not what I meant, Wendy. You see, I recognised straight away, as soon as I walked into your office that you are a submissive, like my Bess.

'I am not a submissive,' Wendy countered fiercely, indignant, and then was immediately scared and regretful. 'Mrs Larkin, sorry, again.'

'So you should be, and you will be punished. Not by me...'

'What do you mean, Mrs Larkin?' Wendy's inquisitiveness got the better of her.

'I mean this, my sexy darlin',' Maude answered whilst straightening Wendy's skirt before standing up and leaning over her prey. 'My Bess likes it when I cane her.'

Wendy was aware of this sort of relationship, but still it shocked her, the fact also of these two lesbian gangsters and their private lives. 'I am not like that, Mrs Larkin. I do not desire...' and she drew that word out, '... to be caned.'

Maude grinned and moved in very close, and Wendy thought she was going to kiss her, then she did, and Wendy was surprised by the softness of the hard woman, and again sensed a thrill. 'You do. I know.'

'How?' Again curiosity got the better of Wendy.

'You will see, sweetie. When you get home, I will have a cane delivered. It is not for you, but Flora to use on you. When Flora gets home, you will tell her you allowed me to tantalise you intimately and you loved it. You will then ask Flora to punish you. I would say twelve strokes should do it.'

Wendy's head was buzzing. She did not know what to say, just said, 'Twelve?'

Maude leaned in again and snogged her for what seemed like an age. 'Would you like more then?'

'No, please. Mrs Larkin.'

'Good. I will check that you have obeyed me, and if you have not done as you are told, I will visit you for more anger management. I might anyway, it has worked wonders for me, and you too, yes?' Wendy nodded, again. 'So, you are going to be a good girl and do as you are told?'

'Yes, Mrs Larkin.'

17

A LADY IN WAITING?

RUTH GOLDING HAD FINISHED THE BOOKS. THEY LOOKED
healthy, even after she had creamed off her take. 'You look
happy,' she said, and he ignored her as he so often did. Just
lately Ruth had begun to question if she did love Tanner or
even desire him. He was a handsome devil, of that there was no
doubt, tall and svelte, well-groomed black hair that set off his
devastating five o'clock shadow that reinforced his shady look.
Well, Tanner was shady, and nobody knew this better than
Ruth Golding, accountant to the Tanner Empire. Ruth was
more than an accountant. She was the *Bookkeeper*, and that was
a much darker role. Many said it suited Ruth's delphic, Jewish
looks. Black hair, natural, none of this wig-wearing for her. She
had eschewed her shietel. Her *arranged* husband had insisted
she maintain her orthodox form of clothing also, but this was
the sixties and she had wanted to follow the *Mary Quant*
imagery. This did not go down well with her husband's friends
who all wore their big hats that would be racy if not worn by
such dour men with unkempt straggly beards, dressed in drab
clothing to match their crabbed and stringent attitudes to

women. Fuck sake, this was the sixties, and the seventies looked like they may be even better.

Ruth had a strong independent streak and her arranged marriage to a Tottenham cowboy Jewish man did not suit, other than it gave her contacts in the Borough which had come in useful when Tanner wanted to form an alliance with the George family. Of course, Tanner thought he had made the alliance, and Ruth allowed him to think that; after all, she owed him one. Tanner was dashing, everything a man should be, and well, he had arranged for her fucking husband to have a fatal accident. Ruth was free and she owed this to Tanner, and he wasn't half bad in bed.

Much to the disgust of her orthodox family, Ruth now dressed in short skirts, skimpy tops and leather boots, her trademark. She was a beautiful butterfly, free of her previous saturnine life. She lived life to the full, away from Tottenham, her late husband's borough, which, if Ruth had her way, would become a part of the Tanner Empire, once the George family had completed their arranged tasks, namely, blitz the East End. If only she didn't love Tanner, it would all fall in place for her, as Queen of the East, West, and North, along with her already firm grip of the expanding South. She would be happy to be consort to Tanner, but he only had eyes for that cockney tart, Blossom Temple. She knew that Tanner planned to kill off Chas Larkin, which was strategically sound if he was to wrest control of the East End, but Ruth knew in her bones that if Chas was done in, it would free Blossom for him. How blind men could be. Blossom had no interest in Tanner and never would, not if Ruth had her way.

'Why would I not be happy, babes?'

Tanner called her babes. Ruth liked it at first but now she found it irritating. 'Please, don't call me that, Arthur, I don't like it.'

'It's a sign of affection, sweet'art, babes...'

Tanner was distracted, so Ruth thought going to bed was likely off the cards. 'Tanner, please.'

'Don't call me Tanner.' He was alert now.

'What, don't you like it... babe?' Ruth wiped the scowl from Tanner's face.

'Take that smirk of yer boatrace, it don't suit you.' Tanner was irritated himself now.

Ruth had been attracted to Tanner's cockney accent and his use of rhyming slang when they first met up, and strangely, he had been attracted to her mode of Yiddish dress. This fascinated Ruth. Now she was, as many said, drop dead gorgeous and sexy, he seemed to lose interest. Well, she wished at times he would drop dead, brown bread like her late pot-and-pan, old man, husband, and this made her titter behind a masking hand; she knew Tanner could be volatile if he thought she was laughing at him.

'What?'

'What, what?' Ruth responded, now openly enjoying herself.

'What you laughing at... babes?' The grin had now been lost on Ruth's boatrace. In fact, she was angry and Tanner could see it. 'What were you laughing at, sweet'art?'

Better, but not much better. Ruth went in for the kill, metaphorically, but she knew this would wound her lover, and funnily enough, at this moment, she did not care. 'I was laughing at how you found my shite box clothes I used to wear sexy, but now I am drop-dead desirable, you hardly give me a second look.' Ruth stopped there. She could have gone further, but even though her Arthur could be a bastard, she could see he was hurt, and this made her feel guilty. Why was that? she thought.

'You're me bird, ain't yer...'

'Yes, I am your WOMAN...' she emphasised, not liking being called a *bird*. She looked at his face and headed off his smart-arse rejoinder. 'I am not your twist and twirl, mother of pearl, squeeze and definitely not your fucking tart. What of it? What is your point?' She knew what his point was. She was his possession, and he did not like other men lusting after his property. Ruth at first liked this quality, but now it irritated her.

Tanner was riled. 'You are, my, WOMAN, and I don't like you dressing like a Sloane ranger tart.'

'Is that why you lust after drop 'em Blossom then? Because she wears drab flowery hippie dresses?' Ruth had gone in for the kill and saw that she had struck at the heart of the matter.

Tanner turned to leave but spun back and flat-handed Ruth across her boatrace so hard she was knocked across her desk. He had hit Ruth before, but never this hard. She saw him approach through the stars floating across her eyes and she brought her knees up into the protective foetal position. Was he going to give her a kicking? He grabbed her hair. It was thick and naturally curled, she didn't like it, but Tanner did, maybe because it wasn't sexy. He liked her wearing the shietel. He pulled her to his face and, spitting bullets, 'You, are, my book-keeper, and for your information, you are no longer my tart. I want you outta the flat before I come back. Sort yourself out, babes, and I will see you in the office in the morning, got it?' Ruth nodded. 'Say it, have you got it?'

'Yes, Arthur, I've got it...' Tanner dropped her head, and it thudded on the floor as he turned and strode from the room, likely to go to one of his pubs to get pissed, and that was when Ruth decided she had to have him killed and she may even do it herself.

———

'Oi, Dorothy, slow the fuck down, I forgot me skates,' Flora shouted after Detective Danny Boy. People turned to see the source of the contretemps and saw this robust dusky lady shouting down the man with the fulminating Irish gypsy looks. Paddy stopped in his tracks and once again Flora bumped into him. 'Don't say it...'

But he could not resist the rejoinder. 'I suppose you fink that's funny,' he said, snuffling like he had a severe cold and couldn't say plub jam and bunday borning.

'Leave the jokes to me, Paddy, you ain't got what it takes,' she responded, shaking her head but struggling not to laugh. She grabbed him by the sleeve of his jacket so he could not make another run for it. 'Okay, now. In a slow walk, tell me...'

'What?'

'Are you thick or something? Tell me about yer skin and blister.' Paddy was smiling, oh how he loved winding her up. 'And take that poncey grin of yer boatrace, or I'll knock you from Monday to Sunday. So, Paddy, your sister...?'

'Yes, you'll love her...' and he turned and recommenced his fast-striding walk, and Flora sighed. She knew she should have had a tighter grip on his arm, but resigned, knowing she could always knock his block off later, she pursued him, looking like an idiot chasing an eejit.

The Two Chairmen pub is like a hideaway drinking hole, except it is beautifully ornate and loved by the regulars, mainly because tourists rarely find it. Opposite Cock Pit Steps, at Dartmouth Street and Trafalgar Square, the pub dates back to the early seventeen hundreds, and despite its name, it is missed often by the businessmen also. The chairmen refers to the men who used to lug a sedan chair around town, and this had been their pub.

Flora knew the pub, liked it, and she'd had many a drink here with some of her Met police colleagues on a night out in the West End. One time she had brought Wendy; she loved it too. "So ornate," she had said, the dozy cow, Flora thought, but she was her dozy cow and she loved her. These warm thoughts caused her to slow her pace and was irritated at the blarney bastard calling out to her from the pub door and spoiling her amorous reverie.

'Come on, slugalugs,' Paddy called, 'we have things to do...'

Flora reached the door. 'We do?'

'What?' Again the Danny Boy cheesy grin that all the girls loved, even Flora, though she preferred the girls.

He went to enter the pub, she stepped in front of him. 'Paddy, what lot do we have to do?' Flora looked nonplussed at what she had just said; was that right? And this pause enabled Paddy to ease her to the side, which was more of a shove, and he was able to get around her to enter the Two Chairmen.

18

A MYRMIDON POW-WOW IN INCUBATOR STREET

BACK IN INCUBATOR STREET, IN THE TWO-UP-AND-TWO-DOWN terraced house that was Blossom and Tommy's, and now, more and more the home of Chas Larkin, it was to be pow-wow time.

It was also lunchtime and the enlarged kitchen that had been knocked through to the back living room (the front room, the parlour, was only used on special days, it was posh you see) and it was crowded. The Stepney Myrmidon gathered while Blossom warmed through a shepherd's pie she had made earlier. The veg was already steaming on the large refectory-like table.

'Get Tommy in, sweet'art,' Blossom called, and Chas went down the tight stairway corridor to lean out of the front door. It was warming up and so the door was open. Most doors in the street were open. This was a street full of villains so nobody would steal anything. It was not difficult to spot Tommy, he was bouncing backwards on his *space hopper,* a new-fangled toy, just out in the shops that Chas had bought the boy. It made Tommy a firm favourite with the street kids looking to have a go, except they would go forwards. Tommy always went backwards, even walking. Chas did not know why, maybe it was to *watch his back,* to look out for bullies? Chas liked this quirk in his stepson, but it worried Blossom. She worried all the time for her little boy with the little thalidomide legs. She needn't have caused herself so much stress as everybody loved Tommy. He had the kindest nature and Chas knew he allowed the other children a go on his hopper. Chas loved Blossom and he loved Tommy Little Legs.

'Tommy, dinner,' Chas called out, and Tommy bounced backwards to his front door, left his hopper on the street, and rushed backwards into the house; he was always hungry. Chas derred and collected the hopper to bring indoors, not that anybody would take it, and not just because they liked Tommy, which they all did, but he had protection.

Tommy walked backwards to his place at the head of the table. Chas insisted Tommy was the man of the family, and Tommy took his place with pride, a puffed-up pigeon chest, and Blossom, looking on, loved her boy and Chas even more.

'Tommy, why don't you walk forwards? You nearly knocked Aunt Bess over and she's as big as an 'ouse what wiv the babe an that,' mum chastised her son.

Bess leaned in as best she could with her distended belly and ruffled Tommy's hair and planted a cherry-red kiss on his cheeks. 'He's alright, Blossom darlin'. Aren't you, Tommy. My favourite boy?' and she kissed him again.

'Oi, Aunt Bess, yuck, stop kissing me...' and this brought a hearty laugh from Bess, and even more so as Blossom took her hankie, spat on the corner and rubbed the lipstick from her son's cheeks. 'Mum, stop it, you're rubbing the skin of me boat.'

'Shush now, let me get it, my lubbly jubbly babes, so you are.' And Tommy sighed, looking to Chas whose face told the lad to suck it up and take it like a man. Blossom turned to Chas. 'And you can stop it as well. I know you're making faces behind my back,' and as Blossom returned to scraping the skin of Tommy, Chas gurneyed for the little boy, who giggled in his cherubic way. Sighing, Blossom said, 'That'll do,' and she kissed her boy and walked to Chas, a friendly punch on his arm followed up with a loving kiss.

'Gawd blimey, Blossom darlin', leave 'im alone and give us me dinner, I'm Hank Marvin' (in the East End, dinner is lunch – don't worry, you'll get it, but by then the dinner / lunch will be cold).

'I take it you're all starvin', sorry,' and Blossom shouted out to the garden for Flan Milkman to come in and get his beans on toast; the rest dived into the huge shepherd's pie. Flan was sitting out in the garden with Rinso. Nobody would be able to eat if he was in the room; he even left a trail of odour as he passed by to the garden, helped along by Blossom's boot up his arse. The garden table was beside the window, so Flan and Rinso could hear what was said. This was allowed as the wind was in the right direction, away from the house.

After the dinner, (lunch), had been eaten, the plates cleared and the apple crumble and custard polished off, it was time to start the meeting. Chas kicked off with a comment to Blossom. Stretching his arm out, he waited as Blossom nestled in and Chas hugged her waist. 'What a blow-out, darlin', loved it almost as much as I love the chops of you.' Blossom smiled a beatific smile that the Mona Lisa would be jealous of, and she leaned in and gave her man a big kiss.

'Get a fucking room, will yer.' It was Bess, who else. For a demur gangster, she had a bit of a mouth on her. Well, how else could she keep control of Maude, outside the bedroom that is? And this was what the meet was about, Maude.

'Bess, babes, will you kick off? What's latest on Maude? I'm hearing some pretty dodgy stuff...' Chas said.

'Relaxacat, Chas, I've got it 'andled,' Bess said, sticking crossed fingers in the air.

'Not what I 'eard,' Chas responded.

Sighing, Bess answered. 'Well, you know Maude, she can

get a bit enthusiastic, I suppose...' and Bess pinched finger and thumb to show it was only a little bit. 'Getting noticed is she...?'

Blossom stuck her oar in, wanting to get the meeting over, send Tommy out to play and shag the brains out of her pot-and-pan. 'I say. Noticed? I fink the 'ole bleedin' world has 'eard she's gone radio rental.'

'Maybe cool her down a little, eh, Bess. Job done an' that,' Chas said.

'I'll 'ave a dicky bird wiv 'er when I get 'ome. Now, I'll 'ave a gypsy's kiss before I go, wot wiv this bun in me oven, I'm pissing all the time.' Bess looked at Blossom who indicated, tell me about it. 'I'll use the outside khasi, I'll not make it upstairs.' And they all heard Bess head for the back of the garden, telling Flan and Rinso to foxtrot Oscar and not listen in to her having a Jimmy riddle.

Blossom made sure Rinso went directly out through the kitchen, corridor, and into the fresh air of the street. Flan followed up. He'd finished his round and said he would give Bess a lift home on his milk float. Blossom rolled her eyes, but Chas thought it was a nice gesture.

19

THREE PUBS

*The Queen's Arse otherwise known as The Fat Cow –
Tottenham.*

QUEENIE HAD JUST FINISHED HER SAVELOY AND CHIPS BETWEEN
two bread vans, sandwich, the dribbles of brown sauce and fat
still evident on her lardy lady chops. She dragged the back of
her hand across those fat cheeks and stained lips; she was a
stickler for how she looked. Satisfied that most of the dinner
time (lunch, you'll get the hang of it) snack detritus had been
removed, she cleaned her hand on the back of her dress; out of
sight out of mind was her motto, and everyone agreed, it was
quite a sight, revolting, grease stains on a fat bottle-and-glass
was not the best of views, but it has to be said you could not
miss it.

Behind the bar, Lavinia looked and sighed at the revolting
habits of her only daughter. George George saw his mum's look
and grinned. Queenie was a bleedin' nuisance as far as he was
concerned, but relaxed, he knew his mum had the measure of
her, and he chuckled at his unspoken pun.

'What?' Queenie looked at her brother.

'What do you mean, what?' George George reacted, ready to make a run for it, but he was saved by the bell.

Lavinia answered the phone, "Allo, yes...' she waited, 'this is Vinnie, you daft apoth, you can tell me...' and she listened intently. 'Fuck me sideways,' and she looked around the bar and then directly at Queenie.

'What?' Queenie enquired.

'What, to me in my state of 'ealth?' Vinnie responded, holding the phone away and those nearest could hear a squeaky ant trying to get Vinnie's attention. She went back to the phone and addressed the ant, 'Oi, you oily filf, shut it.' So the oily police ant shut it, while Mum informed her daughter and son. 'It's the filf at Arbour Square, they're sayin' 'Opalong Saint was shot twice this morning.'

George George interrupted his mum who looked annoyed, aware her son was probably last in line when the brains were being handed out, and then this was adequately proven: one, he interrupted his mum, and two, he thought, then said, "Opalong has been shot and then later on, shot again?'

Vinnie and Queenie rolled their eyes, Queenie farted, and tempted as everyone was to make a run for it, they knew they had to stay and listen to Vinnie George who was now back on the phone talking to the copper ant, who was likely a grasshopper, not shopping a copper but grassing up coppers for what will amount to a bit of sausage and mash, and what copper didn't need a bit of extra money, it was expected. Vinnie hung up the phone and looked directly at Queenie.

'What?'

'Don't you what me, I'm yer bleedin' muvver.' Vinnie made her intellectually informed response resound around the bar; the slight and slender gangster mum had a mouth on her, and didn't everyone know it.

'What's that got to do wiv the price of fish?' Queenie

answered, thinking she could murder some fish chips right now, with tomato sauce.

'Fish? What?' and before the brains trust George George could say anything or Queenie could stuff her face with fish and chips, Vinnie put her hand up as if to stop the traffic, stuck behind a steam roller. 'Listen up,' and everyone did, wary that Queenie might fart again, but she didn't. "Opalong was apparently shot in the leg and then in the arm this morning. The police took him in for questioning after he was released from casualty.'

'Shit a brick...' It was Queenie, and people looked behind the fat cow because if she did have a movement it would likely be several bricks.

'Yes, darlin', my thoughts entirely, and my source at Arbour Square reckons he was shot by Chas Larkin while Maude and Bess held him at gunpoint, not that 'Opalong is sayin', but it has to be. Stands to reason.'

'Why?' George George, the dozy thug asked.

Vinnie rolled her eyes and tried to think if she had dropped her son on his head when he was a baby. Her other son, murdered only yesterday, was a child molesting priest nonce and would be no loss, except for regular absolution, but she had to get her thinking head on. But first, George. 'Because, you dimwit, he has been saying as soon as he gets out he intended to kill Chas Larkin and, we hoped, do for the two dykes as well. So, that didn't 'appen, did it.'

'No?'

'George, why don't you run and get your sister some fish and chips and a *Mars* bar, she's gonna need it to help her work, rest and play, because she's gonna be getting married.'

'She is?'

'Are you still here George? Fuck off to the chip shop, will yer.'

'Righto, Mum,' and George George disappeared out the

pub, somewhat relieved. He was out of his depth and knew it, but when it came to beating up and killing, he was mustard, and everyone knew that.

'I'm getting married, Mum?'

'You like 'Opalong, don't yer?'

'I do, Mum, he's lubbly, even if he only has one foot.'

Vinnie explained to her fat ugly daughter the real facts of life. 'Sweetie, I hear from the boys in his wing of the prison that in the showers, 'Opalong had a knob to die for, and let's face it, who cares about a foot so long as he can hop to the bed, eh?'

'No, Mum. How do you know all this?'

'What, about his big knob?'

'Nah that he wants to marry me?' Queenie asked, not unreasonably, she thought.

'Because, I hear also he is going to be let out of Arbour Square soon and I will arrange for him to have a lift back here, to us. I think he may be a useful weapon against those fucking Larkin Saints, don't you?'

Queenie couldn't see, but that didn't matter because if her mum said it, she was okay with that, but she was definitely interested in marrying 'Opalong, even more so if he had a decent 'ampton wick. 'Yeah, Mum. How'd you know he will marry me?'

'Leave that to me, darlin'. There are not many men could resist you, sweet'art,' and Vinnie made another phone call to the 'Arf a Sixpence pub and left a message for Tanner before she busied herself around the bar with a massive grin across her boatrace while Queenie took in the fact that she was irresistible.

————

The 'Arf a Sixpence, Kilburn, West London

Cock of the walk and bouncing into his pub, (no, not 'Opalong, he's still in Arbour Square police station – keep up), Tanner felt good, and this was one of many pubs he had acquired along the way, and here, he was hailed a welcome by the regulars at the 'Arf a Sixpence. Loving his adulation he thought about the pubs he would get in the East End, first and foremost being the HQ, Larkin Saint Pub.

The Saint pub, The Dog and Duck, known colloquially as Dad's, was now combined with the Larkin pub, The Bottle and Glass, known as Arries, as in Aristotle, bottle-and-glass. arse. Because the original Dad's had been burned to the ground, and because it was semi-detached with Arries, when it was rebuilt by Maude and Bess, they joined the two pubs and renamed it Dad's Arse, and Tanner wanted Dad's Arse for himself, along with all the blandishments he envisaged that would come with it.

Still, the 'Arf a Sixpence was a good Irish pub in Kilburn, despite the renamed cockney brand. It was where he was steadily building his support. Needs must, and he enthusiastically enjoined the Irish bonhomie, the IRA a substantial part of his funding. He made no secret to the London Brigades as they built and grew, that he was their man to take over the East End, the goal of the IRA. Tanner in exchange provided their fighters living accommodation and warehousing where arms, munitions and bomb-making materials were slowly being accumulated, ready, and it would not be long. This is why Tanner needed to move up his agenda, to build momentum.

In this *Irish* pub, he had to be at least *a token Irishman*. 'Slainte,' Tanner saluted his thanks as a bottled Guinness and a Jameson's was passed to him. He hated the stout and was no lover of the whisky either. In fact, Tanner wasn't much of a drinker, but tonight was to be a fund-gathering night, traditional Irish musicians and patriotic songs, and he would be expected to be there.

'Good man yerself, Tanner.' A man sidled up to him at the bar.

Tanner recognised him; he was a local Brigade leader. He picked up his whisky and toasted the man, 'Slainte,' and Tanner swallowed his pride, making sure he paced himself with the drink; he had to focus on the task at hand. He had the Georges where he wanted them, even though it was like herding a bunch of cats; he had them firmly in his grasp. He'd given Ruth a slap. She was getting a bit uppity lately and a bit too big for her kinky boots. Still, he had sorted her, and tomorrow, Chas Larkin would be killed and maybe, give it a week or two, he could go in and take what was rightfully his, Blossom Temple, and along with this prize came the territory. The despatching of the two lesbian gang leaders would not be easy, but he had agreed with the man beside him at the bar that they would arrange for a bomb for him to plant, and then, bye-bye Maude and Bess and hello Tanner, King of the East End.

Of course, it would not be quite this simple, but he had arranged with the George family to take out the key members of the Saint Larkin family, and when that was complete, the IRA will kill off the Georges of Tottenham. It was a sweet deal, admittedly Ruth's idea, but she was always there if he needed help. She just needed to know her place.

———

The Two Chairmen – just off Trafalgar Square

Following the jostling of Paddy with Flora, trying to squash together to get through the pub door first, Flora looked to berate Paddy but was dumbstruck by a gorgeous woman leaning at the bar, an elegant leg hooked over a slender ankle and seductively waving to them, well, Flora thought it was seductive. Paddy seemed unmoved but Flora's collywobbles wobbled. This was a stunning woman, her most immediate feature being long, fine and glossy red hair, like burnished copper, crowned with an incongruous black beret that on this woman looked, smoking hot; she was a lot like a wartime French resistance woman.

The redhead approached them and Flora's eyes were drawn to the beautiful figure beneath the flowing trench coat that opened as she strode purposefully to greet them. She was wearing a verdant green silk blouse and tight black trousers that moulded to her legs for the benefit of, men she supposed. It left little to the imagination but Flora appreciated the view and allowed her imagination to run wild; maybe she will not mention this to Wendy.

'Paddy, mo bhrathait alain,' the woman said, hugging Paddy.

Flora noted that this gorgeous woman had a much thicker accent than her Inspector, more lyrical, sexy, but she had to allow this may be her imagination on overtime. Flora looked to Paddy and shrugged her shoulders and sloped her head. He looked confused, so she explained for the dozy eejit. 'What did this woman, who I imagine is your skin and blister, just say, you dozy eejit?'

This seemed to amuse the trench coat Goddess, and before Paddy could say anything, he always was a bit slow, Flora was smothered by the fine red hair and all she could see was a pale face with pouting red lips closing in, and Flora was captivated by the sultry staring emerald eyes. This gorgeous woman was like a lioness focused on her kill, namely a half-Maltese detective sergeant with a less fattening centre. Flora was unable to move, resigned to accept what was about to happen, excited in reality. The woman grabbed both of Flora's shoulders, it was a mighty grip as well Flora noted as the woman's whisky breath filled her nostrils and then moistened her ear. 'Mo Dhia do bhean bhoidheach mar sin tha thu, b'urrainn dhomh fuck an-seo agus an-drasta,' and then the crackerjack woman kissed Flora full on the mouth. She stepped back, presumably to enjoy the image of a shocked detective sergeant Flora. Still in a stupor and sucking in the heady vapour of perfume and whisky, Flora noticed this woman's brother was unmoved, as if he was used to this behaviour, when the French resistance returned and in a lilting whisper, 'What I said was, a greeting to my beautiful brother and, to you...'

'Yes, yes, Roisin, enough, please,' Paddy more than suggested.

'No, Paddy, I want to know...' and she looked to Paddy's sister, '... please.'

Roisin offered a broad and most alluring smile. 'What I said, Flora, because you are Flora, are you not, so?'

'I am, and how do you know me?' Flora answered.

'Well, you are first and foremost a beautiful woman, and I've followed you often enough,' and she looked and grinned at her brother.

'You've followed me?' and Flora spoke to Paddy, 'Paddy...?' Paddy just shrugged his shoulders and held out supplicant hands. 'You are most certainly a bleedin' dipstick.'

'Ah, he is that, so. Well-known for it, so he is,' Roisin said, offering a playful punch to her brother's upper arm. 'Now, a drink, a quick chat and I have to be off...' and she looked to Paddy. 'We have a new Mother Superior you know.'

'I know. I'd like to meet her sometime soon,' Paddy answered.

Flora was starting to sway, completely out of her depth, struggling to follow the conversation and still reeling from the smouldering kiss, she followed them to the bar where she saw three glasses of what she presumed to be whisky and, if Flora was to guess, they were triples.

'I thought you'd be wanting a snifter, as you British say, so I ordered *tree* stiff drinks, so.'

Fuck me, more Irish, Flora thought to herself. 'Paddy, I can't drink that. It's the middle of the day and I'm on-duty; besides, I do not have the head for whisky, just so you know.'

Roisin closed in, her lips again brushing Flora's ear, and again Flora was surrounded by flyaway sensual hair. 'Now then, Flora, me sweet darlin'. You want to know what I said to you just now, don't you?' Flora had come over all unnecessary, her legs felt weak, she was all over the place; she just nodded. 'Good, now, drink yer drink and I will tell yer, so I will,' and Roisin allowed her lips to brush Flora's ear; Flora could not avoid being sexually charged.

'Leave it out, Roisin, please. If she doesn't want a drink, let it go,' Paddy insisted.

However, it looked like Roisin took no prisoners. 'Is that right, Flora? You don't want to know what I said to you, eh?'

'I do want to know,' and then Flora recovered enough of her wits for a light bulb moment. 'Hang on. You're Roisin, and I am guessing you are, Roisin O'Neill, yes?'

'I am. Padraig's sister. ' Roisin now focused on the clever bonce woman in front of her.

'I did warn you, Roisin, she's no dunce...'

'Shut it, Paddy,' Flora now insisting that the bog dweller shove off or at least keep his north and south shut. 'Okay. Now, not so long ago, we had a Roisin Dubh here in London, specifically the East End, my manor.' She put her hand up to stop the motor mouth Irish gobshite from commenting. 'You're Roisin and your feckin' eejit of a brother at first led me to believe it was a Chas Larkin, dressed up as the Black Rose. And then, in his hospital bed, after being blown up, a wall falling on top of him, which he unfortunately survived, he said he was O'Neill, not Casey, and was the Black Rose.' Roisin smiled adoringly at Flora and then her brother who was about to be allowed to speak, but only when Flora said so, mainly because Flora had him by his non-existent bollocks; at least, this is what she imagined after she had removed them, that is. 'So, Paddy, what do you say?'

'I didn't say I was the Black Rose,' and he floated his airy-fairy hands about to reinforce his innocence, but it didn't look to him like it was working. 'Well, what I mean to say is, it suited for those gathered around my bed to assume all of that. So, I am sorry, Flora. What I said was O'Neill was the Black Rose and...'

Flora stopped him, she grabbed her whisky and downed it in one. 'Feck, that burnt,' she exclaimed. 'You...' and she pointed at Roisin.

'Flora, it's rude to point.' Paddy said and immediately knew he had encountered a Flora trip-wire and it could explode any minute.

Flora, while she still had her finger out, used it judicially to poke Paddy in his chest and she felt a little better, or maybe she was a little bit tipsy. 'So, Roisin. You are the Black Rose, yes?'

'Shush, Flora leannan, don't let the whole feckin' world know...' and she leaned in, to take up station with Flora's ear once again. 'Leannan is darling in the Irish and what I said was that you are a beautiful woman and I could fuck you right here and now.' And Roisin, picked up her drink and downed in one, practiced and unmoved by the burn. 'Now then, I must go...'

'Wait, I still have some questions.' This delay enabled Paddy to sip his whisky, while he looked on and admired his detective sergeant in full interrogation mode; she always impressed him.

'Fill yer boots, gorgeous,' Roisin sensually granting permission to be interrogated.

'You're going to meet your new Mother Superior, yes?' Roisin nodded, looked to the barman who slammed down another tumbler of whisky and left the bottle: Jameson's. 'You're a nun?' Flora asked, unable to mask her amazement.

'I am a nun.'

'A nun?'

'A nun.'

'Yes, she's a feckin' nun, Flora, okay?' Paddy seemed irritated, and this caused both women to smile appreciatively; job done.

'And let me make another guess. There is a new Mother Superior at the Convent of Clemence, is that where you are going?' Roisin nodded. 'You're catholic, I presume?' another nod. 'But the Sisters of Clemence are C of E?'

Paddy butted in for some light entertainment, 'Church of Egypt,' and he laughed heartily until he opened his mirth-ridden eyelids to see the death stare from two women. 'Sorry.'

'Yes, they are Church of England, but I don't care, do you, Paddy?' He said nothing, just shook his head; no fool that man.

'I know of the Sisters. They do amazing work with the poor in the East End, and take in orphaned girls, educate them, and if they do not take orders, they place them where, as women, they can influence the decision-makers, in business, the professions and even government. Their aim is to pave the way for a full meritocracy for women, so much so that they eventually take over and run the country with empathy and not for money-grabbing war-loving bastards.' Flora phewed and looked apologetically to Roisin, not Paddy; he could look after himself and, she was beginning to realise, so could the Black Rose. 'Sorry.'

Roisin leaned in and gave Flora another brahma of a kiss. 'Paddy said you were good and you are,' she said as she came up for air.

'Look, you should know, I'm in a loving relationship...'

'I know, Wendy, right? Got yerself a cracker there I have to say. I'd give her one for sure...' and Roisin offered a wink.

'Are you not, celibate?' Flora asked, now wondering if the Black Rose had followed Wendy as well.

'Celibate? Feck that for a game lady soldiers. Now, I must go,' and she downed the neat whisky.

Flora shot out an arm, 'I'm coming with you.'

'You are?' Paddy questioned before Roisin could say the same.

'I've always wanted to go, *Sub-Rosa...*'

Now this shocked Roisin. 'You know of Sub-Rosa?' Roisin asked, her glorious head sloping, and Flora finally felt she had the upper hand.

'I know of it and would like to know more, please, Roisin.'

'Okay then, let's get our skates on. Paddy, your shout for the drinks and then, you up for an afternoon in a convent, eh? All those nuns; hubba hubba.'

20

PROFESSOR CHARNEL - WENDY AND TRIXIE

NADIA WENT WITH PROFESSOR CHARNEL TO THE CANCER WARD where they were met by the doctor who had been treating the pathologist.

'Professor,' and he swung his look to Nadia, 'I hear you collapsed? Nadia, I think we should admit Brian to assess where we are,' Dr Green said to Charnel but was looking at Nadia.

'Can you give me a moment with the professor, Rob... please?'

Green responded. He liked Nadia. 'Of course. I will need to speak to the ward sister anyway and brief her, so fire away, he will be okay in the wheelchair where he is for the time being,' and swinging his gaze down to the wheelchair, 'that okay for you, professor, and would you like me to call your wife?' The professor coughed a yes to both questions. He needed to see his wife. He sensed he was closer to death than he had imagined.

Green, a squat man not particularly comfortable in his body, scuttled down the ward and disappeared into the Sister's office. Satisfied they were alone, Nadia sat down on her haunches beside the wheelchair. 'Professor, you say the bodies of the children have not been taken yet?'

'No, not yet. They're in the chilling cabinets, why?'

'I think I may have a solution to all of our problems. Do you trust me?' Professor Charnel nodded, he did, resigned in his fate and seeing Nadia as a beacon of hope. 'Okay, your priority is to protect your family, yes?'

'Yes, but how can you do that?'

'Best you do not know. As far as you are concerned, you always did everything you were supposed to do, what would be expected of you, except today; you were too ill. Agreed?'

He nodded, 'But I had done the autopsies and made two reports... for each...'

Nadia waved the folder containing the full reports. 'Where will I find the single summary sheets?' Nadia asked.

Charnel looked worried and Nadia reassured him with a gentle look. 'The top file, the one they want for the police, is on top of my desk. The detailed report with my findings, you have and there is a backup carbon copy in chiller cabinet six. It has a loose panel to the rear of the door that can be opened slightly by releasing the top two screws, copies are behind there,' and it looked like this revelation had been a huge relief to the professor.

'So, if anyone comes a-calling to ask, this is what you say. You've not done the autopsy yet as you were ill. Stick with that and I think I can free up any risk to your wife and kids. Now, I must dash, I will call in to see you later,' and she leaned over and kissed him on his cheek. 'You're a good man trapped by some bad men, and I promise you, I will bring them down. Bye.' Nadia headed off to the stairs down to casualty to let them know that she would be out of the department for a while and then headed for the basement and the mortuary.

———

Wendy Richards was too distressed to even think about carrying on working. Her encounter with Maude Larkin had shaken her up considerably and she was still trembling when she discovered that Muriel was not at her desk. Wendy scanned the note. So, Maude had done the biz on her receptionist as well, and she had resigned. Wendy could not say that she blamed the woman. A mother of three children, she had other more pressing priorities than loyalty to a loony psychiatrist fixated on research into the gangsters of the East End, and even Wendy was starting to examine her motives. Fear caused her brain to fuzz. She had called Arbour Square police station to get Flora to come and collect her but was told that she and DI Casey were out and not expected back. She asked that should they call, Flora be told it is a family emergency and to come home immediately. Whether the message would get through, Wendy doubted. She knew Flora and Paddy were almost persona non-grata in the Nick, so some of the spiteful coppers may not pass the message on, even if they did call in.

In the event, Wendy decided to leave the hospital and caught a bus. She would not feel safe until she was home, and even then, not until Flora was with her. And then the dreadful necessity, how to tell her what had happened. She would deal with that later, first, she had to get home. Seated on the bus with the comfort and security of other passengers around her, she sensed she was close to tears.

'You alright, darlin'?'

Wendy looked into the kind eyes of an elderly woman sat beside her and staring at her with honest concern. Oh, how she loved the local cockney people. The ordinary people that is, not the fucking gangsters. 'Not really, but thank you. I've had a bit of a scare and it has fair shaken me up. I'm going home.'

Wendy felt the warmth of a feeble arm hugging her and the floodgates opened. 'I'll walk you home, sweet'art...'

'Thank you... there is no need...' Broken sentences from both women, both insistent.

'There is, and I'll brook no argument.'

'This is my stop now anyway,' Wendy said as the bus began to slow down.

The old lady stood, reached up for the cord and rang the bell, so the driver knew passengers were wanting to get off. 'It's only a couple of stops more for me, so it's not inconvenient,' and the old lady and Wendy alighted from the rear platform, the conductor helping them both, thinking the old lady was frail and the younger woman would collapse anytime.

'You sure you're alright, miss?' the concerned conductor asked.

'She'll be okay, thanks. I'm walking her home, she's had a funny turn,' the old lady answered and gestured with her head to the push bell.

He pushed the bell and swung on the pole, leaning out, 'Hope you feel better soon luv...' and the bus was gone.

'Now then, sweetie, where do we go?'

'I'm just down the next street. I should be alright...' Wendy answered still detecting a wobble in her voice and feeling now, embarrassed.

The old lady showed grit and determination. 'Come on, I will see you in and make you a nice cup of tea. I'll stay with you until you feel better. My name's Trixie, and you...?'

'Wendy, and thank you. I appreciate it.'

'Is there someone I can contact for you? There's a telephone box on the corner...'

'We have a phone in our flat, and I've left a message for...' Wendy was not sure whether to say Flora's name but did not need to as Trixie butted in.

'Got a dog and bone eh, Uncle Josh that,' and Trixie giggled like a little girl, and this warmed Wendy. She liked this woman, a real East End character.

'We have a phone because I'm a doctor and my... my, err, partner, is a police detective.'

'Filf is he... well, it takes all sorts, and as I always say to my Bert, that's me pot-and-pan...' and she looked at Wendy the posh woman with a phone, '... *my old man*, husband, sweet'art, get me drift.'

Wendy nodded. 'Yes, I knew that. My partner is a cockney.'

'From round 'ere is he? Well, I 'ope he's not a wrong'en, but as I was saying, we complain about the filf, but if there's trouble, it's them we call, right?'

Wendy nodded. 'This is me. We have the first floor flat. As I said, there is no need to come in...'

Trixie put a hand on Wendy's arm. 'What kind of neighbour would I be if I left you all distressed? I will wait with you, make sure you're alright until your fella gets home, okay. I'll not take no as an answer.'

Wendy retrieved her keys from her handbag and climbed the few steps to the street door, looked at her elderly guardian angel. 'Two flights of stairs I'm afraid.'

Trixie looked at the steep dog-leg stairs. 'No sweat, sweet-'art, I was a dancer in me time and still got it, me an' Bert down the rubbadub on a Saturday night, we trip the light fantastic,' and Trixie showed just how spry she was as she climbed the stairs in front of Wendy.

Wendy and Flora's flat was in a modest Georgian terraced house, divided up after the war to meet the housing demand, and consequently the rooms on the first floor, originally formal reception rooms, were spacious and well-proportioned. Wendy opened the door and ushered Trixie in first and the old girl whistled, 'Blimey babes, what a lubbly jubbly French plait you and yer fella 'ave 'ere, and neat as a pin. Bet that's you though, eh?'

Flora looked at Trixie, questioning, and then it dawned on her. 'Oh, French Plait, flat. Yes, it is nice and I have to keep on at

Flora otherwise it would be a pig sty, but she makes up for it in other ways...' Wendy realised the cat was out of the bag. '... Oh, err...'

Wendy saw that Trixie was not flummoxed and seemed to take the news of Wendy being in a lesbian relationship in her stride. 'Ginger beer are you, sweet'art? Don't worry on my account, I've been round the block a few times. It takes a lot to shock me. I 'ave a nephew who's Perry Como, and we love him dearly even if he is light on his feet,' and she chuckled. 'Between you and me honey, I said I was a dancer, but in truth, I was a stripper, although my Bert says I was an exotic dancer. Blokes, eh,' and she laughed and Wendy liked Trixie more. 'So yer twist and twirl's a filf detective, eh? That's some achievement that is. You must be proud.'

Trixie kept talking and at the same time working her magic. Wendy was feeling a lot calmer although she knew as soon as Flora came home, she would breakdown; how could she not. How could she not tell her what Maude had done, and she knew Maude would take pleasure in grassing her up to Flora, not to mention she may pay a call to Wendy again to check, as part of her *anger management* counselling.

Wendy was so distracted she did not realise Trixie was talking to her from the door of the kitchen, 'Sorry, Trixie, I was away with the fairies, if you pardon the pun...'

Trixie laughed. 'Got it in one sweetie, fairies. Now, I'll make us a pot of Rosie Lea. Where d'you keep the necessary?'

Wendy got up and followed Trixie into the kitchen, retrieving the tea caddy from a wall cupboard that Flora called the Mother Hubbard. The kettle was easy, as was the old brown earthenware teapot. Trixie got the milk from the fridge, with just a flick of the eyes to say she was impressed they had a fridge, and Wendy set out the teacups and saucers, happy to be doing something, a welcome distraction.

21

OKAY AT THE MORTUARY CORRAL?

NADIA FOUND THE CARBON COPIES OF THE REPORTS. THEY WERE where Charnel had said they would be and she destroyed the single-page reports intended to be collected. She had no idea when the retrieval thugs would arrive, but she put the tiny, emaciated bodies of the three boys on separate tables. The tableau was an awful sight, and Nadia felt the bile rise in her stomach; what men would do to children to satisfy their own perverted carnal lusts. She hosed down the tables to make it look as though she had just completed the autopsies herself and added her name to the bottom of the truthful reports that had been left unsigned. Charnel had been thorough, and with the copies of the duplicate reports behind the cabinet door, Nadia felt she had all bases covered.

Satisfied she had arranged things to look as they would be expected to be, and using the mortuary camera, she took detailed photos that showed clearly the diabolical things that had been done to these poor children. The photos would eventually be attached to the report; she removed the film and taped it to the underside of the desk. She was done. If the goons arrived now, it should all look normal, except Professor Charnel was not there to cover up the misdeeds.

Nadia sat at the desk, picked up the phone and swivelled in the chair while the operator put her through to Arbour Square police station. Her call was answered by the desk sergeant, Jim Rayner, someone she now knew she could trust and most importantly, Paddy had confirmed was kosher. Previously the desk sergeant had been *Old George* and he leaked like a colander to whomever would pay the most. 'Jim, is that you?'

Rayner recognised the exotic accent. 'Nadia?'

'Yes, Jim. Is Paddy or Flora back?

'No, sorry.'

'It's okay, but if you can get a message to him and say that I am in trouble and at risk, please.'

'Nadia, I will put out a call, but you know him, will-o-the-wisp. Now you see him and then you don't. Where are you? Let me get help to you.'

'Thank you, Jim. If you can get two of your most trusted to the mortuary at the Royal, I am expecting some ruffians anytime soon...'

Jim cut her off, 'Hang on, Nadia, stay on the line...' and he disappeared. She waited and then he was back. 'Nadia, you still okay?'

'Yes.'

'I am sending Smokey Robinson and Jack Parlance. You will know they are the real deal because Smokey is the only black copper we have and Paddy rates him. Parlance is Smokey's partner, not too sure about him, but Smokey will keep you safe. Can you tell me what is happening, please?'

'Jim, make some notes and draw up a formal report and then record it, so it cannot be... *lost*, if you get my drift? Smokey can take a copy of my autopsy reports on the three young boys found in the mud of the Thames tributary, you may recall. Jim...' there was a catch in her voice, a mixture of fear and sadness, '... they have been used and abused terribly. Those poor children, but I suspect you know?'

'I do, Nadia. Hold up, I have Smokey and Parlance here now. I'll get a patrol car to take them. It'll be quicker,' and she could hear Jim instructing the two uniforms. 'Get to the mortuary at the Royal, bloody quick and be prepared for some rough stuff. Dr Nadia may be in trouble, so, bell sounding all the way, okay?'

"Sarge," she heard a deep baritone voice answer and the sound of scuffling feet; her cavalry, coming over the hill in the nick of time, she hoped.

'Now, Nadia,' Jim was back on the phone addressing her, 'I want you to stay on the line. Just leave the phone receiver off, somewhere discreet, cover with papers or something, just so I can hear that you are safe until Smokey and Parlance get to you. In the meantime, I will step up the search for Paddy and Flora. Wendy has also asked for Flora urgently. What the fuck is going on?'

'It's serious, Jim, and not even Paddy knows how much.'

———

Nadia sat in the swing chair behind Charnel's desk and waited; she wished to appear casual, but she was on edge and not at all relaxed. Waiting? What for? Who would turn up first? Thugs or the police? She had the autopsy reports in front of her and reread them. Charnel had done a thorough job, as she would have expected of a man with a considerable reputation, and then she thought, maybe this will be tarnished as soon as all is revealed? She hoped not, but needs must, and surely most people will see that he was forced into the situation. It was not of his making. She hoped his family would understand. He had only their welfare uppermost in his mind, and then it occurred to her, did his wife know?

The swing doors squeaked and Nadia looked up, relieved to see it was the two uniformed policemen. She looked at the black officer and, with a certain amount of irony, 'I take it you are Smokey?'

'I am,' and he had a wonderful smile, she thought, which went well with his Smokey smoking hot looks and deep baritone voice that reverberated in her chest. Well, she thought, if Paddy doesn't come up to muster, Smokey would be right up there as a replacement, first reserve even. As she continued to gaze into his deep brown eyes, she saw his smile fade. He'd looked over the corpses of the three boys and he could not disguise his emotions; he sighed. He noted Nadia observing him. 'I've seen a lot, especially around here, but this, it grieves me to the core. So much of it, and nobody does anything.'

'I agree, it makes my blood boil...' Nadia answered, her eyes on the other constable, officer Parlance did not seem at all disturbed, or in the least bit surprised.

'It's been going on forever, Doc,' Parlance said, explaining his nonchalant demeanour.

'And that excuses it, does it?' Nadia stood to assert her disgust, and not just the sadness of the three children in the mortuary, but the laissez faire attitude of this policeman.

'I'm not saying that, I'm just sayin', what can you do about it?' Parlance seemed taken aback by the reaction of this lady doctor.

Smokey rounded on his partner in uniform. 'That's why we are here, Jack, so we can do something. Someone has to make a stand sooner or later, and Dr Nadia is drawing the line, making the stand, and we must back her up and keep her safe.'

'Thank you, Smokey. I...' She halted as the doors squeaked again and two thugs entered and walked two paces before standing still; momentarily stunned? The police officers were not expected. It took a while, and Nadia was not encouraged that these were particularly bright thugs, and as the doors squeaked shut behind them, it was like they made a decision, one thug following the lead of the other. Legs spread, adopting a threatening body pose, the suited and booted men, sunglasses and malicious grins, scanned the room before focusing on the three tiny bodies.

Smokey took a step towards the goons. Both men, reacting in practiced and slick movements, removed guns from inside their jackets; the looks on their faces said they meant business, if the guns alluded you. The fact they made no effort to disguise their faces, apart from sunglasses, told Nadia that they had establishment back up to get them out of trouble, if anyone dared report them.

One of the gunmen spoke. 'Where's the prof?'

Nadia answered. 'If you mean Professor Charnel, he collapsed this morning and is in the oncology ward upstairs and...' she shook her head, '... I'm saddened to say, his condition is bad. The prognosis, he does not have long to live...'

She was halted as the gunman spoke again. 'Prog... what? And who are you? And what the fuck is oncology?'

'I am Dr Naadhira Khalid, and oncology is the treatment of cancer. The prognosis is our understanding of his condition and his chances of survival. The professor is riddled with the disease.' She kept her answer simple and direct, presented in a professionally clipped tone. She had faced interrogation at gunpoint before now and the Israeli troops were more gung-ho than these thugs who clearly did not want trouble, here just to collect the bodies, the accompanying paperwork to settle any administrative issues and get out of there. But now the police were present and it was an unexpected and additional complication, though this would not likely bother them either; the police were in their pockets, or their bosses' pockets, it was just a complication they could do without.

The lead gunman nodded to the bodies. 'We need to take them, and I will take the paperwork as well.'

'I'm sorry you can't do that. I have done the postmortem on these poor children, and they have been seriously abused. I have reported it to the police...' and she nodded to the uniformed constables.

'You've done what?' the first gunman was now reacting and he shuffled on his feet, a nervy reaction complete with a hair trigger hand, waving his weapon.

Smokey could see this developing, and not in a nice way. Still, he had to state the case even if these gangsters had no decision-making powers. It might at least delay them. 'The incident has been logged down at Arbour Square and I am here to look at the bodies, collect the reports and get back to the station. It will then be taken up with CID. I am sorry to say that these bodies are going nowhere other than back into the fridge.'

Nadia was impressed with the bravado of Smokey but was not sure if he could stand up to these two thugs, and in her opinion, Parlance would be no use at all, not sure he would have the spine or the ability to fight his way out of a wet paper bag.

'Stan, get the paperwork and bring that trolley over here...' the lead gunman ordered his confederate, who did as he was told. Flicking his fingers, thug number one indicated he wanted Nadia's reports. She passed the paperwork to him, nine pages of foolscap. 'What's this, it should only be one page?'

'That is a detailed autopsy report on each child, and what would you know about it? Have you collected bodies before from Professor Charnel?' Nadia pressed and saw Smokey roll his eyes; he was worried. Paddy had told him that his squeeze was a bit strong minded; well, this bore that out.

Smokey walked towards the man now with the levelled gun aimed at the policeman's chest. 'I think you should put the gun down, sir...' There was a resounding click in the stultified atmosphere as the gunman cocked his weapon. Parlance dived for cover rattling a trolley full of equipment, which masked the sound of the squeaky doors opening. Ruth Golding stepped in and shot both gunmen.

'Fuck me,' Smokey exclaimed.

Nadia could hear a tiny voice and realised that the phone was still connected to Arbour Square police station. She picked up the receiver whilst at the same time, with a finger to her mouth, indicating for Ruth to be quiet. 'Jim, we're all okay,' and she stopped to explain what was happening. 'I have had the phone line open all the time to Jim Rayner...' and for the benefit of Ruth, '... he is the desk sergeant at Arbour Square.' She went back to the call, 'Jim, noted. Yes, okay, you can call the cavalry off. I'll explain all later,' and she hung up, leaving a spluttering sergeant Rayner not at all satisfied. He despatched an armed team anyway.

Smokey asked the question that Nadia wanted to ask, directed at Ruth. 'Okay, we are no longer being listened to, so please, just who the hell are you? And by the way, thank you.'

'You're welcome. I am Ruth Golding.'

'I feel like I should know that name,' Nadia said, 'but I don't.'

'You're the *bookkeeper* for Tanner, right?' Smokey showing he had a grasp of not just East End gangland politics.

'I am, and I need to talk with Chas Larkin and your fella, Paddy Casey,' she answered Smokey whilst looking at Nadia. 'Lucky I decided to come and see you first. Your colleagues in casualty told me where to find you. Now, I suppose we will have to think about how to deal with this little mess, eh?'

'You may have a point there, Ruth,' Nadia answered with a smile and evident relief in her voice. 'I am sure Paddy will know what to do, but in the meantime, Smokey, maybe get back to your nick and say that someone unknown to you killed these men and then ran off?'

'Sounds like a plan,' Parlance said, breaking his silence at last, keen to distance himself from the carnage.

'Before you go, and after I photograph the scene, can you help me get the children back into the cabinets, and these thugs up onto the tables, if you wouldn't mind.' Nadia, demonstrated a professional attitude, disguising just how scared she had been.

22

BOYS' CLUBS – CLUBS FOR THE BOYS

CLARISSA HAD FINISHED ALL OF HER BISHOPRIC CLERICAL DUTIES for the morning, principle of which was besmirching any other candidates who might have set their sights on the Bishop of London job; that was her Smiffy's post to have, and Clarissa would stop at nothing. He would have to get it, or it would be the end of the gravy train for both of them. It was getting harder to lean on people these days as the public were becoming scandal hardened, but Clarissa had a few cards up her sleeve. Choir boys are, of course, always in demand, even more so if they could sing, and with her network they were ten-a-penny. The youth clubs were always there as well, but it was the Church orphanages and homes-for-boys that were the pay dirt.

Ordinarily, today wasn't the day that the Bishop did his rounds. However, Clarissa had received a call from the scaredy cat wimp of an MP, little Willie. He had rambled on about a visit from the IRA, the fucking turnip, Clarissa thought. However, Willie was a lynchpin to the whole game she had planned. He had been instrumental in getting the planning consent for the new Orphanage and Youth Club in Incubator Street School, despite robust opposition from the locals. More importantly, he had used his position to shut down police enquiries into *shenanigans* in the other *Home*s and *Boys' clubs*.

Clarissa retrieved the Bishop's Raleigh three speed out of the shed of Christ at the back of the garden, gave it a wipe over so that it sparkled; very particular was Smiffy about his Bishop cycle and all other matters of cleanliness, to the extent that he insisted Clarissa have a bath every fortnight, whether she needed it or not. Her bike, unlike the Bishop's new cycle, was a veritable bone shaker that she had had for ages, since her days at Canterbury; tight-fisted bastards were the upper echelons of the clergy. However, Clarissa considered this bone rattler of a bike wonderful to cycle around the East End and she deliberately steered their course so she had to ride over the cobbled roads, particularly satisfying. She even lost concentration once or twice and would bump into a parked car, and the Bishop would calm an irate owner with a sprinkle of Holy puddle water; he would never waste the good stuff on the plebs. He would then immediately forgive Clarissa, so what could anybody do about that? Nothing.

The bishop always followed Clarissa, not just because he had no clue where he was in the East End, even though this was his Diocese, because he had no interest in the area or the people, except some of the little boys were so charming, after he had bathed them, naturally. And anyway, he had bigger fish to fry, thinking to himself about the Bishop of London Palace and maybe they would have fish and chips that night; yum. Clarissa swung her bike into Incubator Street, looked at the new building works, now complete, barring a few snags she had been told by the builder. She was so focused on the new building she almost ran into the red and white striped road-work's tent. Must be for the connections to the utilities in the road, she imagined, ignoring it until she heard the bishop hit the tent. The fucking idiot she thought, looking back at Bishop Smiffy sprinkling Holy puddle water on an irate builder.

If she had thought about it a bit longer, or moved closer for a better look, the fact that the man was carrying a machine gun should have alerted her, but she was as short-sighted, physically and emotionally, as the Bishop; they made a right pair, and parishioners wondered that if they had decent eyesight and could see each other, whether they would have a relationship at all.

Smiffy picked himself up from the road and collected his bike and passed it to Clarissa to inspect for damage; she couldn't see any, obviously. In the meantime, the Bishop thought it a bit odd that a road worker should gesticulate holding a big stick and thought it even stranger that the two men inside the tent wore decent clothing, not scruffy work overalls; must be foremen, he thought. He dismissed his prejudicial myopic observations and wondered if the nuns had moved into the orphanage yet and whether they could kiss his grazed knee better. It was a good idea of Clarissa's to have some nuns on site as an extension to the local convent knocking shop. They were very busy these days, and he was forever forcing the nuns to comply with God's wishes that they keep the Diocesan coffers topped up, stepping up the extracurricular activities. Well, what was he supposed to do, the sisters made so much money for the Church. It would be okay, so long as the Sisters of Clemence did not hear about it, because if they did, there would be hell to pay. The Clemence Brigade were a deadly sin all of their own, and they were untouchable in their Royal Peculiar.

No nun being available, Clarissa rolled up the bishop's britches, kissed his grazed knee better, sprinkled it with Holy puddle water and all was well. Smiffy stopped crying and remounted his bike and followed his housekeeper into the school playground, ignoring boos and hisses from some of the residents in the street; this was normal, puddle water off a plebs back to Clarissa and the Bishop. He, of course, sprinkled them anyway because he was generous like that, but everyone knew it was just puddle water and not the good stuff, so they told him to fuck off, which he didn't hear because he was short-sighted and assumed it was Clarissa, who frequently told him to go bugger himself. There were times his housekeeper was temperamental and he never understood why as he was a good boy, after he had sprinkled himself with the good stuff and forgiven his sins, that is.

Entering the school hall, Clarissa could see the blur that was little Willie nervously pacing. His bodyguards were equally nervy, not understanding what was happening; they should have left by now, heading for the Houses of Parliament for the debate on Northern Ireland, even though nobody cared about that. Willie relaxed when he saw the bishop and Clarissa bearing down on him. It was mainly Clarissa bearing down, and you wouldn't want to be in the way of that; she looked mean, and a tad cheesed off.

'I'm glad you came...' Willie started off. It made him feel better, talking always did, even more so if he was leading the conversation.

'Oh, right, so that's okay then...' Clarissa replied.

Was that a sarcastic tone? Willie thought. 'I hope you didn't have plans because this is important.'

'Oh, no, just today is the day Smiffy has off, and well, we usually spend it in bed if I can tear him away from his altar boys.' Clarissa said with a sardonic smile and a brief glance to Bishop Smiffy, who looked like he'd got off homework, his mind drifting to a nearby Boys' Club that they could maybe call into for a random inspection, so to speak. 'Well, we're here now. You said you had a call from the IRA...?' Clarissa spluttered, thinking this was hilarious; the IRA, in London, how stupid was that.

'He is the Secretary of State for Northern Ireland, dearest,' Smiffy interjected, and Willie and Clarissa saw him splash himself with Holy puddle water; needs must in times of crisis, and Clarissa was a crisis.

'I know what he fucking is, bozo. He's a bleedin' nonce.'

Oh dear, Smiffy thought, Clarissa has likely been in Stepney too long, she's even speaking like the locals.

'I'm not a nonce,' Willie insisted.

Smiffy had a questioning look, likely wondering what a nonce was. 'Not a nonce?'

'No, not a nonce!'

'Not a nonce?' Clarissa repeated, unbelieving, raised eyebrows drawn on with a pencil.

'What's a nonce?' Smiffy asked, and both Clarissa and Willie burst out laughing at the dipstick bishop.

'Shut it, Smiffy. You nonce.'

'Am I a nonce, dearest?'

''Ave you fiddled kids?'

The bishop tried hard to look shocked. 'Clarissa...!' he almost shouted (told you he was shocked) as he looked around. Was anybody listening in? Willie sat back, enjoying the show, relieved Clarissa had a new target.

'Well...?' Clarissa tapped her hoof.

'A nonce?'

'Yeah, nonce, you.'

'Well, it doesn't count as I sprinkled myself with real Holy Water and forgave myself, so there.' Smiffy most sincere with his innocent smug face.

'Shut it, you child molesting, fucking nonce, or I'll kick you in your ecclesiastical bollocks.' So Smiffy shut it. Clarissa turned to Little Willie, 'What makes you think the IRA called on you?'

'Credit me with some intelligence, woman,' and Willie looked like he had overstepped the mark, and when Clarissa gave him a right-hander, he knew he had. Rubbing his cheek to sooth the soreness, Willie answered with as much bravado as he could summon. 'Well, for your information...' he looked and appeared to have got away with that, '... a woman with long ginger hair under a black beret and wearing a trench coat came into the hall and she spoke with a thick Irish accent, that's why. And, if I was still not sure, she showed me her pistol.'

Smiffy started giggling like a twelve-year-old. Clarissa turned on him. 'He said pistol, not Bristol, City, tittie, you jeffing moron.'

'You have lovely Bristols, Clarissa, my darling...' Smiffy, trying to make up lost ground, and it looked like he had scored as she sported a wide salacious grin.

Licking her lips and pointing a headmistress finger at her bishop. 'See me later.'

Little Willie interrupted the foreplay of the Bishop and his tart, 'What do I do?' Little Willie building a head of panicky steam.

'Nothing, Willie. You do nothing. She was probably just putting the frighteners on you, marking your card, you know.'

'Well, it worked. I am frightened. She mentioned the money the IRA had put into the youth club and orphanage, via Tanner and the George family, so I'd say she was the fucking IRA. Oh, and she left this note...' he waved the paper, '... and she said just before she left, "The O'Neills say hi."'

There was a stunned silence and all three looked scared now. Everybody in the East End knew of the O'Neills. Not who the O'Neills were, but what they were.

'I need to think about this...' and snatching the note, and after reading it, she turned to Smiffy and said, '... to the bikes, Batman.'

―――――

They would have had even more to think about if they knew about Byng lurking in the shadows, and what he had heard was prime intelligence, but who should he share it with. He knew Tanner was thick with the IRA and so was likely aware of what had just happened. He decided his best bet was to go to see the Georges. They also pay well, and he maliciously chuckled to himself, this would also screw with the Larkin Saints if the IRA were known to be now on their manor; how could they deal with that, a trained army on their patch. So, Georges it would be, and as they contributed spondulics, they may even allow him to be on the podium at the opening ceremony. Maybe they would even take him in and respect him; he deserved respect. He would have to live out in Tottenham which would be just as well as it looked like it could get a bit tasty here in the East End. If only he knew what the note said.

―――――

The Fat Cow pub

Lavinia put the phone back in its rest and shouted for George before she even looked around.

'What mum?' George was behind his mum.

'Jesus you made me jump, you bleedin' arse, and how did you know it was What?' Vinnie rebuked her son to the great amusement of the burgeoning bar, the locals enjoyed that but soon applied serious frowns when they saw that Vinnie could not see how funny it was.

'What, Mum?'

'Yes. What. You know, Bing... What Bing.'

'Oh...' George cottoned on, or at least gave the impression he did.

'George, the Bishop and that fat cow, Clarissa was given a note by little Willie at a meet this afternoon. I need someone to go into the Bishop's home and get it, quiet like. You have a man?'

'I do Mum, I do.'

23

SUB ROSA

'Back door, gorgeous?' the master of ceremonies, black cab driver, who had talked non-stop since leaving Trafalgar Square, interrupted his entertaining monologue to ask a question.

'You talking to me?' Paddy asked, eliciting great mirth, even from the cabbie who was the professional comedian.

Roisin answered the man after giving her brother an old-fashioned look. 'Yes, please. The Rose gate.'

'Gotcha, sweet'art, sub-Rosa, it is,' and the cabbie swung into a narrow lane and about fifty yards up on the right was a simple carved stone archway leading into a masonry shelter with a studded wooden door beyond.

The cab pulled up, and they stepped out while Paddy continued his joke with the driver whilst rattling loose change in his pocket, a manly gesture as a prelude to paying.

Flora, in the meantime, looked up at a carved insignia tracing the line of the stone arch. 'So, what does that say,' Flora said, speaking to herself, focusing her eyes. The stone was ancient and crumbly in parts, making the inscription some-what indistinct. Roisin was about to say, when Flora made a stab, reading it out in a passable French accent, recalling her languages at school where the teacher wanted her to take French further, but where would she use that in the East End, her father had said, '*Odre Ancien de La Mort noir des Soeurs de Clemence...*' and she translated for the benefit of her dozy bog dweller, DI Paddy, who now gave her his attention, the driver forgotten. 'The Ancient Order of the Black Death of the Sisters of Clemence. Bleedin' 'ell, that's cheerful.'

Paddy raised his eyebrows to his female company as he decided he'd played pocket billiards long enough and went to pay. The cabbie waved him away. 'If you have biz with the Sisters, this is free. They do such good work for the orphan girls where I come from.' There was no need to ask where he came from, his cockney accent said it all, and when you're ready to leave, I will collect you.'

'Thank you, I will be sure to tell Mother, and Sister Porter...' Rosin said as she muscled her brother out of the way and leaned in to read the name badge, '... Ron,' and she planted him a big kiss on his whiskery rough cheeks, leaving a strawberry imprint of red lips on a cheeky cockney chappy, grinning broadly as he drove off.

Flora followed Roisin through the arch, looking up to the ceiling in the loggia to a projecting carved rose. 'Is this the rose referred to in sub-Rosa? We are under the rose, after all?' Flora asked Black Rose.

Roisin was serious, the exotic mirth now mysteriously fading, maybe because she was a nun about to enter a convent? Not her convent, Flora presumed, but a holy establishment, nevertheless. 'Well, it symbolises the importance of the Rose to this Convent, but the true sub-Rosa insignia is a flat five-petal rose,' Rosin answered as she pulled on an iron rod with a looped handle that Flora presumed rang a bell somewhere, but she couldn't hear it. 'It is best that we meet the new Mother

Superior and she can decide if she wants to share the importance of the rose with you.'

Just then a tiny hatch in the solid timber door opened and there was a squeal of delight from a young face pressed against the metalwork grille. 'Sister Vagi-Sicarius, welcome, it is so good to see you. Mother is expecting you, oh...' she had spotted that the Black Rose had company, '... can you tell me who these other people are, please? I will have to check if I can allow them in. It's a busy Mother today, she already has one guest with her.'

Rosin responded looking to silence the young nun, presumably a postulant who might give away too much information. 'This is my brother, Detective Inspector Padraig Casey, and this is Detective Sergeant Flora Wade.' The nun closed the hatch and presumably went to inform the Mother of her additional guests.

'Sister Vagi-Sicarius?' Flora queried, keeping her distance from the Black Rose. As much as she had been titillated by the brief intimacy they had shared in the pub, she loved Wendy and did not want to betray that love.

Roisin answered, 'It's Latin...'

'Getaway wiv yer, I'd never have guessed.'

Flora's sarcasm fell on deaf Black Rose ears. 'Indeed.'

'Well, what does it mean?' Flora pressed, but the door was opening and she noticed Roisin's reaction. Her persona automatically displayed now a solemn countenance, so Flora copied her, not knowing how things worked in a Royal Peculiar convent. Paddy seemed immune, or he knew more than he was letting on; his passport everywhere, it seemed, was his Irish wide-boy grin.

As they were being ushered in by the excitable young nun, Paddy whispered to Flora, 'Vagi-Sicarius, it means, *Wandering Assassin.*'

Flora was about to offer a shocked retort but responded to the stern look from a more senior nun who had joined them, the implication clear; Sister Porter frowned. Flora hushed and dutifully followed the porter, Paddy, and a racy Black Rose across a garden laid mainly to growing produce. Nuns laboured in the mid-afternoon sun, and as the guests were shown inside the convent and the door closed behind them, there was a refreshing and welcome coolness within the stone corridor. Flora had no time to take in the architecture or even the tempered cool air as the nun had taken off at a fair lick, reached a door, spun and looked back, awaiting the train of visitors to catch up. As they gathered outside a door she said, unnecessarily, 'Mother Superior's office.' She knocked, opened the door, and with a flourish swept them inside, closed the door behind them and she was gone; she was not a part of this meeting, even though Flora sensed an inquisitive nature in their guide, and thought, she was a serious nun, but the postulant might not be taking orders, and wondered what career she would take up at the behest of the sisters?

Flora would have liked to take in the atmosphere at her leisure but was surprised to see that the Mother's attending caller was none other than public enemy number one, Chas Larkin.

Chas stood as they advanced on the large oak desk behind which sat the Mother, a petite woman of about thirtyish if Flora had to guess, and an attractive face; the rest was covered up and dressed as a penguin. She lifted herself out of her chair and stepped around the desk to gather some additional chairs.

'Roisin...' and Chas held his arms out and the Black Rose went into them.

'Chas. You're looking well, so,' and she hugged him in return and then planted a full-on kiss, that Chas took in his stride. Flora saw that it was passionate from both Chas and Roisin, and she had to presume that this wandering assassin nun batted off both feet; interesting. Chas then shook Paddy's hand, looked across to a stunned Flora, and strode to her, still with just the hint of a limp she noticed, and wondered if this was a psychological memory of his club foot? 'Flora, I'm pleased to see you again.' He shook her hand and held onto it causing the detective sergeant to blush; was he going to kiss her? There had been too much kissing today. 'Sit...' and Chas waved his free hand to three additional seats that the mother had set out in an arc around her huge and impressive desk before returning to her own captain's swivel chair. Chas dragged Flora to sit beside him and Flora wondered if Chas had sensed that she was making like a statue, she had been so stunned with Roisin, her revelations, her kisses, and now this amazing convent.

The Mother leaned across her desk and Chas pulled Flora's hand and planted it into that of the Mother; they shook a greeting, 'Flora Wade, so pleased to put a face to the intelligence that we have. I am Dame Adelaide Pimple, simply Mother Adelaide now.'

'Intelligence?' Flora asked unable to disguise her dismay, ignoring the naming ceremony, amazed at how young the woman was to hold such high office, and then recalled that this was an inherited title and position; privilege made her sick. However, Adelaide may be young but she had an intelligent face, and was, fit, from what Flora could see and imagine beneath her stilted garb, and imagine she did; she couldn't resist.

The Mother waved away Flora's query and intensive visual assessment to complete her greetings. 'Paddy, been a while, how is that lovely lady doctor of yours? Have you married her yet?'

Paddy answered, clearly frustrated. 'I keep asking, and she keeps saying, no.'

'Well, maybe if you were a little more honest with her, she will say yes. Yes?'

Mother had hit the nail on the head, Paddy's head, but it

was Flora who drove the nail in further. 'Yeah, and when you tell her, you can then tell me...'

'Now, now,' Mother chastised as she sat back in her chair, spread her hands and arms out onto the desk, and demonstrably leaned in to speak to her guests. Flora was taken in by the desk, almost black, it must have been polished so many times over the centuries and wondered how old it was. Adelaide provided the answer, 'I see you observing my desk, Flora. It has been with the Order since the late fourteen hundreds. Seen some action...' Adelaide said, and she gave a saucy wink to Roisin, who chuckled like a naughty assassin nun.

When they were all seated and the offer of tea declined, Mother opened up. 'It is fortuitous that you join us now...' and she swayed her head, '... there has been a lot happening and things may be going more speedily than we all anticipated.' Flora raised her hand to interject and this elicited tittering from Roisin and her brother, but a warm embracing smile from the Mother Superior. 'There is no need to raise your hand, Flora. It is, after all, time you were fully briefed,' and she looked to Chas and then Paddy. Both nodded and this infuriated Flora. It was noticed. 'You are angry, yes?' Adelaide asked.

'Yes, but toss pot, here...' and Flora brought herself up sharply, covering her mouth with a hand, worried she had offended the Mother Superior who spoke in such a refined way; she already knew Adelaide came from an aristocratic family and she was trying hard to conceal her natural resentment, '... sorry...'

Mother offered another beatific smile; must be a trick of the trade, Flora thought, and it worked, Flora was mollified and then angry that she could be so easily mollified. 'Please, do not worry, we are not precious here, and many of our flock swear. You may have heard some ripe language from Sister Blende here,' and she tilted her head to Roisin.

'Sister Blende?' Flora jumped in, looking first to Roisin then Mother and back to Roisin via a scowl to Paddy. 'How many fucking names... oops, sorry, hail bleedin' Mary and all that tosh... do you have? Black Rose, Roisin Dubh, Blende, and whatever that Latin malarkey was that meant watch out or I will walk around a bit and then kill yer?'

Mother Superior took over the conversation, the trademark smile spreading again in an appreciation of the humour of Flora's retorts, and Flora thought she was warming to the Mother, before she pulled herself up so as not to be suckered in. Who does she think she is, the bleedin' Virgin Mary, and that thought made Flora match the smile of Adelaide; posh tart, not from Nazareth?

'Maybe someday you will tell me what thought just crossed your mind just then,' the perceptive Adelaide said to Flora. 'Okay, the names. Officially Roisin was given the name Sister Blende when she came to us from Ireland. There has always been a Sister Blende in our Order...' and putting her hand up to halt any enquiry from Flora '... the name means, *cover*, from a Germanic root. We like to have a nun that we send into the community, to, err, observe...? However, the true root of the name, as far as the Sisters of Clemence are concerned, is that Blende means *Ore*, and at each rebirth of the name the sister is entitled for a precious metal: Gold, Silver etc. The current Sister Blende...' and she looked to Roisin, '... is Copper, quite appropriately because of her hair. Historically, a Sister Blende has skills beyond her calling, a *Gift*, if you like. We spot this, or nuns in another order find a *special* postulant and they are sent to us; we can protect them within our precincts as a Royal Peculiar, you understand?'

Flora nodded, 'It has been explained to me, but I suspect there is so much I do not know, yet.'

'Yes, there is, but suffice to say...' Adelaide continued, '... the *gift* is ordinarily one of a Seer, and without her nun's habit out in society, she will have a rare ability to *see* what is happening, and in street clothes, blend in. You may have noticed this with the *Black Rose?*'

'Spy, you mean,' Paddy clarified, but Flora had already got the drift of the *gift*.

'Maybe a bit more than that crude analysis, Paddy,' the Mother answered. 'Roisin was brought over from Ireland, err...' the Mother halted, channelling her thoughts, to explain, but not to go too far Flora surmised. 'She has a certain skill set that we felt was needed at the time, beyond the *gift* and other natural abilities. This was in nineteen sixty-six, you may recall, Flora?' Flora nodded, of course she remembered. 'We were concerned about the warring factions of the Saint and Larkin families, and aware also that the O'Rierdons had their eyes on the crown of the East End, and when she was here and taking in the territory, Roisin saw something in Chas here, and she was right, of course.'

Flora interrupted, a confused look on her face. 'I recall all of this, naturally. It's when I began with Paddy, but...'

'You cannot fathom why a collective of nuns should know and why they would act, yes?' The Mother cut straight to the point and looked to Paddy.

'Flora, I will explain fully later...' Paddy interjected, '... but the Sisters of Clemence, as a Royal Peculiar, have always involved themselves in the community, both pastorally as well as politically, and always maintaining a low profile, behind their good works.

'Other gifts, abilities?' Flora asked firmly, and then answered her own question, clearly impressing the Mother. 'Sister Vagi-Sicarius, yes, her skill as an assassin, I presume'

'Indeed, Flora. I can see that Paddy has been right on the button when he suggested you to us as a useful arm of our *Canon Law*. This is a time of great foment...' the Mother continued, '... we have the George family in the north and Tanner in the west, both, we understand, have formed an alliance in order to make an assault on the Larkin Saint territory in the East. This will happen, and when they do, it will not be pretty and even worse afterwards if one or other of them win that war. Add to that the knowledge we have that Tanner has taken over the funding the O'Rierdons enjoyed from the IRA, and we have double trouble.' Flora was going to say something, but the Mother once again stopped her. 'Not yet Flora, I want you to understand that our political view should be seen as neutral, but suffice to say that natural justice would, in our opinion, see Ireland united and the warring faction of Protestants and Catholics in the North concerns us deeply. You see, Flora, we have only the welfare of the innocent people as our objective, and especially the women. You may also gather from this that we will not interfere so long as people are not harmed. Damage to infrastructure, buildings, well...' and she waved a dismissive hand, '... that is a different matter, and if it helps bring politicians to the table...' There was no need to say more, Adelaide had made her point.

Flora leaned on the desktop and exchanged eye-to-eye contact with Mother Adelaide. 'I understand, and now let me guess, Maude Larkin has been going way over the top lately, and along with Bess Saint advanced in her pregnancy. This is all designed to make Tanner and the George family bring their plans forward when they are not truly prepared, and in this, I presume this includes the IRA objectives. However, *we* will be ready and waiting for them, yes?' Flora put up her hand to stop a response. 'Fuck me, are you helping the IRA?' There was no answer, just a stunned silence.

Flora had blown them all away. 'I told you she was a brainiac,' Paddy said, sitting back in his chair, taking the credit for his protégé.

'Take that supercilious grin face off yer Danny Boy boatrace or I'll clump yer. Women can think for themselves, you know...'

and Flora pointed to the Mother Superior and then waved her hand around to take in the whole of the convent. 'So, how about you tell me what has been cooked up, and Mother, you said things were happening fast. What things? And while you are at it, what the fuck is *sub-Rosa*?'

All eyes turned to Mother Adelaide; now was the time to reveal all, or at least nearly all, to this trusted cabal; trusted because Sister Blende had confirmed that they were trustworthy. 'To understand sub-Rosa you have to realise that the origins have become unlawful. In other words, the meaning has been supplanted by, men...' and she rolled her eyes, '... to their benefit, obviously, and side-lining women, naturally, putting them back in their box. Men have always been threatened by women. Why, I cannot fathom, not being a man, but the masculine take on sub-Rosa has been subverted to mean *privacy* or *secrecy*. Convenient, eh?'

'So, what do you believe it means? Or, what it was originally designed to mean?' Flora was engaging with Adelaide excluding the others.

Mother was intent on responding and the others sat back and listened. 'What sub-Rosa really means is *Divine Union*. Make of that what you will, but all life comes from a mother and sub-Rosa means, *The Magna Mater heralds the Dei Mater*, the Mother of the Gods also heralding the resurrection. Well, that was the updated version, naturally.'

'So, what you are saying is that all religion stems from women, or one woman, and that men took it and compromised it, or buggered it up?'

'Well, Flora, I suppose you could say that...'

Flora continued her interruptions, 'And this explains why the Sisters of Clemence look to assert the rights of women by education and eventually, if I am allowed to extrapolate, women will eventually control society, for the better?'

There it was again, Flora thought, the beaming beatific

smile of the Mother Superior. 'Simplistically put, but we also re-establish our own sexuality, yes. Men defined what Women should be and we, naturally, resent this, and aim to change that perception, slowly but surely. Not revolution but, evolution. Not dismissing men, but making us all truly equal in power, yes, but mostly, respect. A long-term goal, but if you excuse the crudeness of the argument, men have fucked up big time. Greed and war, for instance, and it is high time the women took over to sort things out; it is, after all, what we do.'

Flora was impressed by the vehemence with which the Mother Superior expounded the sub-Rosa philosophy as followed by her convent, it defied her age, but Flora presumed she had been groomed from a young woman for this role. It looked like this was all that Adelaide was going to part with, but there must be more. 'There must be more,' Flora stated, clear and standing her ground. 'There is more, I know, and I hope that one day you will share the rest with me.'

'Some time I will, Flora. Maybe if you come on a retreat with us, and bring Wendy, yes? That is a truly impressive woman, and I know she is viewed as meddling, it is the way men describe clever assertive women, putting them down, and I believe your partner in life will be at risk because of this.'

'What? She is?' and Flora stood immediately, ramrod straight, and she excused herself. 'Mother Adelaide, I must go, but when this is all sorted, Wendy and I would love to come to a retreat here and learn more. In fact, I think I would struggle to keep her away.'

And following Flora's lead Adelaide stood and moved to the door. As they filed out, Flora went to shake Adelaide's hand but found herself in a warm embrace. 'Come back soon,' she whispered into her ear, and she stepped back and allowed Flora to open the door; she was impatient to get back to Wendy.

The nun who guided them to the Mother's office was waiting patiently outside, and wordlessly, took them back down the corridor, into the garden and to the sub-Rosa gate. She opened the heavy oak door and there was a cab there, it was Ron. 'Ron,' she called, 'please take these people to where they want to go.' Flora could see a look in Ron's face, and the sister reacted. 'Sister Fleur is well and growing stronger daily,' and then she closed the gate on the world, but the sisters reach could not be contained by walls or a gate alone; they were a Royal Peculiar.

Flora, Roisin and Paddy climbed into the back of the cab. 'Where to?' They gave their destinations and Ron sped off, calling back to offer an explanation as to why he was there waiting for them. 'Sister Fleur is my daughter, Janet. She was brutally raped and left for dead. The Sisters of Clemence took her in when she left hospital, and slowly she recovers. She has also expressed a desire to stay sub-Rosa, and we support her decision, and the nuns call the cab café in Cannon Street, it is how they get me. I was also at Trafalgar Square waiting for Sister Blende, so that explains that, eh?'

Flora was wondering about that coincidence but pushed Ron on his daughter. 'Did the police get her attacker?' Flora asked, softly. Ron was clearly still emotional about the whole episode.

Ron pulled over to the kerb, looked back to Flora. 'Not the police, but her assailant was found dead under London Bridge two days later, stripped naked, his crime written on his bare chest.'

'Really...?' It was Flora who noticed that Roisin and Paddy remained quiet. 'Oh... I see.'

Ron nodded, 'The Black Rose is a friend to the East End people, sweet'art,' Ron's spirits returned and as he drove away, he was back as the talkative cheeky chappy black cab driver.

24

HOME TO ROOST

Roisin had asked to be dropped off at Bishopsgate tube station and there she disappeared underground. Ron delivered Flora, waved a hearty goodbye, and proceeded to take Paddy home to Nadia.

Flora and Wendy:

Flora skipped up the steps to the street door, picked up a brown paper wrapped package with her name on it, tucked it under her arm, stepped into the lobby, slamming the door behind her after she had examined the parcel in more detail; you just never know these days. On the reverse was a sender's name. 'Fuck me gently,' Flora cursed, 'Maude Larkin. What the fuck?'

Upstairs Wendy heard the front door slam and said to Trixie, 'That will be Flora. She's no soft shoed ballerina,' a hint of humour that she did not truly feel.

'Okay, sweet'art, you drink that tea,' Trixie said, and went to the flat entrance door and could hear the clodhoppers of Flora approaching as she turned the dog leg in the stair and Trixie stood with the flat entrance door behind her.

Flora appeared and halfway up she stopped as she looked up to see an old lady where her door should be. 'Christ on a bike, you made me jump.'

'Sorry, darlin'…'

'Who are you and why are you here?' Flora approached more steadily until she was in front of Trixie. 'Oh no, has something happened to Wendy?' Flora had in mind immediately the thought that the Mother Superior had said that Wendy might be in danger. 'Is Wendy okay?'

Trixie stopped Flora from barging past her and into the flat with just a gentle touch with the flat of her hand. 'Let me talk to you before you go in. I know yer filf, so listen, please.'

Flora nodded, stopped but sensed an even greater panic. 'Okay, what is it?

'Wendy is okay, but she's had a scare. I met her on the bus. I could see she was distressed. I brought her home and stayed with her until you got home.'

'What happened?' Flora asked, craning her neck trying to look into the flat through the crack of the door.

'It has taken me a little time to get it from her, but I think she has had a run in with that mad mare, Maude Larkin.'

'What! I'll kill that cow…'

Trixie calmed Flora with a hand gesture. 'Please, be calm. She needs you to be strong, and more of a steadying presence rather than going bleedin' gung-ho. Okay?'

Flora sloped her head, enquiring of this elderly woman. 'Yes, I'm sorry. You're right. Err, who are you again?'

'My name is Trixie, people call me Trix. I live a couple of streets away, so it was no trouble for me to get off the bus with her; she was in a right two and eight.'

Flora was notably calmer. Trixie stepped aside and gave the door a gentle push to reveal a red raw faced Wendy poking her head over the back of the sofa. 'Oh, my darling, what has happened to you?' and Trixie pushed Flora gently, guided her, as best the heavy footed copper could do, and after putting the parcel on the dining table, she went to Wendy who stood to take the embrace of her lover. Wendy sobbed into Flora's shoulder.

Flora felt a gentle hand on her shoulder, and in a soft voice Trixie spoke, 'I will leave you now,' and speaking to Wendy, 'sweet'art, I've left me address on the table so you can contact me, if only for a cuppa splosh, okay?'

Wendy nodded, 'Thank you Trix, you've been a diamond. I'll be okay now I have Flora, and I will take you up on that tea.'

Flora stood and escorted Trixie to the door. 'I don't know what to say, other than thank you. It was so good of you, and fortunate you were on the bus when you were.'

'Look, luv, I know yer the old bill and it must be difficult, but something needs to be done about Maude Larkin, and since Bess Saint got in the club she has lost her grip of Maude and it is getting worse. Everybody's talking about it.'

Strangely, Flora thought with her police head, the plan they had discussed in the convent just now is clearly working, but she was angry that it should impinge on Wendy, but then, is it so strange? Adelaide indicated that Wendy was known, and might be in danger and perhaps, just maybe, Maude was sending another message, but to whom, and strangely could this be protection?'

'Look, I can see yer box of tricks...' and Trixie tapped Flora's head, '... is working away, so I will leave you for now and if I might say, you have a lovely woman there and I know you will look after her.' At that Trixie left for the stairs but called back, 'Don't be a stranger, babes, okay.'

Flora mumbled an acknowledgement and went back into the flat, closed the door and slammed the bolt. Wendy noticed and was alarmed, it was something they never did; this was a friendly neighbourhood, wasn't it?

Flora joined Wendy back on the settee and just cuddled

her, said nothing other than words of love and comfort. 'When you are ready, tell me. Take your time. I love you so much and hate that you've been hurt...'

'Flora...'

'Yes?'

'I love you too, but...'

'But what?'

'Well, if you shut up I will tell you.'

This comforted Flora, Wendy was back asserting herself. 'Sorry, my lovely. Tell me what is troubling you.'

'I've been... naughty...'

Flora couldn't stop herself laughing. 'What're you on about?'

Wendy was back sobbing again and Flora pulled her back into her arms. 'Tell me all about it. Trixie said you had a run in with Maude Larkin.' Flora felt Wendy stiffen. 'Please, tell me. I think I know what is happening?'

'You do?' Wendy was for the first time energised, and this again encouraged Flora.

'Yes, but tell me what happened to you first,' and Wendy told Flora all, with many stops to cry and to look into Flora's eyes to see how she was taking the news. 'So, Maude came to you to seek anger management counselling,' Flora could hardly contain an ironic chuckle, but she did because she could see how traumatised Wendy was.

'She did and, you see, I've been naughty and you have to punish me. You know about the relationship between Bess and Maude?'

'I know that in their domestic set-up Bess is submissive, why?' Flora responded.

'You did? Why have you never told me?'

Flora was stunned, 'Well, it never occurred to me that you would be interested and, most people know.'

'They do?'

'Pretty much, yeah.'

'Well, I didn't and as I said, you have to punish me. Please do that. Maude will ask if you had, she said so, and said she would deliver a cane for you to use on me.' Wendy looked deep into Flora's brown eyes, saw that she looked over to the dining table where there was a package. 'She has delivered it then...?'

'Wendy, my love, there is no way on earth I would hurt you, physically or emotionally. I love you,' and with that she stood, retrieved the package from the dining table, opened it and broke the cane into many small pieces, demonstrably taking out her anger on the stick.

Wendy was aghast. 'Oh my God. What am I going to do now? What if she comes to check if you have punished me?'

'She will not, because I will see that she doesn't, okay? You trust me don't you?'

'Of course. So you're not mad at me. I was too scared to stop what she was doing to me, I... I. I'm not sure how to say this, but I felt a flutter of excitement... I'm so sorry...'

'Listen to me, Wendy. What I am going to say is important.' Wendy nodded, her dry heaving sobs melting Flora's heart even more. 'I should not need to tell a trick cyclist this, but sometimes in scary situations like you were in, it is possible to feel a sexual charge; it happens. I have heard of it and seen it, so I could never blame you, and if you need forgiveness, then you have it in full along with all of my undying love.'

'Flora, my darling – thank you. I love you so much also, even more now, if that is possible.' Flora stood. 'Where are you going?'

'To the phone, it is important I tell Paddy, because I also think Nadia may be in danger and he needs to know just how real this is.' Just then the phone rang, Flora picked up 'Paddy, yes...'

Nadia and Paddy:

When Ron arrived at Paddy and Nadia's building, there was a police car waiting outside.

'Oh dear, this don't look good, Paddy,' Ron, the master of understatement, said.

'No, but I am a filf, in your parlance, Ron, so I'll love yer and leave yer,' and Paddy stepped from the cab, waved Ron goodbye and walked to the kerb where the police driver had exited the patrol car having seen Paddy arrive.

Paddy recognised the officer but could not recall his name. 'You here for me?'

'Der, yes...' the officer replied, and Paddy thought another cockney joker, and before he could offer up a rebuke. 'Please get into the car, I need to take you to the hospital, Doctor Nadia has had some trouble.'

Paddy felt immediately sick to his stomach as he dashed to the passenger door and hopped in. The squad car launched into a speedy departure with the bell sounding, scaring Paddy even more. 'Is she okay? Tell me, now...'

The driver flicked a glance to the detective inspector with the dangerous rep as he manoeuvred in and out of traffic. 'She's okay, but has been in a shoot-out and two people are dead...' and here the officer offered up a sly grin, '... in the mortuary, sir,' and then he did chuckle and so did Paddy. Well, Nadia was okay, and he also knew she was made of sturdy stuff, but even so, he was scared for her.

The squad car pulled up at the casualty entrance and Paddy was relieved to see two armed uniform officers at the entrance. He jumped out and the squad car pulled away. 'Where do I go?' Paddy asked the uniforms and as they went to point so a black officer approached and stood the men down.

'Inspector, I am...'

'I know, Smokey Robinson, right?'

'Correct, sir. Now if you will follow me,' and he spun on his heel and marched off in double quick time, Paddy following, thinking Smokey must be in the Met athletic team, but then his mind changed to focus on what he might find in the mortuary, apart from dead bodies that is.

As they approached the mortuary, Paddy slowed down and felt inside his jacket for his gun and left his hand on it. He knew that his police station leaked and it would not be beyond belief that he was being set up, but also knew Smokey was kosher. However, he would take no chances.

Smokey noticed Paddy's actions. 'It's okay, sir. The scene is secure...' Paddy looked circumspect. 'Nadia, can you come out here please,' Smokey called, and after a little time Nadia appeared at the squeaky double doors.

'Where the fucking 'ell have you been, eh?' Nadia lost her cool and Smokey retreated, preferring to take his chances with the gunmen, even more so since they were dead.

Paddy took his hand out from his jacket, a movement that Nadia noticed. 'Well, I thought I could be walking into danger and I was right, just not about what,' and he laughed.

Nadia fell into his arms, 'Stone me, Paddy, I've been trying to get hold of you all day. Where have you been?'

'With my sister and Flora, and then some nuns...'

He didn't get a chance to finish as Nadia pushed him away, 'Oh shut up, Paddy, and come inside. We have to sort something out.'

Paddy, feeling more than a bit cheesed off, followed the woman he loved, wondering what he needed to do to get her to take him seriously. Inside the mortuary, Paddy slipped into Ops mode, took in the two suited bodies on the tables, another uniformed officer whom he did not know, and a woman he did. 'Ruth Golding, as I live and breathe, so. You turn up in the most unexpected places, but why here?' Nadia was aware that Paddy's accent thickened, and wondered why, was it for the benefit of this Ruth?

Nadia answered. 'We were about to be gunned down by these thugs when Ruth came in and shot them.'

Paddy stood back, not quite in amazement as he had learned to have respect for Ruth Golding when she had been attached to the O'Rierdons. 'I owe you a debt, Ruth, again...'

'You do, Paddy, and we need to talk, but first off, I believe you have contacts to deal with these bodies?'

Paddy crossed to the desk and picked up the phone, dialled, waited, then spoke, 'Hemmings, I need a clean-up squad at the Royal London hospital mortuary, as quick as you like...' paused, '... not me, Nadia. Yes, you heard right, now, please. Thank you.' Nadia went to Paddy but he put up his stopping the traffic hand, guaranteed to annoy his twist and twirl, and he took some pleasure as he walked on the wild side and dialled again. 'Flora, sweet'art. We need to meet up now...' he listened for a little time. 'Fuck me, really? I think the Mother Superior must have had a sense of what was happening. She did say things were moving on a pace. Listen... I said listen. Nadia was attacked and I am coming over to your flat now with her, and Ruth Golding... Yes, you heard right, Ruth Golding. We will see you in a minute.' Paddy replaced the phone and turned to the two uniformed officers, 'Smokey, you and your mate, droopy draws...' Nadia laughed and Paddy was encouraged, '... these bodies will be collected soon. Stay with them and allow nobody in, do you understand?' Both officers nodded, and Paddy made to leave, Ruth and Nadia were already halfway out. 'Oh, and you can take the sunglasses off the bodies, not to sure they will be that worried about the bright light now,' and Paddy chased up the ladies.

———

Chas, Peanut and Blossom:

Chas didn't ride in Ron's cab, he had a lift from one of the grocery suppliers to the convent. He much preferred to travel in the van with Peanut. Nobody knew his real name, it was always Peanut since he sold peanuts when he wasn't delivering groceries. He could especially be heard at Millwall football club, shouting, "Poiyerut, tanner a bag, roasted," least this is what people thought he said.

Peanut picked up a lot of gossip on the streets and he had been friends with Chas for a long time, not close enough to be a Peanut Myrmidon, but close enough. What Peanut had heard, Chas already knew; the Georges were tooling up and Tanner was in cahoots with them, but what Chas did learn, however, was that the Georges were intent on picking up 'Opalong. It was a good plan working out, and he felt good and looked forward to dinner with Blossom and Tommy: stew and dumplings, his favourite, but first he had to mark some cards.

25

THE ARF A SIXPENCE PUB

IN THE 'ARF A SIXPENCE PUB, TANNER HAD DONE HIS SOCIALISING, his schmoozing with the Brigade boys, securing his position as a favourite of the IRA. He'd even joined in with a chorus of *The Fields of Athenry,* a favourite ballad about a Galway man in the 1840's famine, caught stealing food for his family and being transported to Botany Bay. Tanner could not understand the popularity of the song, but he had learned it and enthusiastically sang along with the others.

The barman nodded to Tanner and gestured with his head, he was wanted in the back room. Tanner knew what this meant. There were likely senior IRA men wanting to meet with him. Frankly, he was getting a tad fed up. They were always so impatient, but they had given him a lot of money, so he supposed it was not unreasonable for them to expect a bit of the old Tanner flannel. He was good at making things up on the spot and things were more or less on programme; his programme, that is. The Georges were primed, the only difficulty, curbing their enthusiasm until the time was right; for himself? Well, Chas Larkin will be no more from tomorrow and then it would be up to the IRA, via the Georges, to blow up the fucking dykes.

He ducked behind the bar and through to the back room. There were two men dressed in black fatigues and wearing black berets guarding the door. This told Tanner two things: one, there were some high-ranking men inside, and two, the feckin' guards were not exactly discreet, almost announcing to the world they were IRA soldiers. Oh well, he thought, not his problem, apart from they were in his pub.

The sentries recognised him and with a nod, one opened the door and the other ushered Tanner in with a shove. This alerted him. Something was up; this was not going to be a polite meet and greet. However, Tanner put on his cheeky chappy cockney boy face and began with the spiel he had practiced so often; it never let him down, 'Whatcha me old cock Robins...' His bravura soon departed. If the guards had him rattled, when he entered the room, he was faced with three people all wearing full black balaclavas, just eye holes and one for the mouth. It was clear there were two men and one woman. The woman had the head of the table and spoke. 'Tanner, sit...' and with a stilted military flourish she pointed to a seat at the other end of the table. Tanner sat, like a good little boy. 'We're getting impatient,' the woman continued, 'so far you've had our money and you have expanded your Empire with no pay back for us. We had anticipated getting a foothold in the East End by now...' The woman left a menacing pause, '... have we picked the wrong man, Tanner? And we are not overly comfortable with some of the investments you have made.'

'What...?' Tanner was alerted. How would they know what he had used the money for, apart from the obvious?

'We know that you have invested in the new Orphanage and Youth Club at Incubator Street School, which in itself is not a bad thing, but you must be aware of the abuse that goes on in those facilities. We are not happy about that.'

'I did that so people would know that I care about the

people of the East End, and I am told this facility will be kosher, if you get my drift.' He was more relaxed now. 'It is so, when we make our move, I, as a King of the area would be welcome.'

'And the George family? You gave them some of our money, which we understand, but you also recommended they invest in Incubator Street school facilities, why was that?'

Tanner was earning his corn this evening. He hadn't expected to be challenged and now was relying solely on his quicksilver tongue. 'I recommended that for the same reason. It is known that the George family want the East End for themselves, and I imagine you would not worry who wins, just so long as they keep up their end of your bargain, yes?'

The woman seemed to accept this touché moment with a nod. 'You do realise that we will watch this closely and any hint of abuse and you and the Georges will pay.'

'Naturally,' Tanner agreed as they likely expected he would and he felt more at ease. His modus-operandi throughout his life had been, buy time, confident he could always think of an idea to get out of any scrapes.

'So, when will we see results for our investment in you? And I ask again, have we picked the wrong man?' The body language of the woman had changed, she leaned into the conversation and this was something that Tanner noted.

'No, no, definitely not.' Tanner shuffled back in the chair, draped his arm over the back rest to over emphasise a casual demeanour, convincing nobody; he was, not unreasonably, scared. 'You will see progress tomorrow.'

'We will?' It was one of the men. 'What will we see?'

'As I have said many times, my motto is, never spring a trap until it is well and truly set.' Tanner was feeling a little better, confident his smooth tongue will get him through this situation, for sure.

'So, this trap, it is set?' the woman asked, a no-nonsense

tone in her voice. Clearly she doubted what Tanner was offering them. Tanner decided she was in charge, furthermore she asserted her command; there was threat in her voice. A menace she then demonstrated by pulling out a gun that had been resting in her lap, laying it on the table with a thud, the muzzle pointing at him; there was no mistaking the message.

Tanner pulled himself upright in his chair and with defensive hands up, he set about defusing something that had seemed to get out of hand, and fast. 'Hey, there's no need for this...' Tanner was jittery, but felt the situation needed him to counter the gesture, to assert himself. 'The *plan* is... set. Chas Larkin will be killed tomorrow and this will rattle the two ginger beer lady gangsters and...' Tanner halted as the woman stood. It was the first time he had been able to take in the stature of this woman, a woman who carried her command with a natural air: tall, slim, and with a body language that suggested she knew what she was doing.

The woman picked up the gun and walked purposefully around the table to where Tanner sat. With the dangerous end of the gun now pressed to Tanner's temple, she spoke harshly. 'You have a problem with women do you, and lesbians in particular?'

Tanner could see now that he was not talking to a dipstick in one of his bars. He was faced with a feisty woman who not only knew her business, she had to be one of them there feminists. 'No, not at all. It was just a way of talking an' that, you know, like...?' Tanner was scared. The pistol was cold against his head and he had no doubt that this woman would use it if the mood took her. Then the conversation took another tack, the woman steering it elsewhere, but possibly on the same theme, it was hard for him to tell.

'Where is Ruth?' the woman asked, now pacing the floor and slapping the gun on her thigh in an unreal casual manner.

Tanner allowed his imagination to roam for a second, a

thought that the woman might shoot herself in the foot, and this amused him.

The woman picked up on Tanner's sly grin. 'Something amusing you, Tanner? I see nothing funny here, so I ask again, where is Ruth?'

'She's at home...' Tanner wiped any grin off his face; he had to be careful.

The commander returned speedily, again the pistol levelled at the side of Tanner's head, interrupting him. 'At home, eh?' and she paused, to build the tension; this woman knew what she was doing, a mistress of interrogation. Tanner was starting to feel out of his depth. Ordinarily he was in charge and had others to do the intimidating for him. 'Not feeling well, is she?'

'No, just a bit tired, you know, got the decorators in, time of the month... you know?'

The woman pistol swiped him. 'You disrespect women and I, that is me, personally, do not like men who abuse women. You know what I mean?' Tanner was still seeing stars but nodded, his head hurt. 'Want to know what I do to men who are violent to women, because we know you knocked Ruth around before coming down to the pub for this meet. A meet that we expected to see Ruth attending... well...?'

Tanner was lost, not sure how to answer. 'Well, what?'

The woman closed in again and Tanner could feel her warm moist breath through the balaclava in his ear. 'I kill them, so I do.' And she paused. 'Ordinarily I would kill you now, but we need you, you see. Otherwise, you are dispensable. You do understand that don't you; dispensable?'

'Yes,' Tanner replied. Well, what else could he say, but he did resolve that should the situation arise, he would kill this woman and her two comrades.

'Good. Now, of you trot, you feckin' arse, and get this plan going and remember this, we will be watching you. Now be a good boy and get us some results. I have another meeting so why don't you fuck off you cockney spiv.'

———

Eyes down at Flora and Wendy's home.

Paddy, Nadia, and Ruth exited the patrol car and climbed the stairs to Flora and Wendy's flat.

Flora was there to greet them, 'Ruth, long time...'

'No see...' Ruth, accustomed to the abbreviated discourse she would have with Flora; they went way back to Flora's West End policing days.

'Now you've had your meet and greet, have a kiss and a cuddle then let's get in, we have a lot to talk about.' Paddy was all business, so Flora tripped him as he passed. 'Oi...'

'Watch that step there, it's a doozy...' and Flora laughed. It was even funnier because Paddy seemed not to be amused. 'Sorry, bog dweller, had no control over me plates of meat...' Flora said by way of an additional amusing aside for Ruth's benefit.

'Shall we go in? Paddy, I can step over you,' Ruth said, showing she was more than a match for Flora and equally, Paddy.

Once inside they all sat around the table, no beverages were offered, a bottle of whisky and glasses placed in the centre, but nobody imbibed, this was serious, and action may be needed tonight? It was difficult to tell, but things seemed to be spiralling and, speedily. However, they were prepared, weren't they? At least, Paddy and Ruth were.

Flora described the experience Wendy had had with Maude Larkin and this received a sympathetic response all round, and then Paddy explained the subterfuge scheming that Maude was to be seen as going off the rails, while Bess was seemingly unable to control her wife, and why this was happening to tempt the George family and Tanner to act before they were truly prepared. This news was received with mixed responses.

An irate Wendy said to Flora, 'You knew about this and never told me?'

'To be fair, Wendy, Flora only found out this afternoon at our meeting in the convent...'

Nadia interrupted Paddy. 'You weren't kidding about being in a convent and meeting your sister?' It looked like Paddy was about to come to his own rescue, but it was clear Nadia was not finished. 'So, your sister was, is, a sister, a nun?'

Paddy thought for a moment, before treading on the gorgeous Palestinian land mine, but Flora answered for him, he looked like a lost soul. 'Nadia, Paddy's sister is a nun and a whole lot more that I do not know if I can say, can I?' She looked to Paddy who shook his head.

'His sister is the fucking Black Rose for Christ's sake, if you forgive the religious undertones...'

'Ruth, that was not for you to reveal...' Paddy asserted and immediately backed down; Ruth was formidable and armed, of course. 'Paddy, all sitting around this table are up to their necks in this stuff, so they had better know what they are dealing with and know that they are not alone.'

'I know, there is MI5, I presume?' Nadia said, looking to Paddy to make sure that the security services did have their backs.

Ruth laughed. 'Yes, well, I suppose we have them, but I was thinking more of the Sisters of Clemence and they weigh in for more than an army, an army we will need if there is to be a war.'

'Stop...!' Wendy asserted herself, tears welling up, and Flora could see she was about to burst out crying again and rushed to her lover.

'It's okay darlin', I'm here,' Flora said, her arm around Wendy's shoulders that she shrugged off forcibly.

'Fuck off, Flora. Did you know Maude Larkin was targeting me as a part of your Machiavellian plan, Eh?'

'No, darlin'. I only found out about the plan this afternoon, but...'

Wendy halted her lover. 'But... if you had known, you would have approved of the scheme, and don't forget I know you better than you know yourself.'

Flora was stumped. Wendy was right in everything she said, especially knowing her so well. 'Well...' and she sloped her head, a form of supplication. 'It is a good plan, and if I had known, I would not have been allowed to share it with you. However, if I had known Maude was going to visit you I would most certainly have stepped in, but I am assuming she saw that you would be the last brick in the wall. It is obvious to me now, and I am so sorry; it was meant well.' Wendy's next fusillade was halted with a ring on the doorbell. 'Who the fuck can that be?' Flora said, standing to go downstairs to the street door.

'No, Flora. Let me get that,' and Paddy felt inside his jacket to remove his gun from the shoulder holster. 'Ruth, you have a gun, Flora?'

Ruth withdrew her gun and Flora looked circumspect. Wendy of course saw. 'You have a gun?' Flora acknowledged that she did, went to the bedroom and returned with a gun and shoulder holster. 'Maybe I don't know you as well as I thought I did. We will talk about this later, but in the meantime...' The bell rang again, twice. Whoever it was had little patience.

———

Arbour Square police station.

'Opalong Saint was processed, given a couple of aspirin for the pain; there was not much sympathy for the one-footed gangster before he was released from custody. He left the police station having revealed nothing other than he had been shot, twice, something the police already knew, but they did not know who had pulled the trigger, suspecting Maude or Chas Larkin though not truly bothered.

'Opalong was ushered out and left to fend for himself, knowing he had to, somehow or other, go to see the George family and meet his fate worse than death, Queenie George. As his head hit the cool night air, he responded to a car horn, tooting rhythmically, and then a saloon pulled up and the back door opened. He walked to it, he was feeling despondent and did have it in the back of his mind he would be shot again as soon as he leaned into the car but discarded his recently acquired caution. He bent down to look and his heart sank.

Taking up nearly all the back seat was Queenie. "Allo darlin'. Get in and I'll take yer 'ome.'

'Opalong thought this cannot be happening, it was fortuitous, but did think he might have a chance of a few days respite first. However, he had a mission and so tried to look pleased to see the woman he was supposed to woo, and then marry; heaven help him. 'Queenie, didn't expect to see you?'

'Just get in 'Opalong and cuddle up.'

Jesus wept, cuddle up, 'Opalong thought. Well, he had not much choice, he was between a rock and a fat soft, *cuddly*, hard place, and not much room left on the seat. So, he got in. 'Back to your place?'

'Well, sweet'art, you can 'ardly 'ang around 'ere and get popped again, can yer?' Queenie answered, and 'Opalong squashed in, felt his bum and removed the sausage sandwich he had sat on. 'Oh, well done, babes, I wondered where that had got to,' and Queenie took a big bite, and munching noisily, she leaned into 'Opalong. 'Now give us an 'eavenly bliss, lover,' and 'Opalong prepared himself for a sausage sandwich with tomato sauce kiss; he felt sick, but his life depended on this.

———

Paddy pressed his back against the wall, his gun ready as he responded to yet another press on the bell. 'Who is it,' he called out.

'It's me, yer dozy Irishman...'

'Chas, is that you?'

'Yes, now open the bleedin' door will yer.'

Paddy opened the door cautiously, his gun ready, but it was Chas, and he was alone. Chas entered and Paddy leaned out, looking to make there were no followers; there wasn't and he closed the door and followed up the stairs. Chas was already at the dogleg and face to face with Ruth's gun, Flora backing her up from the door of the flat.

26

IT ALL HAPPENED SO FAST…

THE CAR PULLED UP OUTSIDE THE FAT COW PUB. GEORGE George was first out of the pub to greet their guest. He opened the back door of the car and 'Opalong popped out like a champagne cork, bundling into George and knocking him over and into a lady bystander. She had a white trench coat and a beret and a green silk scarf covering her face; nobody noticed her amongst the now crowded pavement of regulars from the pub, all gathering for this happy occasion, because Vinnie said it was, greeting Queenie and her fiancé.

Two shots into George's head.

There was shock at the noise, people ducked, looked to run, and after the initial panic, returned as a crowd in order to gaze upon George; the light gone out of him. The agitated talk eased to a murmur as the crowd stood back to see a paper aeroplane glide into the centre of the ghoulish melee.

'Outta my way.' It was Vinnie, elbowing a route to stand beside her dead son.

Queenie was struggling to get out of the car to see what was happening; 'Opalong helped her, whispering into her ear, 'It's your bruvver, George. Brown bread. Sorry, Queenie.'

Some of the heavies from the pub began ushering the crowd away. Vinnie took charge, 'Alf...' she picked out the barman, '... ring the filf and tell them what has happened,' and she bent down, uncaring for her son, to retrieve the paper plane. She unfolded the wings and read the note and then informed those attending what it said; it was clear she was horrified. 'The O'Neills say hi.' Vinnie scoured the area looking to see if the shooter could be identified, but there was no sight of anyone suspicious, and nobody could recall seeing anyone pull the trigger.

———

Clarissa was in her bell tent flannelette nightie. She knew she looked sexy, but it seemed to her that the man pointing the gun, and Smiffy, did not agree. 'This your bird Vicar, bleedin' luv a duck, good luck with that. Odd though, cause I did hear you were one for the choir boys, maybe a bit of dodgy info that?'

'I am the Bishop, not a vicar, and yes this is my, err, bird... so, dodgy information, yes.'

'Bad luck, as I said. Anyway, a little dickey-bird tells me you 'ad a note from an IRA tart this morning, yeah? I say this because the George family would like to know what it said, especially as they contributed money to your Orphanage and Youth Club.' The gunman didn't feel like messing around, and wondering if they got the not-too-subtle message, he shot out a lamp that was beside the bed; he didn't do subtle.

Clarissa feinted with a thud on the floor and the Bishop thought it best he told the man. 'The note said to gather all the sponsors and funders for the works for the formal opening. I imagine it is because we understand that via circuitous routes, they put money into the pot and want the people to know who to be grateful to, yeah?'

'But you've not invited the George family, 'ave you?' The

gunman, aware of what was what, not what What Bing had said, but he was a trusted man and knew what was what.

Clarissa was coming around, it was only stage fright and she was acting, badly, so she heard and answered for Smiffy. 'It may be an oversight. Please tell the Georges we apologise and they will receive a formal invitation tomorrow, and they will be welcome to join a select few later on, here at the Bishop's Palace.'

'Right, well, I will tell Vinnie that. I am sure she will be right pleased, the top table an all,' and the gunman turned and left, as un-stealthily as he had arrived, but that was deliberate; he was told to scare the crap out of them, and this he had done; Clarissa may need a change of nightie.

———

The gathering around the dining table was disrupted again, this time by the phone ringing. Flora answered it, listened, and then replaced the receiver. Walked slowly back to the table and to Paddy, she said, 'George George has just been shot dead outside the Fat Cow pub...'

'Jesus wept...' Paddy responded but could see there was more, '...and?'

'And nobody saw who did it, despite there being a crowd of people there to greet 'Opalong...' Flora said.

'And...?' Paddy seeking the clincher, '... what else that is significant to this evening?'

'Apparently, as people crowded around the body, a paper aeroplane floated in and written on it was "The O'Neills say hi".'

'Fuck...' Paddy was knocked back.

'Your sister... Paddy?' Flora pressed.

'His sister?' Wendy was shocked, still reeling from what had happened to her, and to Nadia, and seemingly was still going on.

'The Black Rose, Wendy,' Flora whispered although there was no need, everybody knew.

'Oh...' Wendy replied to her caring lover who, just at that moment looked like she was ready to spring into action. Wendy put a steadying hand onto Flora's wrist.

The phone went again and Flora lifted Wendy's hand from her wrist and went across the living room to answer it. She listened, gasped, 'Oh no... oh no, please say this is not so...'

Paddy was up. 'What is it?'

However, Flora was focused on Chas Larkin. 'What?' Chas said.

And crying, Flora went to public enemy number one. 'Chas, I'm so sorry, but it seems that the kids of Incubator Street were on the street playing, and from what I can understand, Jack Diamond came out of your house heading to the pub, when he was gunned down and in the fusillade, Tommy was shot...' she paused as the immensity of the news was taken on board.

Chas was panicking. 'How is he...?' He could already tell by the look on Flora's face, 'No...'

'Chas, he's dead.'

————

In the 'Arf a Sixpence Pub, Tanner was trying to show he was not intimidated by what had happened in the meeting with those IRA commanders. He needed to share some bonhomie with the patriotic customers and to get out as fast as he could. He had to find Ruth.

The phone behind the bar rang. 'Arf a Sixpence,' the barman said. "Ang on...' and he looked around, then shouted out over the merriment and hubbub, 'Tanner, it's for you, sounds serious,' and he waved the phone as Tanner approached to take the call. The patrons hushed. The barman looked on as Tanner listened. He had never seen Tanner look so shocked before, ever, as he put the phone down. 'You alright, Guv?'

Tanner said nothing, just left the pub, as white as a sheet and his tail between his legs.

————

'This will be Tanner,' Ruth said as the shocked company sat back down to take in the news, all except Chas, who was on the phone.

'Ruth...? What do you mean, this is Tanner?'

'Flora, I am here to tell you and Paddy that Tanner was planning to assassinate Chas, but I got distracted in the mortuary. I didn't worry as it was meant to be tomorrow. Chas was expected to go home sometime today and leave for the West End in the morning, but Jack Diamond, in the dark, I suppose, could pass for Chas, and the thicko gunman must have taken their chance.'

'Ruth, you will need to go back to Kilburn. Find Tanner and react like you do not know what happened and assess the situation. Message either Flora or me. We will be in Arbour Square first thing, so there, or if you have news tonight and can call, Flora will be here.'

'Where will you be, Paddy?'

'Me, I will make sure Chas gets home safe and see what I can do, but then, I need a word with my sister. Flora, you need to stay with Wendy, no ifs, no buts.'

————

The phone rang again and Flora answered, again. 'Jim, yes, she's here...' and she looked to Nadia, and gesticulating with the phone, '... it's for you, Jim Rayner the desk sergeant at Arbour Square.'

Nadia collected the phone. 'Jim?' She listened. 'Thank you, Jim, tomorrow I will go to see the family, and yes, I will take Paddy with me,' and she hung up, turning to face her man. 'Paddy, Professor Brian Charnel has just died. He was seriously ill anyway, but I want you to come with me to his home in Wapping tomorrow. He has told me where he keeps his autopsy reports that date back years, cataloguing the child abuse that has become institutionalised. I understand he even points fingers, so this will be valuable intelligence and I want it before the goons get there.'

Flora was still standing by the phone. 'I will call Jim back and ask him to arrange for a police presence for the family.'

'A good idea, they can pick the family up at the hospital. They are there at the moment.'

———

The flat was quiet. Everyone had left. It was a traumatic silence, so much had happened in such a short time. Flora and Wendy stood as statues. 'Let's go to bed and hold each other...' Wendy said, '... and then, please, tell me everything. I need to know in order to process this day. What happened to you? You met the Black Rose, and she is Paddy's sister? I would love to meet this woman...' Wendy was research-distracted. Flora had seen this before and knew the crash would come, probably later in the night; she would be ready.

'I love you, Wendy,' and she sealed that with a kiss.

27

THERE WAS TO BE NO SLEEP IN CHAS AND BLOSSOM'S HOUSE, NOR anyone on Incubator Street. This was a devastating evening, beyond all comprehension, and in a neighbourhood used to violence. The locals were traumatised. Some wailed, others kept a silent vigil. The neighbours were out, candles lit and offering each other a shared comfort. There was an arc formed around the front door of Blossom's house, no crowding in, out of respect, but also because Rinso was standing sentry.

All the Myrmidons were gathered inside; this was an attack on them. Blossom was a Myrmidon and Tommy was Blossom's child, and in times of great trial, they had always stood together.

The crowd parted as Chas was seen walking down the street. Slowly he walked into the melee of his neighbours, his allies, his friends, hugging the occasional person, unable to disguise his tears; it was as though all latent feelings he had from his childhood were released. He knew why, it was because it was Blossom who had been his angel. It was she who cared, she who shielded him, hid him, and nurtured him when he most needed it. It was Blossom who grew into the tart with the heart, and then a wonderful loving mother to Tommy and partner, wife, to Chas. It was she and Tommy who gave Chas something that he never imagined he could have, unconditional love, and over time, he had returned that precious gift to Tommy and Blossom; they were a family.

Indoors, in the posh parlour, Blossom stood taking support from the mantelpiece. She was unsteady on her feet, yes, but as Chas entered and as she looked at him, he saw that she was standing to be with the photos displayed over the fireplace, of Tommy, of Chas and all three of them as a happy family. And now, it was gone, and he had not a clue how to comfort Blossom. He went to her and she folded herself into his arms and together they wept.

'Why, Chas...?' Blossom choked out a question, not unreasonable, and Chas knew not how to answer. 'Chas... what will I do? What will we do without Tommy?' Chas had no answer, he just held the woman he loved tighter and let her talk. He sensed that she needed it; he was running on instinct. 'I was, am, and always will be prepared to hear that you have been killed...' and she looked up to him

He returned her gaze, both of them with raw, red-rimmed eyes. He knew exactly what she was talking about. He lived in a dangerous world. But never a child. Never, never, her child. To Chas it looked like the unwritten code had been broken this night, but what would it mean? For a so-called unfeeling gangster, Chas felt it, and not just for Tommy. He had been slowly setting up safe havens, with the able assistance of the Sisters of Clemence, but now. Now, what was he going to do? He knew people would look to him to act. Blossom would look to him to act. 'My love...' was all he could say to Blossom, and she showed him it was enough, hugging him tighter.

It was a gentle and lyrical voice that broke into the couple's mutual support. 'Chas, do not think on revenge right now...'

And Blossom looked up to Paddy. 'Why? Why the fuck not? I want the bastards strung up.'

'Of course you do, Blossom, and my heart goes out to you and Chas, but please take this night, just for you and Chas. In the meantime, I will dig around and tomorrow morning, we will talk. Can you do that, please?' Paddy talked to Blossom but directed his comments to Chas because he knew how Chas was feeling right now. He had experienced these feelings himself when his father and a sister had been murdered back in Ireland, and he wrapped his arms around both Blossom and Chas. 'I share your grief, and, Blossom, Chas will tell you that I know what you are feeling, have felt it myself and someone helped me rise above my natural instinct to kill anyone and everyone.' Blossom looked up to Chas, who nodded, not sure what else to do. Looking at Paddy, Blossom pleaded with her eyes. 'I promise you this, Blossom, you will have your revenge.'

———

Ruth returned to her flat in Golders Green. She had no desire to go to Tanner's flat and anyway, he had kicked her out, hadn't he? She knew he would expect her to return; this had happened before and always, she came back. She knew she was obliged to come back, it was what she was supposed to do; a bitter irony that. Her brain fuzzed. Whatever. She would deal with the fall-out in the morning, and knowing what she did about Tommy Little Legs, she knew Tanner would be running around like a headless chicken, not knowing what to do. He would seek her out. He would look to her to sort it all out for him like she always did. Well, she would most certainly sort it.

She looked forward to the sanctuary of her own apartment as she opened her front door, thinking she would treat herself to a long hot bath, but it was not to be. She was met in the hallway by Tanner, and mindful of the beating she took earlier in the day, she called him Arthur. There was no need to make things worse than they already were. 'Arthur, what are you doing here?' and she backed up against the door as he approached.

'Ruth, where have you been? I've been looking...'

She stopped him with a hand gesture. She could see that he was not in an attacking frame of mind, so she eased past him and went into the bathroom. He followed and just stood behind her. Ruth turned on the taps and began to run her bath, swirling her hand in the water to check the temperature; the water was hot, but she was cool, she was determined, and she was ready; the devastatingly sad cards had played her a decent hand. She turned to face him and this time called him Tanner. 'What business is it of yours where I went, Tanner? You kicked me out if you recall, after assaulting me...'

'I'm sorry, Ruth. I will never hit you again, I promise.'

He looked contrite but Ruth knew he was a consummate actor. 'Why should I believe you, it's not the first time you've hit me. Well, I've got news for you, I am no longer your punch bag. I will work as your bookkeeper, but it will be strictly business from now on. Do you understand?'

'Yes, Ruth. I understand... I...'

'What is it, and why are you here?' I know you Tanner and you have that look on your face that suggests you've fucked up somehow and need me to sort it. So, what have you done? Spit it out,' and she stood, legs akimbo, ready to stare him out, but had to turn around to stop the bath water from overflowing. She felt the water, casual as you like, though she did feel a sense of trepidation, but then anger. The bath was just right and here was Tanner, a man she thought she had loved, however crazy that sounded to her now, preventing her from relaxing; so no change there then. She faced him. 'Tell me what you've done and then I want you to leave.'

'Seriously, you've not heard?'

Tanner did look shocked, and Ruth took some pleasure in this because, of course, she knew exactly what had him so scared. 'Heard what?'

'Honestly, Ruth, where have you been? Tommy Little Legs has been killed, accidentally, of course. The men I had in the road repair tent thought Jack Diamond was Chas coming out and walking down the street and...'

'Please, do not tell me they shot Jack Diamond and killed Tommy at the same time? What the fuck? Tanner?' Ruth shuffled past Tanner and went into the kitchen and poured herself a large glass of red wine, gestured with the bottle to see if Tanner wanted some. He certainly looked like he needed a drink, and Ruth took pleasure in that also. She should be feeling sad because of Tommy, and inwardly she did, but this was a first, she had the upper hand over Tanner and needed to play this carefully.

'Do you have whisky?'

'You know where it is,' Ruth answered in a casual manner as she again slipped past him and went into the living room to take up an armchair. She took a long draft of the robust red wine; she'd had it since Passover. She didn't drink much, didn't like the sensation of being out of control. She heard the chink of glass and after a short while Tanner appeared and took up the other armchair, looking disappointed she had not sat in the settee so he could be beside her. It was what they normally did when he stayed over.

Tanner opened up as it was clear Ruth was staying schtum. 'What should I do?'

Ruth laughed under her breath, discreet but deliberately audible. 'You're asking me?'

'You always know what to do...'

She stopped him, 'Yes, I do, and if you recall I told you that setting up in Incubator Street was a stupid idea, but oh no, you wanted the drama. Well, you will have more than enough drama now,' and this time she laughed, right at him; he deserved it. She sensed something else was amiss as well, something she did not know about, as if the murder of Tommy Little Legs was not enough. She sighed, 'What else have you done in the few hours I took to get medical treatment?' She thought she would give him a little extra to think about while she was at it.

'You got medical treatment, what for?'

'You fucking arsehole. Because you hit me, several times, you bastard, in case you can't see the bruising around my eye?'

'I'm so sorry, Ruth...' and he began to lift himself from the chair.

Ruth knew he was going to attempt some physical comfort, probably expecting her to invite him to her bed. No chance, mate, she thought. She put up her hand. 'Stay where you are. I don't want you anywhere near me. Just tell me what other trouble you are in, and, if I feel like it, I will advise you before you go...' she made a show of thinking, '... come to think of it, tell me, then fuck off. I will talk to you in the morning.' She waited and it looked like Tanner was stunned into inactivity. 'Come on, cough, and then get the fuck out of here. I have a bath waiting for me.'

'Well, Ruth, you see...'

He was evidently nervous and this put Ruth on edge. 'Jesus, Tanner, what have you done?'

'I think I may have upset some big wig IRA people, in particular a woman who seemed to be a commander. Personally, I think she was being oversensitive, you know, not getting any of my jokes, an' that...'

Ruth rolled her eyes. He noticed, and this would ordinarily rile him, but not tonight; she had the edge over him and needed to play this carefully. 'What did you say?' and she puffed out a bigger sigh.

'Nuffing really...' Ruth thought it was likely more than nothing, but she bided her time and sloped her head to suggest he get on with telling her. 'Well, turns out this woman is a rabid feminista, and don't ask me how, but seems she'd heard that we'd a little falling out, you know...'

'You mean she heard you beat the shit out of me and she didn't like that? I might like this woman, when can I meet her?'

'That's just it, she was upset you were not at the meeting in the pub this evening. She seemed to think that she would get a straight answer from you. I don't know why she would think that when I was there to tell her all what was 'appening, and our plans an' that?' and Tanner looked genuinely mystified. 'I think she must be a lesbian, had to be, 'cause I switched on all me charm, you know.'

'Yes, I do know, and it is time you realised that not every-body is a sucker for your famed cockney banter and good looks. So, let me guess, you told these serious IRA people that every-thing was going to plan and that tomorrow Chas Larkin will be assassinated and then the lesbian leaders, Maude and Bess, will follow up in short order. Yes?'

'Yeah, that's it, but this woman got the hump because I seemed to denigrate lesbians. That's why I think she must be one too... see?'

'When will you learn that if a woman takes offence at you for impugning women and especially their sexuality, or even more so, hitting another woman, they may express a desire to kill you, and not because of their sexual leanings. Just wondered if that ever occurred to you in these supposed enlightened times?'

'How did you know she threatened to kill me? She even put a bastard gun to me loaf of bread?' Tanner looked more and more mystified and impressed at Ruth's insight into matters surrounding him.

'Oh, just a hunch...' and Ruth got up from the armchair, '... and now I am going to insist you leave. Perhaps we can meet in the morning and I will have thought what to do. I suggest you find somewhere else to stay tonight, maybe a hotel, and then call me in the morning and I will come and meet you.'

'A hotel?'

'Tanner, you fucking turnip, all and sundry will likely know or have guessed that you were behind what happened to Tommy Little Legs, yeah? There will people out looking to kill you, so if you survive, call me in the morning, okay?'

'Oh, okay, yeah, a hotel, good idea.'

Ruth ushered him from the flat and returned to her cold bath. 'Fuck it,' and she pulled the plug and went to bed, mixed feelings.

28

THE NEXT MORNING

Nadia telephoned Jim Rayner at Arbour Square police station, he acknowledged her and asked how she was. 'I'm okay Jim, thank you. A lot happened last night and I wanted to let you know that Paddy and I will be going to see the wife of Professor Charnel in a moment, so he will be late in. I am not sure about Flora, she may be staying with Wendy; she had a spot of bother also, did you hear about that?'

'No, is she okay?'

'Best Paddy briefs you, I wanted to check that you had officers at the Charnel house overnight, and they had no problems?'

'Yes, we have an officer there now and I've had no reports of any difficulties.'

'Good, we should not be long, and Paddy will bring you up to date when he gets in, and Jim, it was so sad about Tommy Little Legs. Paddy has ideas about that as well,' and she could hear the sigh of despair from Rayner as he closed the call.

Ruth took the call at about eight am. She was expecting it but not quite so early. Tanner was not a morning person, but she imagined he had not slept well and this amused her. 'Bit early for you, isn't it?'

Tanner answered as she expected, 'I didn't sleep well, combination of stuff really but this flea-bitten hotel in Paddington didn't help matters either.'

Ruth laughed hard, this was better than she had ever hoped it could be. 'You went to Paddington? I thought you would go to a swanky West End hotel?' and she continued her audible plea-sure at the discomfort he was feeling. 'Well, listen up, I am not meeting you in Paddington. Make your way to the Dorchester and you can buy me a lubbly jubbly breakfast. See you there in a bit.' And she could hear him complaining as she hung up, and she made a call to Paddy to inform him. 'Yes, the Dorchester,' and she enjoyed hearing him laugh. She hung up, intent on prettying herself up, trying to disguise the bruising mostly for her own vanity, and wearing her most provocative outfit because she knew it would wind him up; she needed her lover, turned nemesis, irritated. The tables were now well and truly turned; she had become his *bette noir*, not that he knew this yet, and she intended that he would never learn this until it was too late.

———

Nadia and Paddy were greeted at the door of the home of Professor Charnel by Smokey Robinson, not in uniform, but plain clothes.

'Smokey, what are you doing here?' Nadia expressing her surprise, looked to Paddy, 'Did you know...?' Paddy shrugged his shoulders.

'Jim Rayner thought it best I be here. I met the widow and

her children at the hospital last night, and...' It appeared Smokey was unclear how to tell the rest.

'And Jim knew he could trust you, right?'

'Yes, err, Paddy... that's about the size of it.'

As they stepped into the hall, Paddy continued his questions. 'I take it you are weapons trained and have a gun?'

'I am, sir...' and he opened his jacket to reveal his shoulder holster and gun.

'Right then,' Nadia interrupted, 'that's enough boys talk. How is Mrs Charnel?'

'We talked a lot last night. The children are fifteen and seventeen, old enough to know what is happening. It was expected. Not quite as rapidly, but they each told me they were prepared and in a way, it seemed a relief. They knew their dad, her husband, was suffering.'

Paddy followed up, 'And the autopsy stuff? How much did the widow know?'

'Well, that is the interesting part. After the kids went to bed, Mrs Charnel and I talked more, in fact, she didn't sleep at all.'

'And...?' Nadia wanted in on this conversation.

'You were right, Nadia. She knew everything. It seemed that the professor confided it all with her and...'

'What...?'

'Nadia, let him tell it in his own time. Carry on, Smokey...' Paddy was trying to finish his sentence but had not bargained on how interfering Nadia would be; he should have known.

'Where is she now, Smokey?'

'She went to bed about an hour ago, although I would guess she will get no sleep.'

'So, what were you going to say?' Paddy was impatient, he had a lot to do this morning and wanted just the bare details, but clearly Nadia had other ideas. Again, he should have known; she had a lot invested in this.

'Did you find the autopsy reports?' Nadia asked.

'I didn't even have to ask, Mrs Charnel took me to the airing cupboard and showed me the hidden panel. I was able to open it and retrieve many reports. We took them downstairs and across the dining room table we discussed them one by one and before you ask...' and he looked first to Nadia and then Paddy who was becoming more interested by the minute. '... yes, I took comprehensive notes.'

'And...' a perceptive and excited Nadia pushed.

'Well, here is the most fantastic bit. Mrs Charnel is a council welfare officer, and between the professor and her, they investigated each autopsy. In many of the cases, they were able to trace back from where they came: orphanage or boys' home. Not all the names though, but, enough to nail the bastards who run the places.'

'Jesus wept,' Paddy uttered on an exhaled breath, just realising he had not allowed himself to breathe while Smokey was talking.

'Indeed, Inspector...'

Nadia, Smokey and Paddy turned to see Mrs Charnel on the stairs, incongruous in her neat as a pin dressing gown, but with the woman looking like she had been through the ringer.

'Mrs Charnel, I offer you my sincere condolences.'

'Thank you, Nadia. You gave my husband such hope in his last days and I thank you for that, and please, call me Edith.'

'Thank you, Edith. My last conversation with Brian was to tell him that I understood and that he was a good man trapped by bad people.'

'Yes, Brian told me, and I thank you for that kindness and most of all, I know you risked your life for him. Now, shall we go into the dining room and I will run through all that I know and then, please, decide what happens next and how you can keep my family safe.'

As they were nearing a first-cut summary of the findings, it was clear that Edith was flagging and Nadia had ants in her pants.

'Nadia, what is it?'

Nadia looked at Edith but was talking also to Paddy and Smokey. 'You may not know that a child was shot and killed last night...' She paused to allow Edith a moment of grief shared.

'Oh my God, the poor mother,' Edith said, and Smokey confirmed that they had heard nothing.

'Smokey, it was Tommy Little Legs...' Paddy said.

'Jeez. Oh God, all hell will break loose now won't it?' Smokey talking out loud his thoughts and noticed Edith didn't know Tommy. 'Tommy was a boy from Incubator Street...' everybody knew Incubator Street and the school. '... and, Tommy was the stepson of Chas Larkin.'

Smokey didn't need to say anymore, it was clear on Edith's face that she knew of Chas Larkin. 'What will happen...' and she put up her hand, '... silly question, of course I know.'

Paddy stepped in. 'Edith, it is important that you know that I am MI5...' Not only was Edith shocked at this revelation, Smokey looked astounded. 'I would appreciate it if you could keep that to yourself, and you also, Smokey.' They both nodded. 'Edith, I say this to you because I want you to know that although I am a detective inspector out of Arbour Square police station, I am arranging for you and your family to be taken to a safe place until we have a full measure of the situation, and in that I mean, from the autopsy reports and the response regarding the young lad Tommy. You can feel assured that no coppers will leak your whereabouts and you can trust Smokey, but you already know that don't you.'

'Yes, and thank you.'

'Paddy, talking of Tommy, I want to get to the hospital. Blossom and Chas will want to go and see Tommy's body and I want to make it as presentable as possible, please.'

Paddy stood straight away, he understood what was important to Nadia and talking to Smokey, 'Don't let anyone in unless they give the password, do you understand? Now, Nadia, I will get you dropped off at the hospital.'

'Err, Paddy.'

'Yes, Smokey?'

'What is the password?'

He chuckled, there was just so much going on. 'A chap called Hemmings will call you in a short while, okay?'

Smokey nodded and Paddy and Nadia prepared to leave, but Edith stepped in to take Nadia into a hug, 'Thank you again. You are a good woman.'

Releasing the grasp, Nadia looked seriously into the eyes of the grieving widow. 'You know this is just the start of it?' Edith nodded. 'You need to know that we will have you and your family's back. I can see you are a strong woman, and you will need to be,' and Nadia went back in and kissed both of Edith's cheeks and left with Paddy.

———

Ruth looked herself up and down in the full-length mirror just outside the entrance to the Dorchester hotel dining room. She knew she looked good and she's managed to conceal most of he bruising, but did she look nervous, and would that be a bad thing?

Madam, if I might be so bold, you look sensational.' It was the Maître d'hôtel who had stepped away from his post beside the restaurant lectern.

Ruth was embarrassed, and she could not remember the last time that had happened, but this debonair man did it for her. 'Thank you for your boldness, your compliment is both welcome and reassuring.' The man gave a slight bow. 'I am meeting a Mr Arthur Schilling.'

'He is already here, Ma'am. If you follow me,' and he turned on his toes but Ruth called him back. 'Ma'am?'

'Since we are being bold, Mr Schilling is an ex-boyfriend and not a particularly nice man. I have to meet him to give him some home-truths, if you get my drift?'

'I do, Ma'am. Would you like me to be nearby, just in case? I can be discreet.'

'I bet you can...' and she leaned in to read his name badge, '... Stanley, and I would appreciate it. I happen to know he is a little...' and she wobbled an outright hand, '... unstable at the moment, and my name is Ruth.'

'I understand completely, Miss Ruth. Now, if you would follow me, please.'

Tanner saw Ruth approaching behind the stuffed shirt of a man who was so uncle josh it got right up his fireman's hose. He was like a coiled spring. He recognised this and counselled himself, he needed to calm down, at least until he had what he needed from Ruth.

She reached the table and although Tanner indicated a seat beside him, Ruth appreciated that Stanley pulled out the opposite chair. 'Thank you, Stanley,' and she offered the man a beaming smile; guaranteed to irritate Tanner, and she saw that it did.

'Thank you for coming, Ruth...' Tanner was interrupted as Stanley had returned with a menu. He handed it to her, and making an inordinate fuss of the starched napkin, he flicked it open in the direction of Tanner, and then, with a gentle ease, he folded it into Ruth's short skirt. 'Oi, mate... what the fuck?'

'I'm sorry, sir, we do not allow that sort of language in the restaurant...' and he gave Tanner a brahma of a stare, totally impressing Ruth.

'Thank you, Stanley,' Ruth said, countering any response that Tanner might make, and looking across the table, 'have you decided Arthur?'

'Decided what?' He was fuming. Wonderful, Ruth thought.

'I believe the lady is asking if you have decided what you would like from the menu, sir.' Oh God, Ruth was falling in love with Stanley.

'I don't need you to tell me what me bird is saying, you toffee-nosed...'

Stanley leaned into Tanner's ear. 'Shut the fuck up, sir. I have warned you, now...' Stanley stood, '... your order, sir?'

Ruth tried, but she could not contain her enjoyment of the situation. 'Stanley, I will have two egg on, please,' and she laughed at the intimation.

'Two eggs on toast, Ma'am, poached?' and Stanley made a note, 'and, sir?'

'He will have a full English with monkey tea. I will have a double espresso and a glass of iced water please.'

'That's PG Tips, you posh turnip,' Tanner said.

'Indeed, sir, I had already understood this being as how we have televisions in the hotel, and occasionally we see the adverts for PG Tips tea with the monkeys.' And he looked to Ruth. 'Most amusing, Ma'am, I shall tell them in the kitchen, on account as they enjoy a tin barf,' and he offered a cheeky smile as he had demonstrated a perfect cockney accent, so much so, there could be no mistake that it was the posh accent that was uncle josh, not the man.

'I'm gonna bop that bloke on his fireman's hose when he comes back,' Tanner said, displaying bravado now that Stanley had left the table to tell the kitchen staff about the twat at table eleven.

'You will?'

'Yeah, what of it?'

'Only that he looks like he can handle himself and you would not be the only gangster to eat at the Dorchester. Now, you want my advice?'

Tanner tried to look anywhere but at Ruth, but Stanley had

returned, following up a waitress who set out their breakfasts, and Maître D'hôtel and gangster, exchanged scowls.

'Thank you,' Ruth said to the waitress, 'and thank you, Stanley.'

The waitress and Stanley departed although it was clear that Stanley was keeping a close eye. 'Okay, Arthur, I have thought this through. You have two problems, the most pressing being that it would not take a genius to work out who planned the incident last night, Jack Diamond and Tommy Little Legs gunned down. There are many who would leap at the chance to see you given up, not least the George family. So, it's back to the Paddington Hotel, and I will ring you regularly with updates.'

'That's it, is it?'

'Of course not, you banana.'

'What then...?'

'Eat your breakfast, which should keep your mouth occupied while you listen to what I am going to tell you.' Tanner squashed a sausage in his mouth, and Ruth wondered what on earth she saw in this fella, whereas Stanley, well, he was a whole different kettle of fish. 'First off, lie low, as I said, until I can get a feel for what is happening on the ground. I will go and see the IRA. You met in the Arf a Sixpence, yes?' Thankfully Tanner just nodded. 'Okay. I will leave a message that I want to meet them.'

'What will you say?'

'Not a bleedin' clue, but I'll have to take the heat off somehow or you are totally dead meat.'

Tanner stood and approached Ruth and out of the corner of her eye she saw Stanley, closing in. 'Is everything okay, sir?'

'What?' The politeness threw Tanner.

'The breakfast, sir. You are not happy with it? Maybe I can get you something else?'

Tanner displayed his ignorance. 'What? No, the only problem I 'ave is you, mate.'

Stanley was aware that the other diners were becoming agitated. 'Perhaps we can take this outside the restaurant, sir. If you have a complaint with me, I can take you to the manager?'

Frustrated, Tanner just humphed, and as he went to leave, he shouldered Stanley, who, it turned out, was a brick shit house under his penguin suit, and Tanner rolled off, only to steady himself and tell Stanley that he had marked his card, not that Stanley seemed at all bothered by this.

'I am sorry, Stanley, he has gone off without paying. I will pick up the tab, don't worry, and, err...'

'Ma'am?'

'What time do you get off?'

'First of all, I will arrange for the breakfast as complimentary, and I finish at lunchtime, say one o'clock?'

'I might do some shopping and perhaps we can go somewhere for a light bite, in Shepherds Market?' Ruth asked, offering a saucy smile so he got the message.

It was a message received and understood. 'I will meet you in the Grapes pub.'

29

CHAS AND BLOSSOM ARRIVED AT THE ROYAL LONDON HOSPITAL and were shown down to the mortuary where Nadia had Tommy prepared as best she could. Fortunately, no bullets had hit his face. Aware of how distraught Blossom still was she respectfully lowered the sheet to reveal Tommy's face. It was like he was still asleep, no fixed face as to the shock of what had happened; he still had that most adorably innocent look.

Chas was holding Blossom but when Tommy's face was revealed, she broke away and fell onto her child. 'Tommy, Tommy, oh Tommy, you're so cold...' she looked to Nadia, '... he's cold.'

Chas muscled in and once again held his *wife*. 'Thank you,' he said, choked himself, and Nadia had a sight of the boy she had taken into casualty and operated on seemingly such a long time ago, but had been only three years. He had grown into his age and face, but just then, it was his vulnerability she saw. 'Can we sit with him for a while, please?'

'Of course, take as long as you like,' Nadia answered. 'Would you like me to leave you both alone?'

'Yes, please. Oh, do you know where Paddy has gone?'

'I do, Chas. He was going to see Flora, and if she was up to it, he said something about meeting his sister...' and Nadia could not disguise her frown.

'Right... and you are not best pleased about that, but let me say, I think if he is meeting her at the convent, then this may be the best thing.'

'I know, Chas. He has all the autopsy reports. You know, what we talked about?'

'I do...'

Blossom looked up. 'Chas, go to meet them.'

'But...'

'No buts, the sooner you are back in the saddle the better for getting revenge on whoever did this, okay?'

Chas understood completely but was reluctant to leave Blossom until Nadia nudged him. 'Go, Chas, I will stay with Blossom. I already have told people I am taking some personal time.

Chas kissed Blossom, then leaned in and kissed Tommy. 'My lovely boy. I will miss you terribly,' and his tears fell again. 'Thank you, Nadia... for everything,' and he kissed both of the Palestinian's cheeks.

The doors squeaked and in walked Paddy

———

Lavinia looked at the gold embossed card *invitation* to the opening of the youth club and orphanage on Saturday 20th June, revelling in the sensation that they, the George family, had been invited to an establishment event.

'Mum, it's the undertaker, wants to know when you want George's funeral and he still has Father George.' Nobody called the nonce priest son by his given name, Peter, or as he wanted to be called, St Peter. He liked the idea that the choir boys would be called to kneel before St Peter. His mum despised that son of hers, and if the O'Neills had not done for him, she would have. He only had one good idea and that was to invest in the building of homes for boys, orphanages and youth clubs, and she knew why. Vinnie could live with that because they made money and she saw it also as a bridge to the East End, but after that, enough was enough. Now if Queenie can make a go of 'Opalong, he would be a good enforcer to replace George George, God rest his soul; not that this bothered her either, he was as thick as mince; took after his dad.

'Mum? You okay?'

'Steve, sorry. What did you say?'

'The undertakers want to know about timings for the funerals, Peter and George. The police have not released George's body yet, but I imagine you can arrange for that, yes?'

Vinnie's mind kept turning over. Steve was her youngest and was never thought to be strong enough for the family biz, but Vinnie had seen more than a spark of intelligence there and maybe it was time to test that, to see? 'What do you think, Steve?'

'Me?'

'Yes, I'm interested to hear what you think I should do.'

'I'm not you, Mum, but I do know you.'

Vinnie's curiosity was peaked. 'You know me, eh? So, what would I do and then tell me what you would do?' Steve was always considered the runt of the litter; not strong, tall and skinny, Vinnie's husband always said he wasn't his. Well, he wasn't, but then who cared, her husband, George and Saint bleedin' Peter were all gone now, so what did it matter? 'Well, cat got your tongue?'

Steve had always learned to control his temper but he was close now. 'First off, Mum, I don't like the way you talk to me, nor the rest of the family for that matter; those who are left that is...' and he chuckled. He would not miss George or Peter. 'As for what you would do, I suspect you would hold off on the funerals, you truly do not care, but for form they must take place. So, the police not releasing the bodies serves, and I suspect, you have arranged for that.' He saw the smile from his mum and knew he had hit the mark.

'And...?'

'And mum, I imagine you will be getting Queenie married off right away otherwise why let her take 'Opalong to bed last night, the poor sod.'

'And...?'

'And, when Queenie is married, likely in the next couple of days, 'Opalong would be a good replacement for George... yeah? I know I'm right.'

'You are, son. Your father was a clever man and I hated having to kill him after I had given birth to you, but I needed nobody to know, and it was important to me to have a son who was clever. Another of my plans comes to fruition. Yes, Steve, you are right, and you are right for taking the firm forward with me, yes?'

'Yes, Mum, and I guessed I had a different father. Maybe you can tell me about him sometime?'

'Maybe I will, we will see...'

'It is also about time you asked me to join the firm, I can be useful.'

'You can, I know, but how do you see yourself, son?'

'For one, we do not need family muscle. We can buy that in and get rid of it whenever it suits. If it is family, we may think twice about killing them off, and that would be a weakness. I can see by your face that I'm right. I will also say that Queenie is a liability and 'Opalong has too many chips on his shoulder; plus, why would he be here, and more especially, why would he marry Queenie, for heaven's sake. I suspect he is having his arm twisted by the Larkin Saints and we will need to be on our guard.'

Vinnie had a huge grin now. 'Son, you are spot on, and I

want to get Queenie married off and maybe put the both of them out to grass somewhere, who knows, but we will need to keep a close eye on 'Opalong. Having said that 'Opalong really does have a grudge against Chas Larkin, so... who knows how that might play out?'

Both mum and clever bonce son nodded to each other and a bond was made where there was precious little evidence before.

———

Ruth was sitting at the bar in the Grapes pub with a gin and tonic when Stanley arrived. He approached her from behind, not expecting to surprise her, because she could see him in the back bar mirror. What interested him was that she did not turn to greet him. He watched her face in the same reflection when he leaned in to kiss her neck. Her eyes closed for a brief moment and a smile was there before she opened them again.

'I have a flat just around the corner. It's not much, but it is just around the corner,' he whispered and his moist breath made her shiver with anticipation.

'What makes you think I will come back to your flat with you?'

Stanley was stroking her upper arm and she allowed his soft hand to rise to her shoulder, whereupon, it gently turned her head. She presented her lips and he duly obliged. It was a brief kiss, soft with no urgency, the urgency was on her part. He looked into her eyes and they kissed again, exactly the same. 'That,' he said.

'That? What do you mean?' she breathily replied.

'That tells me you will come back with me, and I think we should go now, don't you?'

She said nothing, just turned on her bar stool, stood, leaned in, to link with his arm, 'Fair enough, I will have to make a call from the telephone box on Curzon Street and then, I am all yours,' she said.

'Or, I am all yours, I sense?'

And they left.

———

Paddy entered the mortuary, he was coming to see Nadia, before going to the convent. Blossom was so distraught, it was clear she did not know where to look, at Paddy, at Tommy, Nadia, or Chas.

Paddy opened his arms, following a reassuring nod from Nadia, and the decision was made, Blossom needed no second invitation and she went into his arms. 'Blossom, my dearest one, no words can express my sorrow for you, none more than I said last night.' Blossom responded but it was unintelligible, she was sobbing into Paddy's jacket. 'Blossom, look at me please,' and slowly she raised her eyes, he could see a wet patch on his jacket. He offered his handkerchief, which she gratefully took, dabbed her eyes and blew her nose. 'I want you to understand that I ask this out of great respect, but we have made progress and I want Chas to come with me to a meeting. I would not ask if it were not important, and if you want Chas with you, I will understand and manage on my own.'

Blossom became animated. 'If you have something that will get you to the bastards who did this, then take Chas now, please,' and she turned to face her man. 'Chas, do what you have to, but come back to me. I need you, my love.'

Chas took Blossom and held her tight and after a short while and sensing Paddy's keenness to get moving, he broke away and kissed her goodbye. 'I will come back and I think Paddy knows who is responsible, but not who pulled the trigger?'

'Tanner, yes?' Blossom said.

Paddy answered. 'Yes, but we need to play this cannily, not go in guns blazing. There is more to this than simple revenge, Blossom. I hope you understand?'

'I do, Paddy, now go and do what you have to, please. I have Nadia here.'

30

Wendy seemed recovered but Flora knew enough of her lover's psychobabble to know that this could be temporary. When you have been so scared, for your life even, sometimes you think you are okay when you are just in respite.

'What's this, more bloody tea? I will be weeing for weeks, you know that.'

'Can I watch?'

'Flora, my love, that is not even near funny,' but Wendy gave herself away and laughed. 'I need a distraction, and before you say it, yes, you are a lovely distraction but you hardly challenge my mind, just my body, not that I'm complaining. Well, maybe a little bit.'

Wendy had Flora beat. She could never keep up with her thinking, and although this seemed logical and simple, she was just so tired. She had been up with Wendy since the night before. They had gone to bed and even made love, but no sleep came for Wendy and as a consequence, for Flora also.

'A distraction, you say, and not me watching you pee or making love to you?' Flora said. Wendy laughed, was that progress, Flora thought, and then the doorbell rang. Saved by the bell or an unwelcome distraction, either way, she knew she had to go; it could be Maude.

'Flora, don't go.'

'Why not?'

'Just, don't go, let's just be together...'

'You're worried it will be Maude, yes?' Flora probed with her copper eyes. 'I can see that is what you are thinking,' and going to the sideboard drawer she retrieved her service weapon.

'Flora, no...!'

'Shhhhush, baby. I know what I am doing,' and Flora checked the gun before going downstairs. Before the dog leg, she looked back and saw Wendy looking, concerned. 'Go back in the flat, love,' and she continued to the front door, where she pressed her back to the flank wall. The bell sounded again. 'Who is it?' she called.

'It's me, Flora, and I'm with Chas.'

'Paddy?'

'Yes, open the door.'

Flora steadily opened the door, her gun at the ready and came face to face with her working partner and behind him, Chas Larkin bouncing on the balls of his feet. 'Nobody followed you, and Chas, what's the matter with you.'

'I need a Jimmy riddle, Flora, mind out or I'll piss on your doorstep,' and Flora stepped out of the way and watched public enemy number one run past her, up the stairs to find their toilet for a number one.

———

'Well, Stanley, I have to say you are not just a good Maître D'hôtel. I may have to come back for seconds, but sadly, I have to go. I have a meeting back in Kilburn.'

'Can I come with you?' Stanley looking in the bedroom full-length mirror, stood before Ruth, both stark naked and having a conversation into the reflection, like they had been married for twenty years.

Ruth couldn't resist, circled him from behind and fondled his wedding tackle. 'Stan, with me this evening is not somewhere you would want to be, trust me. However, if you have time, perhaps you can come to my flat in Golders Green for a bit of afters? Do you have to be back at work?' She had Stanley excited, not sure if it was the thought of afters at her place, or her expert fondling; maybe both.

'I do not have to be back at work until tomorrow morning, so I could meet you at your flat. I would like that and then we can finish off what you have just started?'

'That is a deal. I will give you the address, here is a spare key, and I will meet you later, there will be no need to dress,' she said with a lascivious smile. 'Is that okay?'

'Lubbly jubbly, I will see you then,' by which time Ruth was dressed and heading for the door. She stopped, turned and returned, for one last kiss and a cuddle. She liked Stan, not Stanley, but that must be his posh knob job at the Dorchester name; he had a lovely posh knob also.

———

They all heard the toilet flush and Chas finally appeared. He'd washed his hands which impressed Wendy; sometimes she struggled to get Flora to wash her hands.

'You washed your hands, Chas, I am impressed. See that, Flora...' Flora rolled her eyes and Chas noticed.

'Of course I washed my hands, and left the toilet seat down; Blossom has me well trained, even Tommy...' He pulled himself up. He will have to get used to this now.

Wendy went to the gangster and hugged him, 'It's alright,

Chas. It will take a while,' and she took him by his shoulders, looked at his face and passed him the screwed-up tissue Flora had given her. 'Here, wipe away those tears...'

'Thank you, not sure what came over me...?'

'Grief came over you, Chas, and thank the Lord you are man enough to cry,' Wendy said.

'What are you both doing here?' Flora asked, and it was the shakeup Chas needed, and Paddy by the looks of him, sneaking his handkerchief back into his pocket.

Before they could answer Wendy interjected, 'How is Nadia, must have been a scary day for her?' and she looked at Flora for emotional support as her own fears returned. Flora put her arm around her and they all looked to Paddy to answer. However, Paddy looked as though he had no answer, so Wendy pressed him. 'Paddy? You don't know how she is?' and then Wendy stepped it up a gear. 'For fuck sake, Paddy. This is the woman you say you love, and you can't answer this simple question.' She had Paddy in a corner with no exit possible, short of plumbing the depths of his feelings. Flora was once again reassured Wendy was recovering and felt a little sorry for her bog-dwelling partner. 'Paddy?' Wendy pressed and it appeared Paddy realised he had nowhere to go.

'Well, I don't know... I, err...'

'Don't know, I got it.' Wendy did not let it drop while the audience became enthralled. 'Okay, where is she now?'

'She's at the hospital.' Paddy's face had that look hoping he would get through his grilling; Flora recognised it, from her own face so many times.

'How was she when you dropped her off? Confident? Looking concerned? How was she when you woke up? Did you sleep at all last night?'

'Whoa, Wendy. Give the man a break.' Flora never thought she would come to the rescue of her Irish partner, even though she thought Paddy deserved this, and she should be enjoying it, but she wasn't.

'Shut it, Flora,' and she returned to Paddy. 'Answer my questions, this is important.'

'It is?' Paddy answered like a mouse before a hungry cat, and he seemed to have the sympathies of Chas and Flora.

'God, give me strength. Okay, baby steps it is, you great big baby...' Wendy could see Flora had ants in her pants. 'Stay out of this, Flora, this is important.'

'It is?' Paddy again wondered how.

'It is. Now, first. How was she when you got home last night?' Wendy was counting on her fingers and Flora wondered if she had enough hands, she had seen Wendy like this before and never understood how she could think of all of her questions. 'Paddy?'

'Well, she quite surprised me.'

'How?'

'When we got in she all but raped me, and wanted to make love all night and did not want to talk at all.'

'You were bleedin' lucky, I had to talk all night,' Flora said, quite shocking Wendy. 'Blimey, did I just say that out loud?'

'You did, sweetheart, and we can talk all about it tonight, through the night even,' Wendy said with a smile, but Flora half thought she was serious. 'Listen, Paddy, the reaction to shock can take many forms. I would say that Nadia just needed physical comfort, the need to know she is loved and that you are there for her. How was she this morning?'

Gawd blimey, here she goes, Flora thought and then checked herself to make sure she hadn't said that out loud also; she hadn't and she sighed, out loud, which got an old-fashioned look from Wendy. Oh well.

'As soon as we were up and dressed she wanted to go to see the professor's wife.'

'And you went? How was she when you got there?'

'Nadia was enthusiastic, totally energised. We got the records and blow me down if the wife knew all about it, works for the Welfare in the council and together the professor and she had worked out where most of the children came from and even some of their names.'

'Fuck...'

'Yes, indeed, Flora,' Paddy respecting that Flora was bringing the conversation back to a level he understood.

'And then?' Wendy still had the bit between her teeth.

'Well, I talked my ideas over with her as we walked along the embankment from Wapping to her hospital. We needed the air and privacy to talk this through. She said she should go into the hospital...' and he looked to Chas, '... to prepare the body of Tommy for viewing...' he looked at Chas again, '... sorry, Chas.' Chas acknowledged Paddy and could not disguise his tears as he raised the ragged tissue once again. Flora passed him a clean one, went to take the screwed-up one, but he wanted to hold it; his comfort tissue, she imagined.

'She wanted to come to the convent with Chas and me, but she had things to do, and I thought it best to let her go her way. Was I right to do that?'

Wendy answered. 'Yes. She is a strong woman, and after you fucking her brains out last night, I hope, she was back on track, and, Flora, stop sighing, and see me tonight.' Flora's hopes were raised only to be dashed again. 'So, why go to the convent, and are you here to take Flora with you?' She gave no chance for an answer. 'I want to go with you...'

'Why?' Flora realised as soon as she said it she had stood on a Wendy baited trap.

'Because, my gorgeous lover, I want to see this Black Rose sister of Paddy's and give her a piece of my mind, kissing and feeling up my woman.'

'You told her...?' Paddy was astounded.

Wendy settled the Irishman. 'Yes, of course she told me, we

talk to each other and share our lives, and, if you did the shame with Nadia, maybe one day she will say yes to your umpteenth marriage proposal.'

'She told you that?'

'Paddy, she did. We also talk.'

'You do?'

31

A CLASH

APART FROM THE SMELL, 'OPALONG ENJOYED HIS NIGHT OF lovemaking with Queenie, it was a lot like rolling around on a Lillo air bed, but then he had been in prison for three years. He just feared what would happen if ever she wanted to go on top. But the good news was, she wanted breakfast; saved by the *full English*.

As 'Opalong watched Queenie stuff her face across the kitchen table, it took all of his willpower not to be sick, and then Vinnie appeared and dropped a piece of paper in front of him. He looked up at the stick-thin powerhouse, still handsome woman, 'What's this?'

'What it says.'

Even Queenie stopped eating to have a look, snatching it from a stunned 'Opalong. 'Mum, it's a wedding licence and it has my name and 'Opalong's on it,' and she passed it back to 'Opalong who tried hard to look pleased, not easy when you have that sinking feeling in your stomach.

'I arranged it yesterday. It's a special licence so you can get married this afternoon.' She looked at her watch, breakfast was more lunchtime. 'Maybe tomorrow, that will give you time to get your hair done nice, eh?'

'Lubbly jubbly, Mum.' She looked to her, fiancé. 'What do you think, 'Opalong?'

'Ah, yeah, lubbly jubbly, darlin'' 'Opalong knew he was done for, but it looked like Vinnie had more good news. 'Vinnie, is there something else?'

'Yeah, and it is brilliant, and please, you should call me Mum, after all, you are marrying my little girl,' and Vinnie offered her best devastating smile that said, agree or I'll 'ave you bumped off.

'Of course he will call you Mum, Mum, won't yer, my handsome lover?' Queenie was so made up with love she even stopped eating for a while. 'And, if we are not getting married until tomorrow, we can go back to bed after we've eaten, wouldn't that be nice?'

'Yes, darlin',' and 'Opalong looked to Vinnie, 'what was the good news, err, Mum?'

'You mean the additional good news, after all the best news is you are marrying my lovely daughter, yes?'

'Opalong was done up like a kipper and he knew it. 'Sorry, Mum. What is the other good news?'

Vinnie was pleased to see 'Opalong had comprehended the underlying message, much as he would be under lying with Queenie soon, and this made her laugh. 'The good news is that since you will now be a part of the family after tomorrow, you can represent us at the opening ceremony for the Orphanage and Youth Club on Incubator Street on Saturday.'

'Oh lovely, did you hear that 'Opalong, it will be our first formal public appearance as husband and wife... now, give us an 'eavenly bliss, will yer.'

While 'Opalong summoned up the strength and stomach to give his fiancé a kiss, Vinnie added the cream on the top. 'The good news for you, 'Opalong, would be that you will be at the opening and Chas Larkin will have to watch and swallow his pride. 'Opalong, you will be back where you belong, and when we take the East End, as we plan to do, my Queenie will rule with you by her side. So, what do you think of that?'

'Brilliant... Mum,' and he wasn't kidding. This was the only ray of sunshine he could see: the Saints back and ruling again.

———

It was agreed that Wendy would go with them to the convent; there was no stopping her and this gave hope that there would be something more than talking when they went to bed that night. 'Okay, lover. You come with us and we can have beddie byes with little talking tonight, eh? Lubbly jubbly...' Flora stopped talking. It looked as if she was painting herself into a corner, and then realised she had.

'You see this is the point, Flora,' Wendy responded.

Was she tapping her foot? Gawd blimey, she was. 'Oh bleedin' 'ell, what have I done now?' Flora was totally bollixed and she knew it.

'Last night, one of the things we agreed upon is that I would go to stay with my mum and dad in Bristol until things calmed down, didn't we?' and her foot tapping picked up a pace, and then she smiled; thank fuck for that was all Flora could think. 'It's okay, a lot has happened, even this morning, but me packing my suitcase while you were dressing should have been a clue...?'

Flora, of course, could recall, now: how come things like this slip her mind, was all she could think, certainly not an answer, and then she did. 'Sorry, darlin', we can drop you off at Paddington station after we've been to the convent, eh? That would work, wouldn't it?'

'Yes, darling that would work if that is okay with you Paddy, and you, Chas?'

Paddy was keen to get going, they had a lot to talk over with his sister and Mother Adelaide. 'Yes, Wendy, that works. Now, can we get going?'

Wendy answered, looking at Flora, 'Of course, just as soon as Flora gets my suitcase from the bedroom... Flora?'

'Gawd, alright, I'll do it since your arm's broken.'

'Flora...!'

'Sorry, of course. I will be pleased to carry your case for you...' and she gave her gorgeous lover a warm grin, at least she thought it was warm, but Wendy rolling her eyes had her worried, so she scooted to the bedroom while Paddy made a phone call, her mind already distracted; who was he calling?

———

Of course, the local undertakers were keen to assist Chas and Blossom. These were local boys, and although business had not been so good since peace had been arranged, they knew where their loyalties lay, and that was to the Larkin Saint family, and just in case they forgot, Maude had reminded them.

The date was set, a Saturday, a day of no other funerals, a day dedicated to Tommy Little Legs. The day was theirs. The cemetery was theirs for the day. The chapel was theirs. The Sexton was theirs. The roads were theirs; they would be cleared and closed off. The route to the cemetery was theirs and it would be draped in black. There was no effort spared by the funeral directors; this had to go well.

The funeral was to be a local event. In other words, everyone would be expected to either be there or have a visible presence, and after Maude visited Express Dairies, the offer of milk floats had been made; Tommy had loved the milk floats. He loved it when riding with Flan Milkman, and occasionally, Flan would go backwards, just to please the boy with the little legs. People loved Tommy and did all they could for him, his smile was reward enough.

What the funeral directors didn't know, because it was not public knowledge, to avoid remonstrations, was that the formal opening of the Orphanage and Youth Club was also set for that day. It would be bad enough mixing gaiety with such a sad occasion, but the only space available for the wake was the school premises. The school hall if it was raining, the playground if the weather was fine, which it looked set to be. There was one other significant fact that the funeral directors knew of and had asserted was important enough for all authorities to consent to the arrangements, and that was, it was Midsummer's Eve. This was a date etched in the annals of East End folklore, a date that would be told and retold over time, because just three years previously, it was the battle of the East India Docks whereby the O'Rierdon family were annihilated, as were many of the Saints and Larkins. And, if that was not significant enough, it was the day that Chas Larkin found his chutzpah and announced the merging of the two families with the marriage of Maude Larkin and Bess Saint who would lead the family on a day-to-day basis. And what of Chas Larkin? It was rumoured, but never confirmed, that this formally bullied and crippled runt, now ran the East End, but from a discreet distance.

Who knew that this date would clash? Certainly not the Incubator Street residents and certainly not Blossom and Chas. It was only when the builders began constructing a large stage that questions were asked. The builders had been told not to divulge what was happening for fear of resistance. The police knew, of course, they had to be in the know, in order to prepare for security for the invited dignitaries. However, sometimes the leaky colander that was Arbour Square police station did a public service. It has to be said that the discreet leak was mainly from fear of reprisals because, if it was discovered the police knew and did not reveal it to the Larkin Saint family, there really would be hell to pay, and, no spondulics.

The police now had a dilemma, which appeared impossible to solve without outside counsel from those in the know, and that would be with the ear of Chas Larkin and the Bishop of Stepney. In the end, the Commander of Arbour Square consulted Jim Rayner, desk sergeant and font of all local knowledge, including the shifty stuff in the police station, which was even more incendiary because of the Aunty Terrorist Unit, aka, the enigma Padraig Casey and his sidekick, Flora Wade.

The gunning down of Tommy Little Legs was causing so much agitation that it could erupt at any time and that would give the police, who were seriously undermanned, a real problem if the People took to the streets, or worse, took to the playground. Jim Rayner suggested to the Station Commander that the funeral date was set in stone, and he had tried, but the date and the day was significant. The Commander knew this and it was a vague hope he harboured that Rayner could solve it as a rare individual, a copper liked by the people. So it was down to the Bishop of Stepney to rearrange the date of their ceremony.

Jim suggested that the Commander telephone the Bishop's secretary, Clarissa something or other, but her reputation preceded her, if not her name, and that was why Jim was dialling the Bishop with not a little trepidation, the Commander being a well-known scaredy cat.

'Bishop's secretary please.' Jim was using his Sunday best voice.

'Owseyfather,' the woman answered, a supercilious tone that should have had Jim backed into his confessional, but it didn't.

'Alright, sleeps in the outhouse all night.' Jim couldn't resist completing the words of a popular ditty that he regretted as soon as the song was completed.

'I beg your pardon?'

Oh Gawd, Jim panicked but had to explain, maybe it would be alright? 'It's, err, you know, How's yer farver, alright, slept in the out'ouse, all night.' Jim gave the lady his full-on cockney accent to add colour to his musical rendition.

'Yes, I do see, amusing, especially as I am Clarissa Owseyfather, the Bishop's secretary, and I should tell you that the Owseyfather name goes right back to William the Conqueror. The Famille Blousedad came over with William the Bastard and the name became bastardised by the Saxons, the bastards, who had a similar song...' and she sang, holding a remarkable tune, '... Comment va ton pere, d;accord, il a dormi dand la dependence toute la nuit.' Jim wondered if he should lay the receiver down and applaud, but the lady was continuing, not singing, she was back talking down to him. 'Who are you again? Did you say sergeant, because I do not speak with such lowly ranks?'

'Sergeant Jim Rayner, ma'am, of Arbour Square police station.' Jim was trying really hard to control his temper.

Lady Fart-face of Normandy replied from an even greater height and cadence, 'Why is your commander not calling me?'

Jim wanted to say it was because he was scared, but Jim was scared. 'He has a cold, Ma'am.'

'Diarrhoea, more like. Frit, is he?'

Gawd blimey, how to answer? Maybe it was best to move on? 'I am calling to ask if you could rearrange the date for your opening ceremony for the Incubator Street Orphanage and Youth Club, please.' Jim found it hard to disguise the tremor in his voice, but his hatred of posh people carried him through.

It seemed that Clarissa found this request highly amusing, laughing down the phone right in Jim's earhole. 'Oh, sergeant, that was funny...' Jim got that, '... you do know who I am right?'

Should he answer and should he maintain his obsequious tone, even though it was obvious he could never ingratiate himself with the likes of these people and this made him angry, and may have influenced his response? 'You're the tart who sorts the fucking diary for that ponce nonce of a bishop, now, if you don't change the date of your ceremony, I am afraid we, that is the jeffing police, the coppers, the filf, the rozzers, or whatever William the fucking bastard called them, cannot guarantee your safety. I also inform you that I will reduce the number of officers because I cannot risk them getting hurt. Do I make myself fucking clear, you old bat?' Clarissa hung up and Jim said to the dialling tone, 'I'll take that as no then,' and he replaced the receiver gently, wondering if he had upset her, but certainly, he felt a lot better. Now to tell the commander.

Jim plodded the stairs to the top of the police station to impart bad news to the commander. Sabrina, the commander's personal assistant, hushed him, 'He's just taken a call from the bishop's secretary and she didn't sound too happy, but then, does she ever?'

Jim, sighed. 'I had better go in. Can I borrow your tin hat please?' and Jim knocked on the door and went in with the sound of Sabrina chuckling behind him and the sound of the commander explaining that he did not have diarrhoea, just a heavy cold that currently was affecting his arse, if Jim was not mistaken.

The commander hung up the phone, sighed and dramatically rubbed his forehead. 'Jim, I should be angry with you, but find myself full of admiration. You're better man than me Gungha Din.' The two men shared a laugh. 'Did you actually tell her to go fuck herself?'

'I can't recall, sir, but I can't imagine anyone else wanting to fuck her, except the bishop, although I think he prefers altar boys?' and they shared an even heartier laugh.

'Just before she hung up on me she did say that you threatened to reduce the number of police at the event. Is that true?'

'Sir, if they do not reschedule their ceremony, I told her we could not guarantee their safety and I would not risk the lives of my men, just to satisfy their egotistical bastard personages.' Jim felt better.

'Again, I should reprimand you, but I find myself agreeing and applauding you. Do what you feel right, and I suppose we hope for the best,' and the commander stood and leaned across his desk to shake Jim's hand. 'Now, fuck off and send Sabrina in please, she knows just how to calm me.'

Jim knew exactly what the commander meant and so did his p.a. After all, she was stood behind him enjoying the spectacle. 'Sabrina, he needs you...' and he winked and she told him he was a wanker. 'I thought that was your job?' and he made a run for it.

32

HIGH NOON: IN THE EVENING AT A ROYAL PECULIAR

'WHAT'S UP, SWEET'ART? WHY SO GLUM? I SAID I WOULD COOL IT and I did. I take your point and I said sorry, didn't I?' Maude was contrite as Bess came down from using the toilet for the umpteenth time; seemed the babe pressed her bladder, and Maude showed her sympathy by rubbing it and telling the baby to move over.

This amused Bess. 'It's not that, darlin',' and Bess held Maude's hand so she didn't leave her belly; it felt nice.

'Well, what is it then? Is it the heat, summer is brewing up to be a right brahma, are you uncomfortable? Do you need me to massage your ankles?'

'No, thank you. Perhaps later. That is not what has got me perturbed.'

'Per... what, babe?'

'Has me, worried.'

'What is it then?'

'Well, if you will shut up for a minute, I will tell yer.' Maude made like she was zipping her mouth shut, which diverted Bess, but this was important and she needed to be focused and not distracted by Maude's tomfoolery. 'I took the phone call upstairs because you didn't answer it…!' Bess feigned anger, but she knew Maude didn't like answering the phone, and this Bess had encouraged so that her lover did not lose her temper and upset whoever was calling. Maude feigned sadness. 'Come here…' and Bess pointed to her cheek, demanding a kiss, and Maude obliged. 'Don't you want to know who was calling?'

Maude shrugged. 'Don't mind, either way.'

Bess, sighed. 'It was the old Bill.' Now that did get Maude's attention, the police calling them. Bess could tell Maude was intrigued because her glorious eyebrows went up. 'Do you want to know what they wanted?' Maude shrugged again, and Bess gave up, 'It was the desk sergeant we like…'

'Jim Rayner.'

'Yeah, that's him, and he has just informed me that the funeral for Tommy is on the twentieth…' She waited for a response from her lover. 'I imagine this upsets your plans, yeah?'

Maude shrugged again, but with a little more animation in her face; there was something up and she couldn't fathom what, but it had a Bess booby trap and she suspected she had already trodden on it, so this time she answered. 'Yeah, bit of a bugger that, still what can I tell yer…?'

Bess broke the cuddle to lean back and look directly into Maude's eyes while she held her face so she could not avoid her inspection; Maude now knew it was a landmine and likely not a booby. Shit, she thought. 'Well, I suppose since our plans are scuppered by Tommy's funeral, you could tell me what you were going to do for my surprise, eh?' She looked but no response from Maude, but at least she hadn't shrugged. 'I suppose we can rearrange that for another day, eh?' Maude nodded. 'Good, what was it anyway, I am curious?'

Maude looked to the telephone in the living room, hoping and praying that it would ring, but she had been such a bad girl lately it was unlikely God would do anything for her, but then it rang. 'Phone, sweet'art,' she said, unnecessarily, and Bess could see the relief in Maude's face.

'Oh, that's what it is...' Bess responded with a half-smile because she had Maude on the back foot and was enjoying her discomfort; she had not a clue what she was asking. 'Hold that place, I will be back,' and she went to answer the phone. 'Hello, yes, fuck! Thanks, Jim, and yes, I will control Maude. Yes, I said I would, didn't I? Yes, honest injun, and yes, fuck off wiv bleedin' brass knobs,' and Bess hung up.

'Jim?' Maude asked, innocent as you like. Bess liked that face, and when she displayed that side of her, you would never know she was a vicious and violent gangster.

'How did you guess that?'

'Well, you said Jim...'

Bess halted her dimwit, though gorgeous with it, wife. 'I will tell you what he said, adding conundrum upon bleedin' disaster. Shall I?' Maude shrugged. 'Well, he phoned back to tell me that the fucking church was arranging the opening ceremony for the Incubator Street Orphanage and Youth Club on the same bloody day as Tommy's funeral, and they refuse to rearrange it. So, what do you think of them apples, sister?'

Maude shrugged, 'Dear oh dear, that could be difficult.'

Bess slapped her forehead. 'You think?' Maude shrugged again, wondering if this actually was what she was thinking and if it wasn't, what she was thinking? 'Get yer 'at an' coat, sweet'art, it's time we had a chat with the nuns, do you agree?' Maude shrugged, wondering if she agreed, but she followed Bess anyway; she would follow Bess anywhere because she loved her. 'What you doing, it's eight 'undred degrees out there, you won't need yer coat.'

'You said...' Maude saw the look of amazement on Bess's face and decided against the coat. After all, she had her sunglasses. 'Right, babes, no coat.'

———

Flora, Wendy, Paddy and Chas were shown into the Mother Superior's office to be greeted by Adelaide, with a special hug for Wendy. 'Wendy Richards, I presume? Reports of your beauty are severely underestimated as is your reputation. It is an absolute pleasure to meet you.'

'And me you. Flora has told me something about the convent, your work and so on, but I know she left a lot out of what you told her, and I presume you left a lot out of what you told her, yes?'

Adelaide smiled. 'I see we are going to have to be circumspect around you, Wendy. Did Flora mention an invitation to a retreat here?' Adelaide took a little time, enough for Wendy to look across to Flora and for Flora to sink back in her chair. 'Well, never mind, I will tell you later and then you will know, and when you do come, I can reveal much more about our organisation and the Royal Peculiar.' There was a knock at the door. 'Ah, that will be Sister Blende.' The door swung open before Adelaide got to call out "enter", which the Mother said, under her breath after Roisin had already entered with a theatrical flourish, and stepped straight to Flora and gave her a big kiss on the lips; Wendy was shocked.

Roisin observed all. 'Wendy,' and she paced behind the gathered seats to lean over the psychiatrist. 'Didn't tell you, did she?'

'Tell me what?' Wendy was flustered, but it did not prevent her pressing her curiosity.

'Oh, I think it best Flora tells you...' and she looked across to the detective sergeant, '... do you agree, Flora darling...' and then back to Wendy, '... and, if you get fed up with her, I have first dibs, so I do.'

Wendy was about to respond but Mother Adelaide beat even Flora to the jump. 'Sister Blende, I think a little less winding up of our guests, if you please.' Wendy noticed that Sister Blende baulked at the rebuke and there was clear respect for the Mother Superior; interesting, and she never got the chance to burst the Black Rose bubble because Flora had told her about the kissing; she let it go.

'Sorry, Mother...' but she was cut off by another knock on the door.

'Enter,' Adelaide called out, looking around the room to count how many chairs she had. The door opened and in walked a very pregnant Bess Saint followed up by the sleek, darkly dressed, black suit and black open-neck shirt, dark glasses, Maude Larkin. 'Well, this is a lovely surprise. Welcome, Bess, and you Maude, of course...'

Wendy jumped up and her chair fell over as she backed herself to the wall, her face displaying the panic she felt. Flora left her chair to stand in front of her woman, protecting her, even though she knew there was nothing to fear and that the ruse of Maude *off the rails*, was just that. Wendy even knew, but she nevertheless feared the gangster queen; just how much had she been faking? Wendy suspected not much and interpreted that Maude had been enthused by the fear she had displayed.

Maude strolled over, peeked around Flora. 'Ooh, ooh, Wendy, darlin', I believe I owe you a great big apology,' she looked back to Bess, 'okay?' It was obvious Bess had insisted that when they met Wendy Richards she was to apologise, profusely, and judging by the look on Bess's face, it was not enough. 'Alright,' Maude said to Bess, and then back to Wendy and again peeking around Flora, 'Wendy, I am truly sorry. I went too far and I apologise...' looked to Bess, '... profer... err...' and another look to Bess.

'Profusely, she apologises profusely, don't you, Maude?' Bess clarified it for everyone and Wendy, as she leaned in her seat to see around Flora to the cowering trick cyclist.

'Yeah. What she said,' Maude said.

Wendy emerged from behind Flora and looked back to her lover, pleading with her eyes, what to do as Maude had her arms out wide, expecting to hug Wendy. 'Maude, I am not sure a hug is necessary, and we both thank you for your apology, profusely...' Flora said, and Wendy even managed a laugh at that.

'Okay, now that is over please take a seat...' and Adelaide pointed to the last two chairs in the room, when the door knocked again. 'Oh, fuck me gently, who the bleedin' 'ell this time?'

The door opened and a timid nun stepped in. 'You asked to see me, Mother?'

'Shit bang piss. Sorry, I forgot. Everybody, this is Sister Diurnarius.' She waved an arm to encapsulate the guests. Before asking the sister to fetch another chair, the door opened and a postulant entered carrying the extra chair. 'Thank you,' the mother managed to say before the frail-looking girl made to run.

'Wait.' It was Roisin, and she stood and took the nervous girl into her arms. How are you doing Janet, better?'

'Yes, I am, and I have not had a chance to thank you for what you did for me. I know my dad said he was truly grateful.'

'It was my pleasure...' and there was an enigmatic grin on the face of Sister Black Rose, missed by most but not Wendy; she saw all and that was not as benign as the Black Rose may have thought. She also saw that the waif of a girl left more buoyed than when she entered. 'What was that all about?'

Roisin retook her seat, explaining as she went, 'That was Janet, Ron the black cab driver's daughter, you may recall, Flora, and I imagine you told Wendy...?' which clearly she hadn't, and Roisin enjoyed another playful moment, and then she applied her serious face, Wendy thinking her face changes like the wind. 'Well, I did for the bastard who raped and beat her.'

'Thank you, Sister, and it was no more than the dirty bastard deserved. Janet is recovering well within the Order. Now, let me introduce you all to Sister Diurnarius...' Adelaide told the new attendee the names of all present and the new sister made notes, unmoved when Maude Larkin was introduced, but it looked like she had met Chas before. 'Sister Diurnarius is our journalist sister, and she now has a job as a reporter on the *Daily Mirror*.' Wendy looked surprised, so Adelaide expanded upon the introduction. 'If Flora had told you all, she would have told you that if any of the girls we take in do not want to take Orders, we educate them and train them up for the professions: Doctors, solicitors, we even have a Queen's Counsel now, and we hope eventually to establish Chambers at all of the Inns of Court. A slow process, but it is about evolution, not revolution.

'I have invited our journalist because I suspect whatever happens now will be a story, and we want the truth to be written, hence a newspaper with socialist leanings, the *Daily Mirror*. The editor is aware of us and our aims, so he will support whatever our sister writes. Of course, we hope that someday we will have one of our ladies as editor in post, but sadly the newspapers are still so misogynistic,' and she said that as though spitting feathers.

'Blimey...' It was all Wendy could say. She was impressed, and a quick glance to Flora said it all; Flora knew she may have omitted a few salient details.

Bess chirruped, it was her style, a demure ruthless gangster woman. 'It is fortuitous to have you here, Sister Reporter, I am not going to keep saying the Latin name,' and the Mother nodded; she agreed. 'Maude and I are here because I have just taken a call from Jim Rayner, the desk sergeant at Arbour Square nick, and he has informed me, breaching confidentiality I might add, that the Church intend to have a big celebration and ceremony for the opening of Incubator Street

Orphanage and Youth Club, which will be on the same day as poor Tommy's funeral.'

'What...!' Chas was up and there was steel in his eyes; everyone noticed, it was impossible to miss, and Sister Reporter scribbled away, illegibly, unless you knew shorthand.

Paddy followed out of his own chair and put his hand on Chas's shoulder, but noticeably it was Roisin who took Chas in her arms, whispering into his ear, words that nobody could hear, and slowly she had Chas not only calm, but the Black Rose nun and Public Enemy number one shared and evil grin, and then an evil stare for her brother, who was trying desperately to eavesdrop on his *evil* sister.

It was Adelaide who brought the love-in to a close. 'Please, be seated, we had a lot to talk about before this disastrous news that I half suspect, has Sister Blende's mind ticking over with a solution that will no doubt be violent, though satisfying. Maybe when you have formulated your ideas you will share them with me, sister?' Roisin nodded and Paddy rolled his eyes; he knew his sister well, she was not known as the Black Rose for nothing; she will not share with the Mother, but he hoped she would with him. Adelaide turned to Sister Reporter, 'Perhaps, first off, you can run a story talking about the Church riding roughshod over the local people of Incubator Street? It might make them change their minds, but I doubt it.' And turning to address everyone, 'I had invited our reporter to get background on the paedophilia-ridden local establishment, but I think we can use this as a follow-up, but for now, it is time to ruffle some feathers. Now, let us press on, I know Sister Blende has another meeting this evening, yes?' Roisin nodded, she did, and Paddy's antennae twitched.

33

RUTH

Tanner was sat in his seedy hotel room in Paddington. Ruth was right, nobody would expect him to be there, and he didn't mind eating at the greasy spoon café around the corner to the hotel; it reminded him of his childhood, his friends in and around Incubator Street School. He even had a bit of a laugh with the working girls who would call in for a cup of tea and a rest from putting their legs up; it was life going on around him.

He'd received a message from Ruth saying she had arranged a meeting. It was telephoned in to the hotel, but Tanner knew what it meant. She would be meeting with the IRA commander tonight at the 'Arf a sixpence. He reflected, not sure what scared him more, the IRA or Chas Larkin. At least with the IRA, it would be a quick execution... and then he thought, what if it was a kneecapping? They did that apparently. Would this be preferable to a slow and painful death as retribution for the death of Tommy Little Legs; oh Christ, he thought, he really was in trouble. However, he knew Ruth would sort it; she always did.

———

She had Tanner where she wanted him, cowering in a corner and, bonus, she'd found a nice fella who could do the biz in bed. Now, all she needed was for these IRA brigade leaders to agree to what she had planned and all would be well.

She intended to dress smartly, and not slutty so a quick pit stop at her flat, tidy up a bit if Stan was coming. She kissed Stan goodbye and told him, in no uncertain terms, to be in her bed when she got back. She said she would bring something in for dinner and, if all went well, maybe a bit of bubbly; she was in the mood. Stan nodded and got out of bed, stark naked, a move that Ruth appreciated visually, and loved the hug and snog a lot more; Gawd blimey he was a good kisser, and she hated to leave his excitement, she just told him to be a good boy and keep it warm for her, and she left, down the stairs, and hailed a cab.

———

'Are you looking forward to me being Queen, sweet'art?' 'Opalong was exhausted, not sure he had ever held his breath this long before, but with Queenie on top, it was impossible to breathe. 'Baby, don't fall asleep, I'm randier than a rabbit from Sainsburys, so?'

'Sorry my love, what did you ask?' He knew he was buying time before he gave the answer he would be obliged to give, but truthfully, he thought that if the Georges did win the war, he would be fucked if he would let Queenie sit on the throne. He wanted it, and Queenie, of course, could have another heart attack.

'Are you looking forward to when I am Queen and you will be my prince?'

'I long for the day, darlin', and tomorrow we shall be married.' It was clearly what she wanted to hear as she made a grab for what would become his wedding tackle tomorrow. He decided to lay back and think of, not England, not Queenie, but taking over the East End and rubbing out Chas Larkin, and all the fucking Larkins, especially the dykes.

———

'Ruth, good to see yer!' The Irish barman at the 'Arf a Sixpence always greeted Ruth enthusiastically. She half thought he fancied her and, well, he wasn't bad looking, but she knew the truth of it was she was a powerful woman, and in her own quiet way, was scary.

'Sean, good to see you too,' and she smiled with her greeting because she was pleased to see a familiar face before she went into an unpredictable meeting.

'No Tanner? Not seen him in a few days, keeping his head down is he. Can't say I blame him, his meeting here the other night seemed to disturb him, and then there is what happened to poor Tommy Little Legs. Everyone is saying that was Tanner's work, even if he didn't pull the trigger.' Sean gestured with his head to the door at the back of the bar counter. 'They're here.'

'Thanks, Sean, I'll go through.'

Sean lifted the bar flap and Ruth passed through but stopped when she felt his hand on her shoulder. 'Ruth, I like you, and I want you to know that those are serious people in there...' and he pointed to a pistol under the bar counter. 'If you need me, shout loud and I will come. I'm a patriot and all that, but even I think they go over the top sometimes. It's like they think they are untouchable.'

'Thank you, Sean, and I agree with you. However, I think I can calm things down and suggest a way forward that suits everyone, and I come out in one piece,' and she offered a nervous laugh.

'Well, I'm here if you need me.'

'I know. Now I'll go through,' and Ruth passed along the back bar and through the door to see two guards in black fatigues. She thought the same as Tanner, not much disguising who they were. The guards nodded acknowledgement, they recognised Ruth and knew she was expected. They opened the door for her and she thanked them kindly.

In the room sat at the Victorian breakfast table, extended to its full length, she saw three people, also in black fatigues, but with full balaclavas, just mouth and eyeholes. They did look scary and she could understand why Tanner was in meltdown; they meant business and were likely not afraid to assert what they wanted, violently. Ruth took the seat at the opposite end of what was clearly the woman Tanner had mentioned. They both sat, who was titular head of the table to be determined Ruth imagined. The two other brigade men looked like officers but of a lower status than the woman, who just sat and stared through her eyeholes.

The woman remained silent, it was way scarier. It was one of the other officers who opened the dialogue. 'Tanner not with you Ruth?'

Ruth knew she had to play it cool and keep her arguments in reserve, to only use them if absolutely necessary. She had been in meetings like this before and Tanner would always blurt out everything and lose all of his bargaining chips in the first few minutes, the bozo. 'No, as you see.'

'Where is he?' It was the other officer, both had cold Northern Irish accents, brusque, grating even, Belfast if she had to guess.

'If I told you that he would be dead in less than an hour, am I right?' First cards played, and now to see how they are received to take the temperature, Ruth thought to herself.

The two men laughed. The woman didn't, but Ruth sensed she was amused, 'Fair enough,' the first officer said, 'we are not best pleased with him. He has fucked up big time.'

'Yes, he has.' That was all Ruth said, and once again sensed approval from the silent woman.

'When he was here last, a few days ago, he told us he was ready to spring his trap and that he would secure the East End for himself shortly after. He told us that he had arranged for the assassination of Chas Larkin and that with our help, or should I say expertise, he would blow up the two gang leaders, the queen Maude and her consort, Bess. Were you aware of this?'

'I was.' Again short with no elaboration. That was motor mouth Tanner's style.

It was as though Ruth had managed to flummox the two men, expecting a diatribe back from Ruth attempting to justify what had happened. They did not know what to say and looked to the woman for answers; typical was all that Ruth thought as she tilted her head to the woman who clearly controlled the room.

The woman did react and it scared Ruth. She removed her gun and slowly, deliberately, screwed on a silencer. My God, she's going to shoot me, and now Ruth was scared. Had she misunderstood how to play this? And then, as cool as a cucumber, the woman shot both the men and while they slumped in their chairs, breathing their last and spilling their life's blood, the woman put the gun away and said, coldly, 'I didn't like them.'

'No kidding,' Ruth said, wondering where her bravado came from, but the woman laughed.

'Now, Ruth, you and I are going to have a nice chat and put the world to rights, you okay with that?' The woman had a strong southern Irish accent and if Ruth had to guess, it was west, and likely Kerry; it was lyrical and she liked it, but maybe she was influenced by the fact she was not dead, unlike the two poor sods before her, blood dribbling from the mouth hole of their balaclavas.

The woman stood and walked to Ruth, pulled out a chair beside her, sat and then another surprise, she removed her balaclava. 'Feck me it's hot in them tings, so.'

Ruth just sat trying not to gape, a combination of shock of all that had happened, surprise that this woman had removed her face covering, and this woman before her, probably mid-thirties, was stunningly beautiful, her immediate main feature being a long mane of copper red hair that flowed free after the removal of the knitted harness. The woman ran her fingers through the fine tresses and Ruth, who is full-on heterosexual, could only think, wow, and this woman could do anything to her, and already had.

'Close your mouth, Ruth, it looks silly on you, a most attractive woman.' Ruth was immensely flattered and blushed. 'If I didn't know you liked men, I would take you over this table now.'

Ruth really blushed now, and it showed, not always visible with her dark Jewish looks, but strangely, she was turned on. However, she needed to answer this woman who was sitting back in her chair smiling, totally absorbed, enjoying Ruth's embarrassment. 'Well, it is not difficult to find out I like men, and at one time, I liked Tanner...'

The commander interrupted Ruth. 'I didn't like the way Tanner treated you, and for your information, I swing both ways, but if pushed I would prefer to fuck you.'

Ruth was completely taken aback by the frankness of this woman, and knowing if she was not careful she would develop a Tanner motor mouth, and that would not do. She did not reply, just looked into the emerald eyes of the woman with copper hair from the Emerald Isle. The woman leaned forward with her elbows on the polished table surface; Ruth could see the pale face reflected in the depth of the shine. This was obviously the start of putting the world to rights, but she was not prepared for the next shock. The woman gazed into Ruth's own eyes, dark almost black, fair enough Ruth thought, but whatever was coming next, it had power behind it.

'Did you like, Stanley?' she had used her gentle voice and had lured Ruth into a false sense of security, at least this is what Ruth thought

'What?'

'Stanley, you liked him, yes?'

'Well, yes I did.' Keeping it short and to the point, Ruth was not sure where this was going.

'I thought you would like him, so much better than Tanner, and the girls tell me he fucks like a demon...' She stopped and looked at Ruth who could not remember ever being so embarrassed before, but this woman had done it to her. Life just seemed easy for this red-haired lady, and she ably demonstrated just now how fleeting life can be. Ruth looked at the dead men, not walking. 'Well, did he... we know you have asked him to stay for seconds, so I am assuming you are pleased?'

'I am.' Short and sweet, but Ruth was not worried, as much as intrigued. 'What business is this of yours?'

'Your business is my business, Ruth.'

'Shall we talk business then?' Ruth trying to change tack.

The woman leaned back in her chair, this was going to be a casual exchange for the time being, Ruth thought. 'We will, all in good time. I will want to talk to you about when we kill Tanner...' Ruth looked shocked, but knew she shouldn't be. It really was inevitable that someone would kill Tanner; if it wasn't the IRA, it would be Chas Larkin. 'We will choose the time and we will ask Chas Larkin to hold off.'

'You will? You talk to Chas Larkin?' Ruth was shocked. 'But Chas Larkin is the de facto head of the Larkin Saint family, as I am sure you are aware.'

'Naturally we are aware...'

PETE ADAMS

Ruth interrupted, her curiosity getting the better of her good judgement. 'But, if you want to take over the East End, why would you, err...' Ruth thought and wondered if she was on the right track, '... why would you talk to Chas Larkin? He controls the East End, with Maude and Bess, his generals.'

'Ruth, whatever made you think we wanted to control the East End?'

'Well...'

'Because that was Tanner's ambition, and the ambition of the George family, yes?'

'Yes.'

'What we need Ruth, is...' and it looked like she was searching for the right word to describe what sham they, the IRA, wanted, '... for want of a better word, we need agreeable allies. A benign partner, if you will. Someone who will support our aims and allow us to get on with our business.'

'My God...'

'Indeed. You see, I made Chas Larkin who he is now...'

'Which is...?'

'Which is, Ruth, his own man. A strong man, with chutzpah and an uncanny ability to see the big picture, and, just the right amount of ruthlessness to back it up.'

'Then why support Tanner and the George family and their ambitions, and you knew my involvement, that doesn't make sense?'

'First off, your involvement we saw was an intelligent force for, shall we say, the right course. You were always going to lose control of Tanner because in our view and the view of the cockneys, he is radio rental.' Ruth laughed and then put on her serious face. 'You have questions, of course – so fire away.'

'Thank you. May I say what I think you are saying and you can tell me if I am wrong?'

'Please do.'

'What you are seeking is, ironically, peace, and I don't mean that in the wider sense, in the unification of Ireland, eventually, and peace in the north between the Catholics and Protestants. I mean, peace in London. Stability. The quarters of London controlled, and I can't believe I am saying this, by your people. Your people who will let you do what you need to do to convince the powers that be to listen to your argument, yes...' and Ruth indicated she had more, '... and, if necessary, back this up with a bit of destruction, maybe not a body count, but hit the establishment where it hurts, buildings and infrastructure?'

The woman smiled and her green eyes lit up. 'Ruth, we have, from a distance, admired you, your vision and intelligence and this is why we have selected you to be Queen of the West.'

'Me? Queen...?' and Ruth allowed her thoughts to roam.

'You are thinking, what about the north, yes?'

'Yes, the Georges are a violent threat,' Ruth pointed out, unnecessarily.

'They were, we have been slowly taking care of that...'

'You have?' and Ruth was almost laughing before she asked her most pertinent question. 'Who have you chosen...,' and she scratched her head in incredulity... delaying too long.

'Who will be Queen of the North, can you guess?'

'I would guess, Lavinia George?'

'My God, but you are beautiful, and if ever you change your mind about men, and Stanley in particular, I want first dibs, eh?'

'Are you saying, I'm right?'

'Yes that, and if you fancied a fuck, right here and now, then I'm up for it. I can guarantee we will not be disturbed. Sean will see to that, and for your information, he has already taken care of the two goons outside.'

'Thank you for the offer, but I would like to get back to Stanley, who I presume is one of your men?'

'No, actually, he is, believe it or not, MI5, and he will not only love you in every way, he will make sure you are safe; he will be your consort.' And the woman smiled a job-well-done grin. 'You see we have had this covered for a while, and Stanley has followed you; he knows you better than you know yourself.

'Fuck me gently...'

'Well, sometimes, yes, but I would not be so gentle the first time...' and she grinned again, this time a naughty girl look. 'So, you would like to get back to your Stan, would you?'

'Yes,' and Ruth stood.

'Wait,' the woman asserted, and Ruth thumped back down in her chair.

'What, now, there couldn't possibly be more?'

'Well, are you not a little curious as to who I am?'

'Yes, but didn't want to push my luck. I half thought I would be killed this evening.'

'Yes, I saw that in your face when you came in, and you demonstrated your metal; most impressive. So, what I need you to do is get Tanner out of hiding, assure him he will be safe, because he will be, because we need him to be steered, by you, to do something for us. I will explain later.' The woman stood, a prelude to leaving.

'Wait,' Ruth, demanding this time. The woman turned. 'Who are you?'

The woman leaned in and almost brushed cheeks with Ruth as she whispered, 'I am Roisin Dubh. You may know me as The Black Rose.' And on that note, Roisin turned and left through a back door, Sean magically appeared and said he would deal with the bodies and he had a car outside to take Ruth back to Stanley.

34

A BUSY EVENING, FOR SOME...

ROISIN HAD LEFT TO GO TO HER MEETING AT THE 'ARF A Sixpence, and following the departure of Chas, Maude and Bess, the Mother stood, stretched and looking to Paddy and Sister Reporter. 'Well, I would say things are moving along if in somewhat obtuse and different directions than anticipated, and speedier than we imagined, but things are certainly moving.'

Paddy also stood and stretched. It was quiet in Adelaide's study, just the sound of Sister Reporter's scratching pencil. 'Quite a lot for you to take in there, sister,' Paddy said. 'Enough for your first article?'

The sister looked up. 'Plenty thank you...' and looking to Adelaide, '... perhaps we can get onto the paedophile ring now, Mother? This was, after all, the purpose of my coming here, not that I am complaining. I think my editor will be pleased when I write this up for tomorrow's paper.'

'Sister, I did read on your file that you may have been too pushy for the obedience of Holy Orders, but I see now that my predecessor had the measure of you and you are in the right place.'

'Thank you, Mother. Now, can we get on?'

Both Paddy and Adelaide offered up a wry smile. 'Yes, we can,' and Adelaide picked up the phone on her desk. 'Sister Hospitium are our guests suitably accommodated?' She listened. 'And they are comfortable?' Listened some more, the smile on her fresh face broadening. 'Well, they are teenagers, can you ask Mrs Charnel to meet us in the board room please, thank you,' and she hung up. Turning to Paddy, 'Shall we go, Sister Hospitium has...'

Paddy interrupted Adelaide's flow. 'Can we skip the Latin please, it's making my head go funny.'

'Did you not learn Latin at school, Paddy?'

'No, Adelaide, did you learn Gaeilge, which you English call Gaelic?'

'Touché, Padraig.'

'I didn't learn French either, so shall we go to the seomra boiurd?'

'To the board room it is and, yes, I am learning Gaeilge. I have a feeling I might need it, a bit like the cockneys use rhyming slang to disguise what they are saying.'

'Tadhaill.'

'Ditto and likewise, touché.'

———

Tanner was sure there were fleas in the carpet of his hotel room; his ankles and shins itched. He comforted himself in the knowledge that Ruth had sorted the IRA, the telephone message left at the hotel reception, they were no longer after him, but what about Chas Larkin? Could Ruth resolve this? He decided he needed dinner and again, it was the greasy spoon café adjacent to Paddington station, where he was now acknowledged as a regular.

Ruth knew this and now, so did Flora.

Flora had just seen Wendy onto the train for Bristol, after

promising for the umpteenth time that she would tell all about the convent and the Black Rose when she returned, and after an emotional farewell and waving as Wendy carried her own suitcase down the platform to the waiting train, Flora kicked her heels, deciding whether to get the bus or splash out on a cab, when she saw Tanner cross the road and go into a café; this was fate wasn't it? She decided it was and so followed, watched him through the plate glass window settle himself down and order his dinner. What an eejit he was, his back to the window and no view of the door. Paddy was right, Ruth actually ran the show, and why was she thinking in Irish, she thought, feckin' eejit.

'Hello, Tanner,' Flora introduced herself as she sat opposite the man.

'Who the fuck are you?'

Flora produced her warrant card and he read it. 'Ah, think I've heard of you?'

'Not bothered if you have or have not. I've heard of you, and I know you are behind the shooting in Incubator Street where Tommy Little Legs and Jack Diamond were killed.' Flora leaned back in her chair for two reasons, one, to see Tanner's reaction and two, get away from the greasy table, still with residue of cheap tomato sauce on it. She tried hard to disguise her revulsion.

'Prove it...' Tanner's bravado not particularly convincing.

'I don't need to.'

'Why?'

'Do you know who I'm going to see in a minute?' Flora could not resist watching the man's diarrhoea moment, followed up with a quick glance to the toilets at the back of the café that Flora would not go near in a month of Sundays. 'Well, I'll tell yer, Chas Larkin. I thought I would call in and pay my respects, personal-like. You do know the whole street is so upset and everyone is pointing to you.'

'Why me? What about the George family? They are equally hateful toward to the Larkins, and especially the dykes.'

Flora was not sure where her rage came from, maybe because she wanted desperately for Wendy to stay and not go to her parents. She knew that Wendy's mum did not like her, and the parents always try to talk Wendy round, to find a nice man. They could never comprehend what they had done wrong for their cherished daughter, in love with a woman. However, the dam broke, and Flora straight arm punched Tanner on his nose and blood spurted onto the table to join the ketchup, and Flora laughed at that until the manager, with a filthy apron tied tightly around his beer gut rushed to intervene and was readying himself to throw Flora out, when she flipped open her warrant card. The manager stepped back and returned to the counter, muttering something about the violence inherent in the system, but this was a woman; had he never heard of women's lib?

'What d'you do that for?' Tanner spluttered, nasally, trying to stem the flow of blood with his handkerchief.

'You know me now, and for your information, I am a lesbian. Now, would you like to say anything funny about that?' Tanner shook his head, distributing more droplets of blood. Flora stood, 'Well, I'll be off now. Reckon I will be flavour of the month in Incubator Street for a while after tonight, unless you can tell me something that might make me keep schtum on your whereabouts. Well, can you?' Flora watched on as Tanner weighed up his options. And tilted her head questioning.

He decided, 'I think you will find that the shooting was arranged by the IRA.'

Flora feigned surprise, like this was news to her. 'The IRA? Why would they gun down Jack Diamond and Tommy Little Legs?'

There was hope on Tanner's face; this was going better than he could imagine, provided the IRA didn't find out he had grassed on them, telling the filf a dirty great big lie. Well, not such a big lie, Tanner thought, as he congratulated himself on how clever he was. Now for the coup-de-gras. 'Because, lady...' he curbed his language as he was sure the queer copper was winding up for another haymaker. 'Sorry. What I am saying is, I know that the IRA want to take over the East End for their own benefit.'

Flora made like she was considering the value of this intelligence. 'How do you know this?'

'One of the benefits of owning pubs where the Irish patriots gather; I hear things.'

Flora thought that this evening had worked out so well, apart from Wendy leaving. 'Okay, interesting. You just bought yourself a few days' grace. I will not split on you, yet,' and she stood, playfully slapped his cheek and left, a huge grin on her face.

———

Adelaide, Paddy and Sister Reporter, entered the convent board room. It was a substantial room that doubled up for lectures and instructional courses but was mainly for meetings such as this. The room already had five nuns sitting down one side of a large refectory-type table; they stood to greet the Mother.

Adelaide headed for the top of the table, flagging her hand to suggest no formalities are needed and they could sit. Paddy took up a seat beside Mrs Charnel who was either nervous of being in such company or was raring to go; it was difficult to tell. The Mother appreciated Paddy sitting next to the woman, offering some whispered comments that were evidently appreciated. Paddy was a kind man, ruthless and sometimes violent, but he had a gentle streak and she nodded her appreciation to him. 'Okay, some introductions,' and she went around the table, 'Mrs Charnel, I hope your accommodation is satisfactory and you have our sincere condolences on the loss of your husband. I have it on good authority that he was a good man, albeit he had run into some bad men.' The professor's wife acknowledged the sympathies. 'I think most of you know that the professor, at great risk to himself and his family, secreted detail autopsy reports of those abused children that came his way. What you might not know is that Mrs Charnel is a senior officer in the Welfare department of the council and along with her husband, was able to identify a lot of the children, what homes or orphanages they were from, and in some cases, the personalities who carried out such despicable acts on these defenceless children.'

Adelaide allowed a moment or two for the power of what she had revealed to be absorbed. 'Now, I think we all know Detective Inspector Padraig Casey, who, I might add, is the brother of our own, Sister Blende.' This was news to the five nuns sat in a line opposite Mrs Charnel and Paddy, and there was an audible sigh; seems the Black Rose was liked in the convent, and Paddy rolled his eyes. 'And now, the nuns here are known formally as the Sisters of Tutors of Liberoraum, translated as protectors of children, and since this is a large proportion of our work here, they are a sizeable team or as we like to refer to them, squad. And, here we have, Sister Reporter, and Mrs Charnel, you may be rest assured your name will be kept a secret.

'Now, the introductions done. Paddy I know has other matters to deal with and Mrs Charnel, I will leave you in the expert hands of the child protection squad. My door is always open if you need me,' and along with Paddy, she left the room.

Outside the boardroom, Paddy and Adelaide had a brief word, before she wished him success and returned to her office. Paddy left, picking up a cab on Cheapside, heading back to the East End and Nadia.

35

RELATIONSHIPS

PADDY CALLED INTO INCUBATOR STREET TO SEE CHAS AND TELL
him of what had just occurred with Tanner, but mostly, to see
how Blossom was doing. He was shown into the parlour where
there were still a few of the neighbours lingering. Empty
glasses everywhere attested to a large gathering and shared
drinks. Paddy knew it would not have been Chas, he had been
with him all day, and he did not drink, least not that he had
seen. Maybe Blossom did, he would not know, but certainly the
neighbours enjoyed evenings down the local pub.

Blossom noticed Tanner taking in the landscape of glasses.
'I haven't... sorry for the mess. Time, you know...'

Paddy hugged her, leave this to me...' she protested, as did
Chas, but Paddy grew up in a large family, surrounded by
sisters and a strong mother, as a consequence he was accomplished in waving away such protests. He began transporting
the dirty glasses and after three trips he'd stacked them on the
draining board, filled the bowl with hot soapy water and was
busy washing up when he was joined by Flan, who took a tea
towel and began drying. The sound of Blossom sobbing in the
other room carried and it was clear Flan was affected by it.

Paddy stopped washing for a minute, took another towel, dried his hands and went to hug Flan. The milkman recoiled, dropped to his knees and cried out, 'No, no, no...'

Paddy stepped back a little, crouched and waited for Flan to look up. 'It's okay. What is it you are feeling? What are you bottling up, and why now, why now do you feel you can let it out?' Paddy had seen this before, back in the auld country, and knew enough that Flan must tell it himself and only when he is ready; he had seen abused children in adulthood before. Flan was ready, Paddy could see, it must be the wrenching sadness of Tommy and seeing Blossom so heartbroken.

'I never had a mum like Blossom.'

Flan opened up and Paddy could see these were the flood gates. 'Tell me in your own time, Flan,' Paddy encouraged the lad.

'I know that whatever the circumstances, she would never have allowed Tommy to be taken into care.' This was it Paddy thought, an indictment of Flan's own mother. 'I was, time and time again, my mum saw it as a convenience...' he was crying again, '... it kept happening, even though I told my mum what they were doing to me and who was doing it.'

More heartbreak, this time from Paddy who joined Flan, 'I am so sorry you had to suffer like that. If it is any consolation, I am determined to bring them to justice.'

Flan looked up, a gentle smile on a handsome face, still down-hearted, despite Paddy's declared plans. 'People like that never get caught, never get punished, never get what they deserve, because they are protected by the authorities: senior policemen, judges, councillors, churchmen, bloody television and film stars. Paddy, they are untouchable, and every night I have the nightmares. Every fucking night...' Paddy put his hands onto Flans shoulders. It was all he could do, words at this stage were useless; he needed only to show Flan he understood. 'The only help I ever had was from Chas and Blossom. Except for Snotty Oliver, who had his difficulties at Eton, well, the others, the Myrmidons, they all suffered as I did, some worse if you can imagine that...' Again he looked into Paddy's face, 'Every day I get up and try to put it behind me, but I can't. Paddy, I can't...' and he broke down sobbing.

Paddy eased Flan to a chair, pulled another so he sat beside the milkman. 'And this is why you are here, why you have not gone home?'

Flan nodded, 'I know I am loved by Blossom and Chas, and Chas suffered himself, and I don't know how he survived to prosper, but he did. Blossom tells me he has his own night-mares. I know she is trying to comfort me, and for a time it works, but I am at a loss. I'm at my wits end. I feel like I am drowning and sometimes I think of throwing myself in the Thames, but who would mourn me? Not those bastards in the homes, and now, a new Home and Youth Club here, right on my doorstep, to rub my nose in it. It is not right, Paddy, it ain't right.'

'No, Flan, but I will try to make it right so you might feel a little better.'

'Paddy, I know you mean well, but I tell you...' and Paddy saw the young man make two fists, '... I want revenge, I want to kill the lot...' and he mock laughed, '... but how, and if I do, I will just be arrested by bent coppers and thrown into clink to be even more abused. I do not know which way to turn, Paddy, I truly do not.'

Both men stood to see a crying Blossom and Chas behind them, and Blossom held her arms out and Flan went into them for a maternal hug, it would help this night, but the hurt will never go away, Paddy knew.

Chas eased his way to Paddy. 'I've seen too much of this, Paddy. It is time we did something and make it big, make it a statement that says, NO MORE. The people here will take no more. You should know I have spoken to Roisin about this. And well...'

Paddy knew this was incendiary news. 'You what?' and Paddy reflected. 'Okay, yes. I can see why and, well, I guess I agree. We will need to keep this in a tight circle, agreed?' Chas nodded his agreement. 'I am meeting Roisin tomorrow, will you join me. The funeral is the day after. Should you not be with Blossom? Paddy asked Chas, who nodded, and both men looked back to Blossom hugging a crying milkman. 'No more Paddy, no more. I will talk to Blossom tonight and I know she will agree.'

————

Following a passionate welcome that involved Stanley removing Ruth's clothes in double quick time, and Ruth reciprocating, whipping his pants down, relieved he hadn't bothered to get fully clothed, they made violent love; it was what she needed and he gave it to her, and as they lay in amongst the aftermath of bedding and shredded clothing, they shared some home truths, not sweet nothings, but real all the same.

'So, MI5 eh?' Ruth asked, recovering her breath.

'She told you, did she?'

'Obviously.'

'So...?'

'Yes, you are a so and so...' he chuckled, it was hard not to; he liked Ruth's sense of humour. 'We seem to get on, don't we?'

'In the day and a bit we've known each other, I do believe we do.' Stanley was using his posh voice, it amused Ruth. 'I, however, know you well. Did they tell you?'

'Who, the Black bleedin' Rose? Yes, she did.'

'So, let's give it a whirl, eh. You never know...'

'No, you don't, but I know one thing...'

'And that is…?

'I can't keep calling you sodding Stanley, it will have to be Stan.

'When you meet my family, you will see they call me Stan…'

She interrupted, 'Stan the dirty old man, yes, I can see that. So, Stan dirty old man, do your business, right now. You will need to serve your queen you know,' and slipping down the bed, he did, and judging by Ruth's writhing and moans, he was making a good job of being the Queen's man-in-waiting.

———

Nadia was home and when Paddy opened the door, she walked slowly to greet him with a wonderfully warm kiss and a tight hug. 'Thank you for today, Paddy. Coming with me to see Mrs Charnel. I have made some dinner, cold cuts and salad. I did not know when you would make it home.'

'That sounds lubbly jubbly, as Chas would say, and I think you will be impressed when I tell you that the nuns have really got a grip on this and will get all the information out via their good offices and keep the Charnels safe.'

'Tell me later, please. Let us enjoy dinner, I have a chilled white wine,' and she guided Paddy to the table, sat him down and kissed his neck before she disappeared into the kitchen, retrieved the wine from the fridge, popped the cork, returned and poured, sat and offered her glass for a chink. 'Cheers, my love.'

Paddy thought his luck was in, "my love". So, like a lemon, he pushed that luck.

'Nadia I love you.'

'I love you too, you Irish tow rag.'

Such loving words encouraged him to dip his toe into shark infested waters. 'Marry me, please?' he asked. He was worried, she could see, and also sensed he was losing patience with her; he'd asked so many times. Nadia said nothing, just looked back at him. He was lost, what did this mean?

She knew his patience never had much substance, and as it wore even thinner, so his Irish accent became more acute, albeit lyrical, endearing even, and Nadia had trouble remaining steadfast in remaining unwedded. She knew her family were disquieted about her being undeniably in a permanent, and more is to the point, a physical relationship with Padraig Casey. 'And what shall I call myself if my brains turned to mush and I consented to be your wife?'

'What do you mean, "what shall I call myself"?'

She sighed, she did love Padraig, but in the three years they had been together, she still had not worked out if it was the aura of danger that pervaded her lover's persona was the attraction she felt? She had been born into conflict. It was second nature, and despite looking for a peaceful and settled life in Britain, the reason for escaping to sanctuary in this glorious Isle, danger was in her; it was a part of her physical fibre. 'Well, let me see...' and she made like she was for the first time pondering an imponderable question, '...would I be, Mrs Casey?'

She got up from the table, and Paddy realised that his timing may have been off. Nadia walked up and down her living room very much as a model would do, traipsing the catwalk, and Nadia was most certainly model like, tall, five ten, slim and elegant, not classically attractive, a strong nose that some in the East End of London had called her beak, or fireman's hose, but she was, especially in these parts, exotic. Paddy thought she was smoking hot, and just the look of her made him come over all unnecessary.

'Well, yes, Mrs Casey...' He knew he was walking into a trap, but Detective Inspector Padraig Casey was a man, first and foremost, and as a consequence was dead meat to a woman like Nadia. He also was a sucker for Nadia, which equated to this very accomplished, not so much detective as an MI5 operative, becoming a gibbering wreck when presented with a question that for the life of him, he could not comprehend.

'Okay then, Mrs Casey...' and she pondered on whilst she contemplated skewering the man in front of her, her lover, although he was not so hot in the picturesque stakes, he did have a striking presence, and combined with his incandescent and latent power, except when confronted by Nadia, she herself had to use all her self-control not to fling herself into his arms.

'Hmmm, okay, that is settled then...' Oh dear, he had fallen into that classic male trap, assuming that was the end of the matter, and made the additional mistake of smiling, for him relief, but for Nadia it looked very much like a victory smirk.

'So your family, the O'Neill's, back in County Clare, Ireland, a place you have not even suggested you would take me, though I have asked a thousand times...' (Padraig thought it couldn't be a thousand, he would have remembered that, but now she raised the matter, he could recall the question being asked once or twice) '... your family wouldn't find it odd that your wife calls herself Mrs Casey...? Eh, Padraig, O'Neill?'

He had to think fast. 'Well, no, of course when we get married, you will be Mrs O'Neill, naturally, but around here, where I am currently obliged to work, you will go by Mrs Casey. There, okay?'

It clearly was not okay, and so Padraig's momentary lapse into self-satisfied delirium, whilst he reflected on the fact that some still called him Brendan, which actually was his name, Padraig being his middle name. Thinking what was so confusing about any of that, and why would Nadia find it a difficult concept to grasp?

Nadia set about explaining the reality of the turbulent bow

wave she was obliged to live in, even within the informal relationship she had with this, spy. 'So, I shall contact the College of
Surgeons and the Medical Council and tell them that when I
am in London my practicing licence will be Naadhira Casey,
but if they could have a duplicate made for me as Nadia O'Neill,
I would be most excessively obliged, as my husband, Brendon,
Padraig, fucking Paddy, Casey, O'Neill, can't make up his
fucking mind just who he is...' She watched her rugged startled
rabbit, and not for the first time wondered how this man of hers
could be such a successful, policeman / spy.

'Keep your professional name.'

'So, I remain Dr Naadhira Khalidi?'

'Yes.'

She seemed to be considering the notion as a possibility,
the ramifications, and for a moment he had her, and for a
moment she did not think he was a dozy bastard man.

Padraig smiled... big mistake.

'Padraig, you dozy bugger, I'm pregnant...'

Padraig smiled, again, wider this time, an even bigger
mistake, but he couldn't help himself, in that moment he was
so happy.

———

Just as Paddy was weeping with joy, making Nadia's face wet,
Flora returned home facing a cold bed and an empty night. She
clopped heavy footed up the stairs, opened the door to come
face to face with Wendy. Her immediate pleasure in seeing the
woman she loved, mixed with confusion as to why she was
seeing her, soon evaporated.

'Where have you been?' Wendy was not a happy bunny.

Flora was almost lost for words, but knew she needed some
time to gather her wits, 'What... err... why? How?'

'I'm here, because I love you.'

Good, Flora thought. Okay, but how to proceed now? 'I love you too.' A good start she thought.

'If you love me, as you say...'

Flora was not at all sure where this was going, and frankly, she was still reeling from the shock of finding Wendy here. 'Yes, I do.'

Wendy became animated. 'Exactly, yes, I do.'

Flora scratched her head, checked for splinters because she must be looking like a dozy woodentop. 'My darling, I... I'm not sure I know what you are saying?'

'Clearly.' Wendy had her arms folded, which could only mean one thing, but Flora couldn't for the life of her think what it might be, but then Wendy continued, allowing Flora a breather. 'So, you love me, do you?' Flora walked towards the woman she truly loved. 'Stay,' Wendy commanded like Flora was her dog. 'So, you love me?'

Flora was now fed up, frustrated at not understanding what she was on about, and she shouted, which she rarely did with Wendy. 'Yes, for fucks sake, how many times do I have to say it?'

Wendy came straight back at Flora, using her soft rose petal-like voice that had Flora going limp with frustrated desire. 'If that is the case, my dearest sweetheart...' and she ramped up, '... how come you haven't fucking asked me to marry you, eh? See, you don't love me, otherwise you would have asked me by now.'

Flora had the wind completely taken out of her sails. 'Well, err... it's against the law?'

Wendy would not be brushed off so easily. 'So it is okay for lesbian gangsters to be married but not a psychiatrist and a fucking spook copper, or whoever you are, a gun-toting frightening woman, who, and this defies all my understanding, I love.'

'I do love you, and if I could, I would get on my knees now and beg you to marry me.'

'Go on then.'

'What?'

'Get on your knees and beg me to marry you... and don't roll your eyes at me or there will be no sex to celebrate our engagement.'

Flora immediately dropped to the floor and, with doleful begging eyes, looked up to her lover. 'Wendy Richards, I love you with all my heart. I want to spend my whole life with you, please consent to be my wife?' She thought about adding 'and go to prison together', but decided not to; it could spoil the mood.

'Oh, Flora, I love you so much, and yes, I would love to be your wife,' and she opened her arms and Flora stood and went into them, but not before Wendy playfully punched her shoulder. 'Took you long enough,' and they kissed.

So they went to bed and made love after which Wendy insisted Flora explain where she had been and why she was late, without telephoning, and she could get the rings in a day or two. Flora's head spun, mousetraps all along the route of responding, so she just told Wendy she loved her and it was okay, at least she thought so. Flora thought she would never understand women.

———

Maude and Bess retired to bed. It had been a long day and the weight of pregnancy was heavy on Bess. 'This has to be bloody triplets.' Maude smoothed the belly, leaned in and told the baby, three times how much she loved them. 'What are you doing?'

'Telling each of the babies that I love them,' Maude answered, and Bess was not sure if she was joking. 'You know what?'

'What?' Bess enquired, keen to sleep.

'If you had the baby Saturday, it would be three years to the day that we got married...'

'And...?'

'Oh... it would be our anniversary.'

'At fucking last...' Bess said.

36

The Daily Mirror - 19th June 1969

IT WAS GOING TO BE TOUCH AND GO, BUT THE EDITOR HELD BACK the front page; this was not only an important story, it was a good one, guaranteed to grab the public attention. This was the working-class struggle against the establishment, the establishment riding roughshod over the working people. The editor trusted his journalist, she had always been proven right and came up with good stories; where from he didn't know, but then he didn't care so long as she continued. He had to admit though, she was a strange woman, never goes for a drink with the others, contemplative, serene, even when up against a deadline as she had been last night.

At first light he had sent a photographer down to Incubator Street to take pictures of the street and the new buildings; Orphanage and Youth Club, of which she had written was a thorn in the side of the local people. This story had everything and promised more as Gerry had advised him; she liked to be called Gerry, not Geraldine, presumably as her by-line would give the impression of being a man, and if she kept on coming up with stories like this, he would call her whatever she liked, Gungha Din even.

The editor was right because the London evening papers, the *Standard* and *News*, picked up the story and both led with it, along with their own pictures, the street, preparing for a funeral and the Church preparing for a celebration. They would all be there, along with the TV cameras and even Pathe News, so it would be screened in the cinemas across the country. It was a fight to get the best position, but the locals were happy to help there; locations on the roof of the school hall, and opposite the playground stage, the top floors of two houses were given over, prime grandstand views for the media.

———

Clarissa read the paper out loud for the bishop; he never liked to read the papers, but he did like Clarissa doing it for him because she cut to the salient points.

'I wonder if we should have rearranged. It does seem as though the local people are not happy,' the Bishop said, tucking into his kippers.

'Happy, what right do they have to be happy?' Clarissa replied, rattling the paper in annoyance.

'I know you are right, dearest, and we have all these busy dignitaries who would not be able to reschedule,' and the Bishop agreed, offering Clarissa a fish face of kippers.

———

'Sister Reporter was staying at the convent. Paddy had arranged for her to interview some of the Stepney Myrmidon, just about all of whom had suffered in the Church homes and they

provided good copy. The sister made notes of how still traumatised as adults they were, telling of their suffering at the hands
of the authorities. She noted also that all of the names
mentioned by them were listed as dignitaries or celebrities to
be on the stage the next day.

Following on from the Myrmidons, she met the panel of
nuns led by Sister Tutor Liberorum, the protector of children.
Sister Gerry had trouble concealing her disgust, which was
blended with an ebullient feeling of justice achieved at the fireworks that would follow her article when published. She had
called her editor and he agreed to run the story, front page, the
day after the ceremony. Fireworks indeed.

———

Paddy telephoned the Convent of Clemence after Nadia and he
had breakfasted and she had left for the hospital. It would be a
day off for her tomorrow; she would attend the funeral with
Paddy. The call was answered after an extended ring that Paddy
thought odd.

It was eventually answered, 'Convent of the Sisters of
Clemence, Soror Telephone speaking.'

'What?' Paddy asked.

'I am Sister Telephone, who is this, please?'

'This is Paddy...'

He was interrupted by a joyous nun, 'Oh, Paddy, Sister
Blende's brother?'

'Yes. Can I ask if my sister is there, please? I need to speak to
her urgently.' There was silence for a while. 'Sister, are you
there?'

'Yes, can you hold a moment, please? I need to check with
Mother if I can tell you. It may be a little while as she is in the
war room. If you give me your number I will call you back.' And
she closed the call, leaving Paddy mystified. War room? If his

sister was anywhere, it would be in there, surely? And then, Jesus wept, what is happening? The telephone rang and Paddy answered, 'Hello.'

'Paddy, this is Adelaide, I hear you want to speak to Roisin?'

'Yes, please.'

'I am sorry, she is behind the veil and that is sacrosanct. I cannot disturb her.'

Paddy was not sure what Adelaide was saying, let alone what this meant, but he did know his sister. 'How long before I can speak to her please?'

'I understand that she will meet you at Incubator Street at the return of the funeral cortege and before the opening ceremony, and Paddy, it is imperative you be there and you follow her instructions to the letter. Now, I must return to the meeting, we have a lot to do, goodbye,' and she hung up, leaving him with a head full of suspicions.

Paddy called Chas, who answered, not Blossom. 'Chas, did you meet my sister?'

'Your skin and blister, not yet, Paddy, I was going to call her later...'

Paddy interrupted, 'Don't bother, she is in purdah.'

'Where's that, it's out in Essex somewhere, isn't it?' Chas asked.

It was all Paddy could do not to laugh. 'Chas, it means she is cloistered not to be disturbed; they call it *behind the veil.*'

'Well, that's a pain, I must say,' Chas replied. 'Still, we can meet her after the funeral stuff I suppose?'

'That's just it, Chas, she wants to meet you and me after the funeral cortege has returned from the cemetery and before the opening ceremony.'

'I see...' Chas pondered. 'I suppose that is okay? What do you think, Paddy? A bit moody?'

'I think it is really odd. She is up to something, and Sister

Telephone said she was in the Convent War Room. Not sure I like the sound of that?'

Chas thought on. 'Is that because she is controlling things and not you?'

Paddy thought Chas knows him better than he knows himself. 'I suppose that is it, but knowing my sister, as I do, she is up to mischief and she has Mother Adelaide's blessing.'

37

Midsummer's Eve – the day of the funeral – the day of the opening ceremony

As the cortege arrived into Incubator Street, Flan's lead milk float was flagged down by a woman school crossing attendant. She spun her lollipop sign to show, "*STOP, children crossing*", and Flan halted; mystified, as were the mourners following his cart; not so much Paddy though.

'Chas, it's my feckin' sister,' Paddy said, in earshot of Blossom and Nadia.

'I would like to meet her,' Nadia said to Paddy.

'Let me speak to her first...' He found he was speaking to himself as Nadia had stepped out of the line and walked to the lollipop lady. 'Nadia...' he called but knew it was useless and so he followed her, along with Chas. Flora stepped out also, but Paddy put his hand up to say no, but clearly she was taking no notice of him either. He did wonder if he was invisible to women these days. Paddy walked back to her. 'Flora, I think it best I speak with Roisin myself.'

'Like fuck...' and she skirted around the Irishman and approached the Black Rose crossing attendant.

'Flora, looking gorgeous so you are, even in black,' Roisin said, Chas watching on as Paddy tried to steer Flora away. 'Hold your horses, Paddy,' and she addressed Flora. 'Flora, if you stay, you will be complicit, and I am not sure you want to be.'

'Complicit? In what?' Flora asked, waving Wendy back, who surprisingly, obeyed; was that the first time ever? Wendy, however, sensed this was a serious pow-wow between three serious people; serious and violent, and it looked like her Flora wanted in.

'We need privacy and I have agreed the parlour in the end house. It is not being used for the funeral, so we will not be disturbed, but first of all, I need to speak to Flan.' She paced over to Flan, standing to attention beside the cab of his lead milk float, relishing his importance, in his best bib and tucker. Blossom had laundered and ironed his white coat and blue and white, horizontal striped apron and bus conductor's hat; he looked the biz, and everyone knew it.

Flan looked nervous as the lollipop lady approached, wondering if he had done something wrong. 'Miss, not sure you should be here. It's not a school day.'

Roisin smiled and Flan was smitten; she had this effect on everyone, and Flora could see it was the smile she had received in the Two Chairmen pub; Flan was dead meat. 'Flan, I will need you to do something for me and it will be dangerous, but it is for Tommy, you understand? And you, I might add.'

Flan was in a dream but agreed, anything for Tommy. 'And me?'

'Yes, Flan. I want you to follow me into the playground and I will show you where I want you to park your float.'

'But, miss, the people are already arriving and they may stop me?' and he all of a sudden realised what else had been said, 'dangerous?'

'I will explain later, but first follow me with your cart...' and Flan got into the cab and watched as she went to Chas. They talked and she then signalled Flan to follow.

Flan followed silently, watching as Roisin and Chas approached the security men on the gate. They went to stop them but recognised Chas. 'Mr Larkin, I am not supposed to let anyone in.'

Chas looked at the name badge. 'Eric, you know who I am, yes?' The intimidation wouldn't take long, this man did not need trouble.

'Yes, Mr Larkin. Sorry, of course you can come in, and the milk float?'

'Yes, milk float as well,' Chas answered as the men responded, opening both gates fully.

Flan followed and parked where directed by Roisin, who then spoke with the milkman. 'I will need you to stand guard by your cab and nobody is allowed to touch it or look at it, do you understand?'

'Yes, miss.'

'Good, now, when I tell you, you are to drive your float and stop it in front of the stage, in the fenced-off part,' and she pointed, just to make sure Flan did understand.

'Yes, miss.'

'And now, this is very important, so listen carefully.'

'Yes, miss.'

When you park it, the red button there...' and she pointed to just below the dashboard, '... press it, then get out and walk briskly away, do not run, just walk at a fast pace, and get the hell out of the playground, because I have put a bomb in your float, do you understand?'

'Yes, miss. A bomb?'

'Yes, Flan. It is payback time for you and all the other children abused by these people and those who protected your abusers. That is good, yes?'

'Oh yes, miss, that is really good.'

'Now, you will have three minutes before it goes off, so do not hang around, okay?'

'Yes, miss.'

'Okay, now repeat to me what you have to do,' and Flan did, Roisin making him repeat several times how long he had to get clear. And then she embraced him and kissed him; she was confident he would do as she instructed. Paddy had said this young man was motivated, and she watched as Flan Milkman stood to attention by his cab, ignoring all the comments from dignitaries as they shuffled around to get a good spot by the stage, looking up to the cameras on the roof and back to the terraced houses where they had been told Pathe News had set up; this was going to be good.

One man tried to bully Flan, but his friend informed him that Chas Larkin had told the milkman to be there, and the man apologised.

———

Chas returned to Incubator Street with Roisin where they met up with Flora and Paddy, and together made their way to the end house Roisin had *borrowed*. Once inside the parlour, she checked that they were not being overlooked or listened to, and satisfied, she asked them to sit in the posh chairs. They all sat.

She addressed Flora first. 'First you, gorgeous. You are here and what you hear now will mean that you are a part of what is to unfold. You will tell nobody, do you understand?' Flora said she did, and Roisin continued. 'Just so you do understand Flora, I will kill you if you tell anyone, including the lubbly jubbly Wendy.'

Flora looked worried, but Paddy could see she was intrigued; she was in. 'I'm in, so tell me what is going to happen.'

Roisin looked around, got nods from Chas and her brother, not that she doubted their willingness to participate. 'What we are going to do, well, me, and my Sorores Sapper-Demolitions, sisters of demolitions. We are going to blow the fucking lot up.'

Flora laughed. 'You're bleedin' kidding, right?' She continued laughing, almost hysterical and then calmed, looked at the serious face on the Black Rose. 'You're not kidding, are you?'

'No, I am not kidding, and you are now in this up to your glorious neck,' Roisin said.

'I presume that your Sapper Sisters planted charges last night?' Paddy asked.

'They did. I got them into the Orphanage and Youth Club last night,' Chas said.

'Isn't this going to blow up the street and the people of Incubator Street as well?' Flora asked, reasonably, she thought.

Roisin and Paddy shared a glance and a chuckle. Paddy answered the question for his detective sergeant, 'Flora, the sisters are experts.'

Roisin followed up with what she considered reassuring detail. 'The team have planted small charges around the new buildings. The explosives are placed so they will destabilise the external structure enough so that it will collapse in on itself, avoiding the street. The mini-explosions will also provide a distraction to enable Flan to get away before the milk float blows up.'

'Christ on a bike...' Flora said, 'what about the people in the crowd?'

'Those people are all a part of the paedophile ring. We checked; however, they are small bit players. We have designed the bomb, within the box that carried Tommy's coffin, with a shield to the audience side, it will direct the charge to the stage. There will likely be some in the crowd injured, but not fatally,' and Roisin waved crossed fingers in the air, not reassuring Flora in the least.

'But...' Flora was tongue-tied. She knew what she wanted to say, but could not get the words out.

Roisin interpreted, 'You want to know how we are going to get away with it?'

'Well, yes, I suppose that is what I wanted to say... err, ask...'

'Flora, did you read the *Daily Mirror* this morning?' Roisin asked, Paddy and Chas following, they were learning as it went along. This has all been planned by the nuns in their war room, Paddy presumed.

'The article on the upset of the locals versus the church and establishment?' Flora answered.

'Yes, that was by Sister Reporter, and she is laying the ground for many follow-up articles,' Roisin stated, matter of fact.

'So, obfuscation?'

'Yes and no, Flora, but you get the drift. I cannot say much more, but when the articles are complete, most people will think the people on the stage got what they deserved,' Roisin explained.

'And this is the nuns?' incredulity in the voice of Flora.

'You have to understand Flora, the nuns work to do as much as peacefully as they can, but, we are looking at the greater good here, and that is the nuns' motto: *Qyicquid capit, ad majus bonum.* Whatever it takes, for the greater good.' Roisin saw doubt in Flora's face. 'These are evil people preying on vulnerable children, Flora. They will never be stopped by the authorities as they are protected by those authorities, and that includes the police. I think you know that, yes?'

'I know you are right... I just...'

Paddy intervened. 'Flora, this is happening and it is a part of a big plan that you will have revealed for you in time, when the dust, literally, has settled.'

All Flora could do was to offer up an old-fashioned look, and then said, 'I suppose this is about to happen now, right?'

'Yes,' Roisin said. 'Chas, you will stand with Blossom at Flan's milk float in the playground. There will be a few of the Myrmidons standing sentry, I have briefed them as much as they need to know, and Flan knows what he has to do. Okay, so let's get to it.'

And Roisin, Paddy and Chas stood and paced to the street door, Flora picking up at the rear. 'Where do I go? Roisin?'

Roisin, calling back, 'You stay with Wendy. If you came with us, she would want to know what is happening and we cannot have her resisting.' Flora could see that and understood, that is exactly what her *fiancé* would do.

38

BANG! MIDSUMMER'S EVE

After the brief contretemps, Blossom watched Tanner go to the stage, mount it and shake hands with the dignitaries. 'Christ on a bike, Chas, I never saw that coming, but I suspect you did... yes?' Blossom knew Chas well, and also knew not to push. Chas had his serious face on and it had nothing to do with mourning Tommy.

'Opalong and Queenie came up next, walked past Chas and Blossom, just a scowl from 'Opalong. Chas grinned, he had learned that 'Opalong and Queenie had been married the day before and were here representing the George family. Blossom, once again saw all, and frowned so that Chas saw.

'Chas, I don't get why we are standing here? Is it defiance?' Blossom asked.

'Yes, darlin', in a way, but I also wanted to deter anyone bullying Flan. I want his milk float here, so everybody can see it and know that we resent what they are doing.'

'So, they ignore the feelings of the people who live here at their peril, is that it?'

'Exactly that...' Chas halted because the ceremony had started with the Bishop standing at the microphone, giving the crowd a blessing and splashing holy puddle water everywhere, like a God fearing lavatory man with his holy disinfectant. Chas thought it would take more than that to disinfect these entitled, perverted people.

Roisin approached the milk float, still in her lollipop lady get up. She leaned in to speak to Flan, 'You okay, Flan?' He nodded, he was focused. 'When you get to the front of the stage, you press that red button, remove the keys and then get out. Walk fast, do not run, and she went to the entry point of the front stage, moved a barrier, and with her lollipop reading, *STOP, children crossing*, she waved Flan in. People looked around, confused, looking for the children, and when Flan had parked, she disappeared along with Chas, Blossom and the remaining Myrmidons.

Flan knew what he had to do, this was his chance. He switched off the motor and pocketed the keys, pressed the red button, stepped out of his cab and mounted the stage. He punched the Bishop in the face, grabbed the mic as the holy man hit the deck. That got the attention of the people. He then gave them the speech he had prepared.

In Incubator Street the lollipop nun, Black Rose, muttered, 'What the feck?' and then listened in as Flan commenced speaking into the mic, his voice echoing around the street.

'My name is Flan and I am one of thousands of children who were abused by these people on the stage. I tried to complain, but always my complaints were hushed up. The people here...' and he waved his hand to encompass the people on the stage, all pompous and full of indignation, '... these people destroyed my life. I have lived in misery because of the acts these people made me do and they did to me. Today, they get their comeuppance and I will find peace...'

At this point the crowd turned to the new buildings as small popping charges blew in sequence. It was in wonderment that they looked on as the first parts of the building fell in on themselves, progressively and steadily, a planned demolition, by the demolition nuns, and, before anybody could act, the milk float blew, the last visible image on the stage was Flan in his milkman's uniform and peaked hat, his arms spread, like Christ on the cross, as he sought and achieved oblivion: a rest in peace.

As the dust settled on the faces of the people standing in awe in Incubator Street, faces, dusted white and grey, red lips, dodgy teeth and sparkly eyes stood out; they could not believe what they had witnessed.

Nadia responded straight away, running to the centre of the playground to see if she could help anyone. Paddy let her go, there would be no way he could stop her and this was his woman, and soon to be the mother of his child. She looked back at him, 'Paddy, come and give me a hand, now.'

He answered her call to arms and knew what he expected to see, he was prepared as he knew Nadia would be, she had seen this in her country of Palestine and he had seen it in Ireland. Not since the war had Londoners seen anything like this though, and they remained stunned as bells resounded from the approaching fire engines, ambulances and police. Nadia stood and scanned the playground, looking at the walking wounded and shocked members of the audience clambering for the exit gates like the kids would do in the playground at home-time. Paddy looked at Nadia, she had an expression on her face he could not read, so no change there then, 'What? What is it, Nadia?'

She looked at him, grime all over her face. She turned to where the stage had been, it was just rubble, with dead bodies, arms, legs, scattered and not a sign of Flan, just his milkman's hat. She stepped in and picked it up and turned to Paddy. 'He knew...' and she looked for a reaction from her danger man.

Paddy knew this was going to be the hard bit for him, how to lie to the woman he loved, but he had to. 'Paddy, he knew. He knew, and he wanted to get his say and he wanted to die.'

'It certainly looks that way. I told you about what he said, when I met him last night at Chas's. He stayed with them all night. He said they were the only people he knew who loved him, and he felt safe only with them and the Myrmidons.' He looked up and in an arc around where the stage had been and the burning carcass of Flan's milk float, stood the Myrmidons: The Rinso Kid, 'Arry 'Orse Collar, Blossom, Silly Boy Eric, Mickey One-eye, Snotty Oliver. They, each and every one of them cried for the loss of their fallen comrade, Flan Milkman, even Snotty Oliver who had lost his mother in the blast, wept for the loss of Flan. The milkman was loved and nobody could help him.

Nadia spotted some audience members wounded and needing attention. She went to them and triaged for the ambulance people as they began arriving. 'Remarkable...' she said to an ambulance stretcher crew, '... the stage was decimated but the audience, so close, got off lightly, nothing serious as far as I can see.'

It was an experienced crew and they mentioned they had seen stuff like this in the blitz, people standing close to a blown-up house, getting off almost unhurt. 'It's a mystery miss,' one of them said, and Nadia had to agree.

She turned to Paddy. 'I had better get into the hospital; it's going to be all hands to the pumps.'

'Agree, sweetheart, I will come along in a minute, but Flora and I will be needed by the police, to help, and then make a witness statement, although there are enough cameras here to have it all recorded.

Nadia leaned in to Paddy, 'Lucky I love you...' she whispered into his ear, '... I hope you have your story worked out?'

'What...?'

'Paddy, I am no fool and I know you well, and I am getting to know your sister, the Black Rose, because this has Sister Blende's fingerprints all over it,' and she smiled, which confused Paddy. 'Relax, I know the motto of the convent. I've been asking around, it goes something like, whatever it takes, for the greater good, or something like that, and in this case, I think this was for the greater good.' Paddy looked, searching her face, this is something he never expected. 'Got you confused, have I lover?'

'You can say that again,' Paddy answered.

'Paddy, this is a war on paedophilia, and whatever it takes, we must win it...' and she sighed, looking around her, then back to Flan's hat, '... we need to win so Flan's sacrifice is not wasted, so that it means something. I think he cleared the way for Sister Reporter's next article.'

Chas was behind her listening in. 'I agree Nadia. Even though Flan was at the end of his tether, he was brave enough to make that statement to the crowd and it will all be on film. I have spoken to the Sister Reporter, who is writing up her first story now, and she will add that. She said also that the street should erect a statue as a monument to mark Flan Milkman, and, we will do that.'

39

The next day

THE PAPERS SPECULATED ON THE CAUSE OF THE EXPLOSION, ALL
missing the lead by the *Daily Mirror* on the morning of the
event. They followed the punditry and so-called experts that
were rolled-out on the BBC and ITV extended evening news
coverage:

Milkman blows up Bishop
Gang warfare claims life of Bishop
Massive explosion in the East End – is this the IRA?

A spokesperson for the IRA denied responsibility so that
panic eased itself from the minds of the public. So it was gang
warfare? Was the milkman a gangster? Was the bishop a gangster, some said that might be it?

Sister Reporter's story was held in disbelief when she
expanded upon her previous story. The people on the stage
were all involved in in a paedophile ring, and the milkman had
been used and abused as a boy in the system. Gerry also

revealed that this included funding by Arthur Schilling, notorious gangster from the West End, aka Tanner, and Queenie George, of the George family in the north, all as agreed in the Convent War Room. She reported that Tanner was killed in the bombing, as was Queenie, recently married to Brian Saint, aka, 'Opalong, who had recently been released from jail for gangster offences; both were killed.

The news story went on to say that the reporter had interviewed many of the people on Incubator Street, as well as some in the Larkin Saint family, known gangsters. She reported that they were as stunned as anybody at the explosion. It was said by the local people that the Larkin Saints looked after those children abused in the State and Church systems, building and providing their own orphanages and youth centres. And then in a startling revelation, Chas Larkin had been interviewed, and she reported his words that: "the institutional abuse of children in the East End had been going on for a long time, and although many of the police in the lower ranks were concerned, every time an enquiry was raised it was crushed by the *big wigs*," and she reported that he had mentioned that upon the stage was the assistant commissioner of police, as well as the local MP, and that said it all.

Sister Reporter stated that she had interviewed members of the George family, now in mourning for a beloved daughter, and Lavinia George said she did not know what her sons or daughter had done, but she did suspect they had invested in the new building works. Similarly, the response from a spokesperson for the Tanner organisation, the bookkeeper, said that Tanner had invested in many projects, and since his untimely death, Ruth Golding could confirm that there had been considerable *off-the-books* investments in projects in the East End, all of dubious pedigree that she had only recently discovered. She did say that her boss was an East End boy himself and always had a desire to return there someday.

And finally, Sister Reporter ended her story by saying that the *Daily Mirror* had been contacted by Government officials and threatened with a D Notice to quash the article, but the editor refused, and the paper stands by their reporter. Further stories were trailed, including one, expected within a week or two, where irrefutable proof will be shown, Institutions named, protagonists named and shamed, and this set the cat amongst the pigeons.

The other news outlets followed this up with even more speculation, and one even said that there was a mythical family living in the East End called the O'Neills and they blamed the carnage on the Black Rose. The public loved this story of a vigilante woman protecting the vulnerable children and taking action, and anyway, didn't these people get what they deserved?

And then it was formalised: The Prime Minister, the Archbishop of Canterbury and the Commissioner of the Met Police each received a note. It said, "The O'Neills say hi."

———

In the North... in the Fat Cow pub, the news had been received with mixed emotions. Lavinia George made like she mourned the loss of her two sons and now, her recently married daughter. However, it was thought that because Vinnie now held the reigns, and she had the soldiers to back up the new, or at least, modified regime, it was wait and see time. All agreed it was a blessing that it did not happen on their manor, and most had no doubts that it was the O'Neills.

On the surface, it appeared to outsiders that the North was now leaderless, but those in the know knew this was far from the reality; they had always had a Queen, and it wasn't Queenie, but the new Queen could be...? And the pub? Well, this will no longer be called the Fat Cow, but what would the new name be... Stick Thin Vinnie?

. . .

... *And in the West.* Stanley returned from the newsagents and burst into Ruth's flat with an armful of newspapers, through to the bedroom, where Ruth sat up in bed looking at her gorgeous dipstick, panting, as he deposited the morning's news on the bed.

'Steady on, tiger, I don't want you out of breath...' and she released a lascivious smile. 'So, these are the papers, does it say what we expected?' Stan was busy taking his clothes off and snuggling back into bed. 'Oi, in a minute...' but his hands had done the biz on her body.

'What did you say, lover?' Stan managed to say.

'The papers, baby. Do they say what we expected?'

'They do. Tanner is dead and the George family is temporarily fucked, and now, I'm going to fuck you, permanently.'

'I would be amenable to that, Stan.'

————

Vinnie was behind the bar in the Fat Cow pub when she turned to see what had caused the sudden hush, and she did a double take. Was she seeing things? Two nuns walked into a bar, not a joke, they really did, and were now standing in front of her.

'Lavinia George?' The first nun was polite but officious.

Lavinia answered, 'Yes, I am Vinnie George.'

'I am Soror Pacificus, and this is my deputy, Soror Sursum. Roughly translated, I am the peacemaker and this is my backup sister.'

Vinnie could not control her laughter and when she calmed and had the attention of the patrons in the bar, she said to the Sisters, 'You're 'aving a tin barf, ain't yer? Is this fucking candid camera...?' and she looked around, saw nothing, '... what's your game then?'

The spokes nun continued, 'I assure you, Vinnie, this is no game. My convent, the Sisters of Clemence, have been retained to broker a peace deal between you, Ruth Golding, and Maude Larkin, with Bess Saint.'

'You what...?'

'You heard, Vinnie, can we go somewhere private please.'

Vinnie had heard of the Sisters of Clemence, who hadn't in working-class London, but she had never had dealings with them. 'Is this on the up and up?'

'Somewhere private please, and you will be fully briefed.'

'I will have to search you for weapons.'

The spokes nun answered, 'If you must, but all we have is our cross...' and she lifted to simple wooden cross from her chest to show Vinnie, '... and we also have a message from Chas Larkin.'

Now this did get Vinnie's attention. 'Chas Larkin?'

'Indeed...' the sister answered, brief and to the point, '... and if we could get a move on, please, because we have to go and see Ruth Golding after our business here is concluded.'

Vinnie's mouth gaped. 'Ruth Golding, Tanner's bookkeeper?'

'Yes. Now please, can we go somewhere private?'

Vinnie showed the nuns through to the ladies snug bar. 'It never has anyone in here,' she said and unnecessarily, telling the nuns she was thinking of opening up to the main bar. The sisters shrugged their shoulders, not their problem. They sat around a small table and the sisters declined the offer of a drink.

Sister Peacemaker opened up. 'This will not take long. I bring a message from Chas Larkin. He says that he will acknowledge you as Queen of the North provided you guarantee to stay in your territory. This will come with benefits to you that will be explained at a later meeting, with you, Ruth and Maude.'

'That mad cow, I'm not going within a country mile of her, she's radio rental.'

The nuns expected this response. 'You will be guaranteed safe passage, as will Ruth, and Bess will be with Maude, who is, after all, Queen of the East End.'

'Are you saying that I will be Queen of the North, no fighting?' and Vinnie's sparrow's chest puffed.

'Yes.'

'Where is this meeting to take place?'

'It will be held on the site of Wapping Market, opposite the Prospect of Whitby pub in Shadwell. You will be told of the date and time. Do I presume that provisionally you agree to the terms?'

'I agree.'

———

Stan took the call. Ruth was having a bath and he intended joining her, which he did. 'Who was on the dog and bone, babes?'

'It was Sister something or other that means peacemaker and she reported that Vinnie has agreed to be Queen and the meeting will be set up; you will be Queen of the West and South, acknowledging Maude Larkin as overall Queen with Bess Saint as her consort,' and he climbed into the bath.

Ruth was warmed not just by the water and soap suds, and the presence of this dazzling man, but by the news that all had gone to plan. The plan devised and carried out by the Black Rose, that is. 'And the IRA?'

Stan shrugged his shoulders. 'I presume the Black Rose will sort them. Who knows, but they will have to be sorted.'

'I have faith in the Black Rose, and I presume we will hear something today. Now, are you just going to sit there...?'

———

Two men trod carefully across the rubble-strewn playground. They were anonymous, but were permitted passage past the crime scene tape, guided by Detective Inspector Paddy Casey; he was recognised. Most of the police around here knew of the detective and his rep.

'We will meet in here,' Paddy said, pointing to the school hall doors. If Nadia had been there she would have noticed that his Irish accent had strengthened, and she would have known that it was deliberately reinforced for the two IRA personnel who walked with him now into the hall.

Inside and still erected was the table that Little Willie MP, deceased, had met with the Black Rose just a few days ago.

Chas Larkin stood and greeted the two IRA officers, shook their hands, and gestured for them to take a seat. 'This will be a brief meeting. All of your arrangements with Tanner are now ended, obviously.' The two officers were stoically unmoved. 'However, I suppose you know that the East End of London, including the docks, are my bailiwick?' The two men nodded. 'So, here is the deal. I will allow you to import your munitions on the understanding that you use them to make your case for fair rights for the Catholics in the North and your argument for unification, all of which I support.'

This seemed to surprise the two officers, but it should not have as they knew that Chas Larkin had risen with the support of the Black Rose and the O'Neills, not that they knew who they were. 'And the terms of this agreement? How much do you want?'

Chas smiled, 'I do not want your money.' He enjoyed the look of surprise on their faces.

'Then what do you want, because you must want something?'

'I do. I want that the imported arms and explosives are used only to target strategic infrastructure, buildings and so on, so you can add *weight* to your negotiations.'

'Negotiations, what negotiations?'

'I have arranged for politicians to meet with both your people and those of the Protestants, and the politicians in the north and south. What I want from you is this; free and safe passage for the negotiators and an undertaking that no innocent people will be hurt in your attacks on the mainland.'

'And that is it?'

'That is it, but know this, if you do target people, all bets will be off, and I can guarantee you this, I will crush you in London.'

There was a smile from both men. 'You think you can do that?'

'I know I can do that. I have more than you can ever imagine. Now, do we have a deal?'

The two men stood to meet Chas as he was already standing, they shook hands and Chas held onto the hand of the man he had guessed was the more senior officer. 'Break our agreement and you will regret it; understand?'

They nodded and still grasping the hand of Chas, the lead officer asked, 'Why?'

Chas smiled. 'Because you have had your revolution and thrown off the shackles of Colonial rule, except for the six counties in the North. Here in Britain, the working class are still being crushed upon the anvil of the elite, the aristocracy and big corporations.'

They broke the handshake. 'So, what you are saying is that what we do could be seen as a taster for what the government here in Britain can expect if they do not act fairly and justly with the people. Yes?' the IRA man asked.

'Yes,' Chas responded, 'and it might be a good idea if the word was spread across Ireland that the Irish people do not have a beef with the people of the UK. The ordinary people are not responsible for what was done to the Irish historically, and as I said, we have always suffered as your people did and, we are still suffering and we must, we will have our revolution.'

The IRA man saluted Chas and stretched out his hand again. 'Good man yerself, Chas, and be assured I will pass the message on...' He paused.

'What is it?' Chas asked and Paddy answered.

'He is worried about the hotheads in the organisation. Every Army has them.'

'Thank you, Paddy, I surmised this, we have them too. So, what I will say is this, if something happens and you can identify the bad apples to me, we will deal with them and our agreement will stand. This will be time-limited, of course, and hopefully, a peace can be negotiated.'

Chas signalled that the meeting was over and Paddy showed the men out. Chas sat and Roisin joined him after the doors closed. 'They think where they are staying is a secret, but I know all of their places and I have left a note for them, saying I can get to them whenever I want if they break the agreement.'

'Good,' Chas said, 'and now we meet with Ruth and Vinnie.'

40

MAGNA CARTA LIBERTATUM – GREAT CHARTER OF FREEDOMS

THE LANDLORD OF THE PROSPECT OF WHITBY PUB THAT FACED onto the Thames and was opposite Shadwell Basin had done as he was asked. You do not say no to Maude Larkin, even if she was accompanied by her heavily pregnant spouse, Bess Saint. Chas liked this pub, good food and he would allow himself the occasional half of ale. He also felt safe here; these were his people and everyone knew him, and despite news stories to the contrary, most locals thought it was the Larkin Saints who blew up the Incubator Street buildings and the child molesters. In any case, if it were not, and it was the O'Neills or even the Black Rose, everyone knew they or she, sided with Chas Larkin.

As instructed the landlord had set up a marquee on the site of Wapping Market, a form of peninsular projecting into Shadwell basin. This meant that the proposed meeting would be bounded by water on three sides and the land side could be manned with reliable soldiers, not that any trouble was envisaged. Vinnie and Ruth had agreed that the arrangements suited them; it was known that Vinnie did not like the plan to take the East End, and Ruth, well, she fed information to the Larkin

Saints anyway, and now, she was in the MI5 fold, folded in the arms of Stanley.

Ruth walked hand in hand with Stanley. They had come by tube to the nearby Shadwell station; they feared nobody here, whereas Vinnie came by car with an armed driver, followed by another with four soldiers, just in case.

Ruth and Stanley waited outside the pub as the two cars pulled up. Vinnie stepped out and Ruth welcomed her with a hug. 'Can you Adam and Eve this?'

'Believe it, Vinnie, because I think this is the best thing to happen to us, and our territories,' Ruth said.

'Well, I always knew you ran the show for that lounge lizard, Tanner.'

'And you ran the show in Tottenham. Got a bit hairy there, and I offer my condolences at the loss of your children. You still have the youngster though, Steve, don't you...?'

'I do...

'He takes after me...'

'The bright one, eh? Heard he's off to university; posh that,' Ruth said as she steered Vinnie towards the tent. Both women were searched as they would have expected. Other than that, the two women passed by unmolested to greet Chas Larkin, Maude and Bess, who stood to greet them.

Chas was master of ceremonies and nobody contested this, not even Maude. 'Ruth, thank you for coming...' and he hugged her, then turned to Vinnie. 'Vinnie, it is good to meet you at last, and I am sorry for your recent losses,' and he hugged her as well, which came as a surprise to her. 'Shall we sit?' Chas drew out a chair for Vinnie and held it as she sat, and did the same for Ruth; most gentlemanly. 'Now, I will tell you what I have agreed with the IRA. I think you know I have sympathies for the Irish, but I cannot stand the violence to people.' Vinnie leaned back in her chair and raised her eyebrows. 'What I mean is, Vinnie, hurt to the innocent people, the bystanders;

the key bastards are fair game and they would know it. However, I have agreed they can use the docks, but the minute they *target* innocent people, I have promised that I will release hellfire upon them.' Chas paused to read the reaction, mainly from Vinnie. 'Maude and Bess...' and he waved his hand to the pair, '... will be the main contacts, and you may rest assured that Maude is now reigned in.'

'I suppose Maude going radio rental was to encourage Tanner and my boys to go gung-ho unprepared, and it worked, yes?' Vinnie said, and she saw the smile from Maude.

'That was the plan,' Chas answered.

'Okay, I can see what you propose makes sense, the last thing you need is a war with the IRA...' Chas nodded, '... and I suppose, knowing you as I do by reputation, you will have arranged that peace negotiations in Ireland can go on safely, am I right?' Vinnie said.

She knew she was right because Chas's grin broadened. 'Vinnie, you are right and I think with Ruth in the West and the limited area of the South and you in the North, we should have peace, in the way that I have managed in the East End...' and he waved his hand and shrugged his shoulders, '... with just a bit of dodgy stuff for good order, you know?'

'I do,' Vinnie said, and turning to Ruth, 'I presume you agree, Ruth?'

'I do, it is good all round, and I have suggested to Chas that we meet regularly with Maude and Bess, occasionally with Chas, just to make sure we are all still on the same page. Does that suit you, Vinnie?'

Vinnie stood. 'It does,' and she held out her hand to Chas, he shook it and so did Ruth and they shook also with Maude and Bess.

It was done. No war, some casualties, but all for the greater good.

The end

AUTHOR'S ADDITIONAL NOTE

Often, I find my books are inspired by pieces of music or incidental events, other books even; 'Rite Judgement', Stravinsky, *Rite of Spring*. 'Merde and Mandarins', Shostakovich piano *Concerto Number Two*, in particular, the second movement. 'Larkin's Barkin' – A midsummer Night's Chutzpah', Mendelssohn, *Midsummer Night's Dream*, and, a burned crumpet at an Arts event. *Road Kill - The Duchess of Frisian Tun, The Canterbury Tales* - did anyone set that to music? Maybe the Minstrel?

This book has had a lift with Kurt Veil's (Bertolt Brecht) *The Three Penny Opera, Die Dreigroschenoper*. I put the name of librettist, Bertolt Brecht, in brackets, because I listen to this piece in the German and I cannot speak or understand German. It is the phrasing and intonation of the spoken and sung word, sometimes grating with the music that I find engaging and it influenced the writing of this book, probably because I allow the music and singing to drift over me as I conjure my own story:

"At any time I can be creative, and there is no limit, so long as I do not have to be coherent."

A quote from somewhere, it is not exactly right and I cannot attribute it because only the words stick in my memory, not the author – if anyone knows, keep it to yourself.

Having said that, Bertolt Brecht said, *"The person who laughs has not heard the bad news yet."* So, what can I tell yer? Further inspiration came from Brecht who attempted to develop a new approach to the theatre. He tried to persuade his audiences to see the stage as a stage, actors as actors and not the traditional make-believe of the theatre. Brecht required detachment, not passion, from the observing audience. The purpose of the play was to awaken the spectators' minds so he could communicate his version of the truth.

I try to do this in all of my books and this book in particular.

Being called before the Un-American Activities Committee, Brecht said, "I feel free for the first time to say a few words about American matters: looking back at my experiences as a playwright and a poet in the Europe of the last two decades, I wish to say that the great American people would lose much and risk much if they allowed anybody to restrict free competition of ideas in cultural fields, or to interfere with art which must be free in order to be art. We are living in a dangerous world. Our state of civilization is such that mankind already is capable of becoming enormously wealthy but, as a whole, is still poverty-ridden. Great wars have been suffered, greater ones are imminent, we are told. One of them might well wipe out mankind, as a whole. We might be the last generation of the specimen man on this earth. The ideas about how to make use of the new capabilities of production have not been developed much since the days when the horse had to do what man could not do. Do you not think that, in such a predicament, every new idea should be examined carefully and freely? Art can present clear and even make nobler such ideas."

Sound familiar?

ABOUT THE AUTHOR

Pete Adams is an architect with a practice in Portsmouth, UK, and from there he has, over forty years, designed and built buildings across England and Wales. Pete took up writing after listening to a radio interview of the writer Michael Connolly whilst driving home from Leeds. A passionate reader, the notion of writing his own novel was compelling, but he had always been told you must have a *mind map* for the book; Jeez, he could never get that.

Et Voila, Connolly responding to a question, said he never can plan a book and starts with an idea for chapter one and looks forward to seeing where it would lead. Job done, and that evening, Spring 2012, Pete started writing, and the series, Kind Hearts and Martinets, was on the starting blocks.

Pete is well into his sixteenth book, has a growing number of short stories, one, critically acclaimed and published by Bloodhound, and has written and illustrated a series of historical nonsense stories called, Whopping Tales under contract with his publisher.

Pete describes himself as an inveterate daydreamer and escapes into those dreams by writing crime thrillers with a thoughtful dash of social commentary. He has a writing style shaped by his formative years on an estate that re-housed London families after WWII, and his books have been likened to the writing of Tom Sharpe; his most cherished review, "made me laugh, made me cry, and made me think".

Pete lives in Southsea with his partner, the children having flown the coop, and has 3 beautiful granddaughters who will play with him so long as he promises not to be silly.

———

To learn more about Pete Adams and discover more Next Chapter authors, visit our website at www.nextchapter.pub.

BOOKS BY PETE ADAMS

Kind Hearts and Martinets – 5-book miniseries:

Cause and Effect

Irony in the Soul

A Barrow Boy's Cadenza

Ghost and Ragman Roll

Merde and Mandarins

The DaDa Detective Agency – 3-book miniseries:

Road Kill

Rite Judgment

Blood Sport

The Rhubarb Papers

Dead No More

Larkin's Barkin' series

Black Rose

A Deadly Queen

An Avuncular Detective, a new series, commences with a 2-parter:

Murder in a Royal Peculiar, Parts 1 and 2.

Book 1: A Choir of Assassins

Book 2: Extreme Unction – coming soon

A Deadly Queen
ISBN: 978-4-82419-792-4

Published by
Next Chapter
2-5-6 SANNO
SANNO BRIDGE
143-0023 Ota-Ku, Tokyo
+818035793528

18th September 2024